Music City

Praise for Sara M. Harvey:

Compared to Jacqueline Carey, Eugie Foster, Catherynne Valente, and Cherie Priest, Sara M. Harvey's work has been called "thought-provoking" by Analog and both "interesting and complex" and "smart and dark" by Hugo-nominated publisher Jason Sizemore.

The Convent of the Pure:

"While Harvey's treatment of imagery is a tad heavy-handed, her language and word choice are impeccable. Most fantasy writers who employ a "realistic" style shun adjectives, but Harvey uses them to great affect without over-saturating the writing. *The Convent of the Pure* reads lightly and unencumbered, with vivid scenes and images as signposts along the way. The hero is called to action, has initial success, sees the undefeatable monster and faces a setback, gets help and defeats the monster, and then returns to the people. Yes, the story is familiar, but it's also well-written, and perhaps most importantly, it's fun." -- Nick DeMarino, SFReader.com

"Readers...will appreciate the mix of heat, horror and humor." -- Publisher's Weekly

"This is a fast, fun read that does a nice job of getting away from the fantasy stereotypes that you may be used to." -- Dandelion Studios

"The world of the Nephilim is both beautiful and savage, one where the ladies wear corsets but as armor rather than under garments. I loved this book, as I loved its sequel and I cannot wait to start the final installment." -- She Never Slept

"A short but enthralling story, *The Convent of the Pure* was a treat for my reading palate. This interesting take on angels and the Nephilim inspires eager anticipation to return to the intriguing world where science meets fantasy, in a time lost in the end of the 19th Century." -- Bitten By Books

"*The Convent of the Pure* is a compelling blend of the numinous and the creepy, with a rich, atmospheric setting. I devoured it in a

single sitting!"
—Jacqueline Carey, author of *Kushiel's Dart*

"An intriguing fantasy novella that will move you to tears."
—Michael A. Burstein, Campbell Award-winning author of *I Remember the Future*

"*The Convent of the Pure* is a beautifully written page turner, dripping with magic and intrigue. I couldn't put it down. A gifted writer and storyteller, Sara M. Harvey is worthy of a rocket to the top!"
—Fran Friel, Bram Stoker Award finalist and author of *Mama's Boy and Other Dark Tales*

The Labyrinth of the Dead:

"The dead want to return to life, but balance must be maintained. *The Labyrinth of the Dead* tells the story of Portia Gyony, protector of humanity who oversees the border of the shadow world and the world of the living. When his lover tries to crossover he finds himself stuck in a conflict. A unique setting with unique characters, *The Labyrinth of the Dead* is a fine and exciting fantasy not to be missed." —Midwest Book Review

"Harvey uses ancient Judeo-Christian mythology imagery, occult traditions, steampunk gadgetry and her amazing imagination to give the reader scenes that range from the achingly sensual and intimate interludes of long-separated lovers to crossbow bolt firing blood-soaked battles amongst angels and demons." — SteampunkChronicle.com

"The author does a great job of sucking you in, and keeping the pace fast enough that I didn't want to put it down, but not so fast that I couldn't catch up to what was happening in the first place. The characters are believable and so is the world they are in. The story feels like it should be a giant epic tale of no less than four or five hundred pages but the author is able to tell it and tell it well at a mere one hundred thirty seven count. The scenes with the necessary exposition do not feel shoe-horned in or forced at all, but I never felt like things had been left out for the sake of page count." -- She Never Slept

"The characters are full-blooded and compelling, even the bad

About the Author

Sara M. Harvey was born and raised in the San Francisco Bay Area and, after many years of being footloose and fancy free, rather unexpectedly settled down in Nashville, TN.

She is the author of *A Year and a Day*, *The Blood of Angels Trilogy: The Convent of the Pure*, *The Labyrinth of the Dead*, and *The Tower of the Forgotten*, as well as numerous short stories. She is a recovering goth (who isn't trying too hard) and Steampunk enthusiast, loves the New Wave 80s station on her satellite radio, drinks Tennessee Brew Works beer, and has recently fallen hard for Agent Coulson and the rest of the Marvel Cinematic Universe.

Sara has a background in costuming and has had as her dayjob: making costumes at Walt Disney World, making costumes for the Renaissance Pleasure Faires in CA and WI, teaching costume history and art history at the college level, and working with Franne Lee as a theatrical costume designer.

She lives at "The House of Golden Leaves" in Nashville with her aforementioned awesome husband, Matt, her daughter, Beatrice, who has more fans than Sara does, and three dogs that also have their own fan club.

Her website is saramharvey.com, you can tweet her @ saraphina_marie, and keep up on her madcap adventures at facebook.com/saramharvey.

guys, who are deliciously evil. Harvey writes cleanly and with style. The story moves at a good clip, but never sacrifices character for action. The love that Portia has for Imogen pours out of every page. But there is more to the story than lost love. Everything, and everyone, comes together at the end for a cliffhanger that has me waiting breathlessly for the next installment. *The Labyrinth Of The Dead* is a great chapter in what could prove to be a fantastic trilogy. Highly recommended." -- Monster Librarian

"*The Labyrinth of the Dead* is a sensual, apocryphal nightmare — an exquisite adventure that manages to be both epic and personal, sweet and vicious."
—Cherie Priest, Hugo Award-nominated author of *Boneshaker, Fathom,* and *Four and Twenty Blackbirds*

The Tower of the Forgotten:

"Each piece is carefully constructed and combined, making the whole story like one of those weird foods that sound so bizzare but taste so good. Like a bacon cupcake, or so I imagine. The first taste leaves you intrigued and each bite thereafter takes you deeper into a world you never imagined could exist but yet here it is, tangible and ready for further exploration. Much like said cupcake, I finished *The Tower of the Forgotten* in record time and it left me wanting more. I give this book 5 out of 5 tentacles and beg Sara M. Harvey to write more of this world and it's inhabitants."
-- She Never Slept

"Sara M. Harvey writes suspenseful, romantic, and exciting steampunk that is not to be missed. An absolute delight!" —Lavie Tidhar, World Fantasy Award-nominated author of *The Bookman and Camera Obscura.*

Other books by Sara M. Harvey:

From Apex Publications:

The Convent of the Pure
The Labyrinth of the Dead
The Tower of the Forgotten

From New Babel Books:

Seven Times a Woman

From Baen Books:

A Year and a Day (ebook only)

MUSIC CITY
BY SARA M. HARVEY

This book is dedicated to the good people of Nashville who took this California girl in and showed her how to love this town. OMG thanks, y'all!

And to my Kickstarter backers, I could not have done this without each and every one of you. Consider yourself honorary Nashvillians and my personal back-up singers!

Side A:

"It All Begins With a Song"

Track 1

The wailing went on a long time, emanating from the grassy mound behind her, a keening song steeped in loss and regret; a song sung for the dead that echoed across the whole of Ireland.

It rose and fell on the wind, from a high, shrill pitch spiraling down to a tone that rumbled the stones beneath the moss and peat. First one voice then joined little by little until an unearthly chorus gave voice to their grief with wrenching, heartbreaking cries.

Keela stood and listened, the tears on her face mingling with the softly falling rain. The song they sang was for her, still living, but dead to them, dead to all of them.

Somewhere else, perhaps the banshees sang a song of remembrance for Michael O'Neill, taken from this life so abruptly and too soon. She had hoped to be invited to their vigil, but knew she had no chance. She was, after all, the one who had caused his death. Not in truth, really, but had she not become involved with him, he would be living still. That was a fact undisputed, even by her. The rest, however…

The silvery horse beside her stamped its hoof and

snorted impatiently. Keela patted its shoulder and looked down the long, perfectly straight path through the wet grass. It was a subtle trail, the only indication was that the grass grew at a different angle there and shimmered just a little.

"I know, it's time, isn't it?" The horse rolled its blood-red eyes and tossed its head. "Long past time," Keela agreed.

She climbed onto the horse's back, hiking up her green wool dress to sit astride. She carried nothing but the clothes on her back: the dress and her grey cloak. The exiled don't need luggage.

The moment she was settled, the horse took off galloping along the trod, its hooves muffled by the wet grass. Keela breathed deeply of peat and rain, trying to commit the odors to memory as perfectly as she could. The keening wail continued, growing softer but no less poignant as she was spirited far away from the only home she had ever known. Around her, in the distance, lights went on in houses and she felt the tickle of warding prayers being said.

Dear little mortals, she thought towards them, *no one sings for one of yours tonight. Tonight they keen for one of their own.*

The night flew by, wrapped in rain and sorrow; the banshees cried until daybreak. But by then, Keela O'Reardon was a world away.

***

Michael had been from Galway.

Their romance was doomed from the moment they first met, at the top of O'Brien's Castle on the Cliffs of Moher, but that didn't seem to deter either of them.

He had been an auburn-haired young man with soft green eyes and a large crow on his shoulder. Keela knew what that meant; she could read the other banshee's clan in the bird's aura and bearing. She was an O'Neill plain as day, in the direct lineage of Ireland's bloodline of kings. She puffed her feathers and stretched her wings, making clear her claim on this young man.

Keela had never had a charge, a mortal whose death was entrusted to her keeping, and she longed for that kind of intimacy, that kind of connection, the forging of soul and song.

Keela sniffed and considered turning herself into a crow as well and perching on the fellow's other shoulder, just to be a pain. She disliked the O'Neill banshees, who were always putting on airs. Nobility was more than the accident of being born into the right family, but there was no convincing them of it. She turned back to the waves far below her, the rush and crash and icy, salty wind. This was one of her favorite places to come and hide out for a while, to be among mortals and not to have to worry about singing for them. And to be among mortals too distracted to take much notice of a specter of death hanging about. Plus, the castle had wi-fi.

Keela's mother had always admonished her against the companionship of mortals. "Do the collies make friends with the sheep? No, because it isn't their job. Their lot is only to guard and shepherd them from one place to the next, and so it is with yourself. Dallying with humans will only end in tears for you both."

Keela had never been one to listen well enough to her mother.

But she moved to the other vantage point, looking southwest toward Hag's Head, to give the O'Neills their space. The pale sunlight broke through the clouds in places, scattering glittering patches across the sea. From somewhere below she heard seals barking. She gathered her cloak tighter around her, but the wind sought every bit of exposed skin. She never did like the cold, even though she'd been born in the cool dampness of the barrows far beneath the peat fields.

She tried to wrap her scarf another time around her neck, but the wind grabbed it and blew it away. Cursing, she turned to catch it only to find that someone already had.

"I believe this belongs to yourself," he said with a triumphant smile, holding the two flapping yards of sage green knit. It was Keela's very favorite scarf, for it matched her dress.

"Yes, thank you!"

"Here, allow me." He stepped close to her and placed the scarf around her neck, winding it twice and securing it with a firm knot. "Won't be getting away now, will it?"

His fingertips had brushed her neck and he didn't even blink. Most humans felt the chilly promise of death in a banshee's touch. That's when Keela knew that he had been a banshee's lover. And likely still was except that the bird was now nowhere to be seen.

She decided to tip her hand. "Thank you, Mr. O'Neill."

He squinted in surprise, making delightful little crow's feet pop out along the top of his cheekbones. He took a half step back and looked her over. "Of course," he said. "Black hair, grey eyes, skin like alabaster wearing a not-quite-fashionable green woolen dress and a sturdy yet antique dark grey cloak. I should have recognized you at once!" He reached out and took Keela's hand, bowing in exaggerated gallantry and kissing it. "Michael O'Neill at your service. Or I suppose you would be at mine, wouldn't you? My funeral service."

She laughed at his joke, and at the ease with which it was delivered. This young man was used to dealing with banshees, that was certain. She could tell by his posture and the tone of his voice that he had no fear of death.

"Not yours, I'm afraid. My name is Keela O'Reardon."

"Ah, well, I suppose I should enjoy your company now, then, shouldn't I?"

She demurred, "You seem to have enough company already."

He made a noise that was half laugh and half cough. "Maeve? Hardly. I sometimes think she follows me around because it makes her look important. It used to scare me; I thought it meant I was about to die at any moment." He readjusted his tweed cap, pressing it firmly down to his ears. "But I, uhh, figured out what her intentions actually were."

He blushed and glanced over his shoulder, looking for either Maeve or mortal eavesdroppers, Keela wasn't sure.

"I see. Well, it was nice meeting you, Michael." She turned back to the steps leading down into the tower. She supposed she could have turned into a crow herself and flap away, but that seemed unnecessarily dramatic.

He touched her arm. "Wait! Please. That came out wrong." Taking a longer look around, he lead her around to the bench, positioned facing west to best see the sunset, should the clouds ever break enough to show it. "What I meant to say," he told her softly, "is that I know what you are. And I'm not afraid. And that was a long time ago, with Maeve. It's different between us now. She's like my *sister*." He made a face, sticking out his tongue in mock disgust. "I'm doing this all wrong. Can I buy you a pint to make up for me being an arse?"

"You haven't been an arse." Keela laughed. "You've actually been quite charming. I'm not used to flirtation, I rather like it." *That was too bold*, she thought, *too bold by half!*

He grinned and his eyes crinkled again at the corners. "You're not like my banshee," Michael whispered, his voice barely audible above the howl of the wind. "They take themselves too seriously. You're more like I imagined a banshee would be like as a youngster. Do you like to dance?" He mimed classic goth moves, clearing imaginary cobwebs with his hands swept over his head and then reaching up and twisting his wrists as if changing an invisible lightbulb.

Keela put the back of her hand to her forehead and leaned back, looking as insulted as she could manage. Then, giggling, she made as if she was handing him a cup of tea, then swished her arm away from him, wrapping it across her chest with a toss of her head.

"It's settled, then! Let's hit Considíne's Bar and then see if we can find a club hosting a goth night anywhere in Galway."

"I like Trad, too, you know, doesn't even have to be the slow, sad stuff, either. I like me some jigs and reels as much as the next Irishwoman! So, any place will do, so long as there's music." She couldn't believe she was agreeing to a date with an O'Neill boy!

"Of course," he smiled, taking her hand in his. His fingers were cold, but hers were colder, she knew. He didn't seem to mind one bit. "So long as there's music."

That was how it began. Such a simple, carefree beginning it was, too. They met for beer, or whiskey, or coffee, or dancing, or just a quiet walk along the River Corrib. She never wanted to leave; it was as if Galway belonged to them, a place stolen out of time just for the two of them. And the mortals around them, usually so susceptible to the presence of harbingers, just shrugged and smiled as if Keela was nothing more than Michael's peculiar girlfriend. The bands played late into the night for them while Michael sang along. Keela never joined in.

It wasn't that she didn't enjoy singing, in fact, she sang constantly when alone. But she'd been admonished by her mother and aunts and sisters over it enough times that she dared not utter a single note in public. Not because she feared losing their good graces, but because she truly feared what loosing that voice might actually do. So, she let Michael sing, and it warmed her heart.

Michael was smitten. Keela was head over heels. She hung around his little flat above a row of shops off of Mainguard Street. He managed a little touristy place that sold hats and coats and faux Galway shawls over on Merchant's Road. He played the fiddle very well and confessed to Keela his dream of performing.

"I'm an O'Neill, you know? That kind of legacy weighs on a man. I feel like I'm destined for more than this."

Sometimes they stayed in and Michael played for them while Keela danced, light-footed, on the hardwood floor. She never sang here either, for fear of terrifying the neighbors. And of accidentally opening up the doors of death.

Neither of them had seen Maeve since that chance encounter on an autumn afternoon, but Keela had felt her watchful -and disapproving- eyes on them nearly every day. She was not about to give her rival the satisfaction of being scared off of her prize. But she was suspicious that it had all gone so well and so easily. Far too easily.

Now it was early spring. The chill in the air was tempered by the brightening sun, and new buds swelled on the trees. It made Michael romantic and philosophical. It made Keela shy and unsure, suddenly wondering what kind of future a human and a banshee could ever hope for.

The night Michael died wasn't much different from any other. They stayed in. He ordered take-out, they sat together making cheerful, fluffy small talk. He pushed aside the half-eaten curry fries and took Keela's hands. He never seemed to mind how cold they were.

"I want you to know, you mean the world to me."

"Michael," she squeezed his fingers, "you know things can only go so far. Humans and faeries…it almost always ends badly for the human."

"*Almost* always." He winked at her. "We just never hear the stories about the ones who live out their years blissfully and dully happy."

"Optimist." She leaned forward and kissed him. He tasted like curry and Guinness.

Michael brought his hands up and ran them along the sides of her throat, then curled his fingers into her hair. He held her tight as she stiffened and tried to back away.

"Shhh," he soothed, bringing his left hand up the back of her head, angling towards the silver comb she always wore. All banshees had one, most wore theirs every day. The combs had power, great power. Mortals were never supposed to touch them. *Ever.*

"I thought you'd like it if I brushed your hair."

"No!"

"Why?"

Keela shook her head. She reached back for the comb. "Let me take this out first."

"Please, allow me." His hand darted past her eyes in a playful manner and she tried to duck her head out of his reach. Michael's fingertip traced the edge of the scrollwork on the comb before he pulled it free with a flourish. "Ah ha!"

Keela's midnight black hair uncoiled from the French twist she'd pulled it up into and fanned out across her shoulders and then swept down her back.

He smiled at her with delighted pride for the span of a single heartbeat before falling over dead.

"Michael!"

Somewhere between his collapse and the floor, he vanished.

The O'Neill banshees, led by Maeve, appeared there in an instant. Of course she'd know. Michael belonged to her. She'd have felt the instant of his death. Maeve had a grimly smug smile on her face, as if this turn of events was far from unexpected. Keela's heart sank even further.

"Why, hello Keela O'Reardon, imagine finding yourself here," she said in a tone that was anything but surprised. "I was looking for Michael, my charge."

Keela's mouth went dry and she dumbly pointed to the empty place on the floor where Michael's body should have been.

Maeve played stupid, still smiling. "Has he gone out, then? I can wait, we all can, can't we?" Maeve and her three sisters sat down on the couch.

Keela stood there, unable to move. Tears squeezed out from beneath her eyelids and her body shuddered from top to bottom. She finally forced a sound from her lips, nothing but a low moan at first. It reverberated through her very bones and in that moment her black hair turned brilliantly silver and her eyes glowed red. The song stirred the other three O'Neill banshees to sing, slinking down off the couch to kneel around the place Michael should have been.

Maeve remained silently sitting, her satisfaction gone now. Keela sang louder, pouring out her broken heart into that empty place on the floor. Keela had never had a charge of her own; as her clan's youngest, she'd always been deemed too green and too brash. The keening had grown to a crescendo when Maeve finally stood.

"Enough! You are a pretending little trollop, playing house with an O'Neill far above your station. And you further disgrace yourself by singing for him." When Keela did not immediately fall silent, Maeve took two quick steps over to her and slapped her as hard as she could across the mouth.

Keela staggered a step back, her tears finally coming in a rush now as the full measure of what had happened sank in. She did not object when the O'Neill sisters took her by the arms and delivered her back to their barrow where their matron was already waiting.

Eimear O'Neill was an imposing figure, tall and lean with elongated fingers and a towering neck. She had the look of an ancient and powerful sídhe, which she was, make no mistake. Keela knelt to her immediately. Keela's unbound hair, still gleaming silver, fell like a curtain that hid her from the matriarch's scorching glare.

"Where is your comb?" The banshee woman asked.

"With Michael O'Neill," Keela confessed. "On the other side."

Eimear growled. "So, it's true, then?"

Keela nodded, unable to speak or meet the banshee's eyes.

"How long had you known about this dalliance,

Maeve?"

Peeking sideways through her hair, Keela saw Maeve pale and turn away. For a moment, she thought she might not bear the full brunt of the blame.

But then Maeve, in an Oscar-worthy performance with lips quivering and tears falling said, "I knew nothing, Mother, until the moment when he was rent from my soul and dragged unwilling into death. How could he have been slumming like that? Who would have imagined he'd fall for such a tawdry little O'Reardon tramp?" She sucked in a breath, as if between sobs. "It was terrible, Mother. There isn't even a body! What are we to do?"

Eimear sighed. "Did you sing for him?"

"Of course I did! He was my charge!"

"No, you didn't." Keela worked past the block in her throat. "I did. The others did. But not you. You never sang."

"Lying bitch!" Maeve lunged for Keela but Eimear stepped in front of her.

"Calm yourself, Maeve!" Her eyes, black as night, flickered between them. "Tell me truly. Did you sing for him? Because it may be a blessing if you did not."

Maeve considered, her face gone calculating and cold. "Why is that?"

"Because we may be able to get him back. Your song is needed to seal his soul to the realm of the dead. If you didn't sing for him, we can get him back."

She threw herself at her mother's feet, encircling her legs with trembling arms. "Oh, Mother! You always can see the truth, can't you? I was so ashamed I hadn't managed to sing for him! That the shock of my dear, beloved Michael dead by another banshee's hand locked the song in my heart!" Fat tears rolled over her cheeks, splashing onto the neckline of her green gown and leaving shining tracks down her neck. "But now..? Now my failure might be his salvation?"

Eimear bent down and took Maeve's hands. "Yes, my darling, it very well might be. Come on, now, no more of this. Dry your tears. It'll be all right."

Keela hated her so much in that moment.

With her arm around Maeve's waist, Eimear turned to Keela. "What you must do, young O'Reardon, is bring him back."

"Me?"

"Of course *you*. You sent him there, it was your comb. So you must bring him back."

"How? Without my comb, I haven't the power any longer to sing open the portal."

She nodded. "But there is another way. There is a song of great power. A banshee song of old. Were you to sing that song, you would have the power to bring him back to the land of the living."

Keela's heart leapt. "Seriously? Yes! I'll sing it!"

Eimear's smile was cold. "Then you must find it."

"Where is it?"

"No one knows, anymore. It was stolen centuries ago. The last I knew, it had gone to Boston."

"In *America*?"

"The very same."

Keela had never left Ireland, and the thought of traveling across the Atlantic alone on the hunt for an ancient song frightened her. "I don't know if I can…"

Shrugging, Eimear said. "I don't suppose it matters where you go. You're not going to return to Irish soil until Michael is brought back."

"I'm not…?

Eimear let go of Maeve and drew herself up to her full height. A blood-dark glow emanated from her, causing her silvery hair to sparkle and lift slightly away from her black-clad shoulders. The words rang out from her, each one as clear as the tolling of a bronze bell.

"Keela O'Reardon, you are hereby banished from Ireland. Your feet may never touch Irish soil again until you find the song, the *Oran na Céle*, and return it to us, with Michael O'Neill."

The *geis* fell hard upon Keela, the words of the binding settling deep into her bones.

"Can I at least say good-bye to my family?" She was ashamed at how small and pathetic her voice sounded.

Maeve sputtered, outraged, but Eimear only nodded curtly. "So long as you are off my shores before sunrise."

"I am grateful, my lady," was all Keela could say.

She rose, finally, on shaking legs and bowed to Eimear. Maeve and her sisters surrounded her and escorted her from their barrow.

They stood outside in the pale moonlight, hair silvered with the night.

Keela stood her ground before Maeve. "Why did you tell him to take my comb, Maeve?"

Maeve cocked her head to one side. "Did yourselves hear that? I thought I heard the cawing of a little crow."

Her sisters laughed.

"Why?" Keela pressed. "He never took note of it before."

"I did no such thing! You are too bold for asking. The very nerve of it!"

"I know you did it. You're a jealous cow, Maeve O'Neill. Perhaps if you weren't such an uppity bitch, he might not have strayed."

That hit a nerve and Maeve came flying at her, fingernails clawing her face. They fell back into the wet grass and Maeve, taller by a hand's breadth, pinned Keela to the peat.

"Spit all the venom you want, you viper. But you can't prove anything. From where I'm standing, you're the traitorous whore spreading her legs for other banshees' charges and then offing them. Was he going to leave you for *fresher* pastures, little hussy?"

"No. I think he was going to marry me." Keela said it with awe, no longer seeing Maeve, remembering only the dreamy look in Michael's eyes as he reached for her hair. Those were the eyes of a man with an idea in his head, a foolish, romantic, impossible, idiotic notion to take a banshee to wife.

She snapped to with Maeve's hands locked around her throat. The other O'Neills were dragging her back, but it took all of them to sever the contact. Maeve screamed terrible things, her howling curses echoed through the night as her sisters hauled her back toward their barrow.

"Never come back," Maeve roared. "Never!"

Keela fled, running just a few steps before transforming herself into a crow and flapping off to find her own family and say goodbye.

The sun would be rising soon.

Track 2

Had it been a weekend night, she likely would have attracted more attention. But it was a Tuesday and the horse knew its business well enough. Pookahs were a canny lot. It deposited her along a mostly deserted alleyway behind a row of businesses in the middle of what used to be the heart of Irish culture in Boston. Southie, she learned the neighborhood was called.

One moment Keela was hanging onto the horse's slapping silver mane and the next she was clumsily — and not fully of her own volition — sliding off its back. The echoing clatter of hooves rang off the brick walls all around her and faded away. A few doors opened, curious faces peering out, but no one ventured out into the alley. She closed her eyes against the weariness and panic that threatened to overwhelm her.

Although it had been nearly dawn when she left Ireland, here in Boston it was only mid-evening. She could hear traffic and voices from the street ahead of her, the sounds of dinnertime winding down. And there was something else, too: an unmistakable melody beneath the mundane city sounds. There were banshees here.

Keela followed the tune, feeling it in her soul, the song of her kin. The omnipresent streetlights and neon advertisements in bar windows kept her hair black and her eyes grey, but her dress and cloak marked her as strange. Someone offered her money but she shook her head, confused.

She wandered up West Broadway, following a song so soft she didn't think any human could detect it. Boston smelled like home. Not in the gritty fumes and greenish-grey odor of the bay, but in the flavor of magic that permeated the place. Irish magic. Yet it had a strange accent. They called their basketball team the Celtics, but pronounced it with an S sound.

She followed the tune that sang to her of her own family ties; not just banshees, these were O'Reardons. She found five of them lounging in a booth at the rear of the Cornerstone Pub, a non-descript locals' spot with a hockey game playing loudly on the television. The song of her own blood brought Keela to them as if led by the hand.

She stood awkwardly in the doorway until a tall waitress came over and began haranguing her, committing frightening atrocities against vowels and abusing the letter R. One of the banshees from the booth was beside her in an instant.

"Here she is, fresh off the boat by the look of her! Lay off, Karen, this isn't some homeless nutjob looking for scraps." The banshee took Keela firmly by the elbow and pulled her towards the table. She plopped her down on the cracked vinyl and ordered her a Jameson. "You look like you've got a story to tell, sister!"

Karen, still looking quite put out, brought over the drink with a frown.

"Relax, would ya?" said Keela's rescuer. The waitress scowled but left without further comment.

Keela sipped the whiskey. It felt good.

The others waited for her to speak, each not-so-patiently fiddling with her own drink, shredding a cocktail napkin, picking at something on her arm, and so on.

"My name's Keela," she said, finally.

Her rescuer smiled, "I'm Fiona." She was the tallest of the lot of them and had the bearing of a natural leader. She pointed to a sweet-faced, young woman with full, soft lips and said with affection, "This is Grace."

Across the table were two banshees with their hair

cut short, something Keela had never seen before. One had a round face and very large eyes and was introduced as Maggie, the other had angular features and a hawkish nose and was called Noreen. The last of them was a waifish girl with earbuds in who wasn't paying any attention to the rest of them. Fiona introduced her as Eileen.

"O'Reardons all, of course," said Fiona.

"I know," Keela nodded. "I could hear you from all the way down the road."

Maggie raised an eyebrow. "How's that?"

Keela shrugged. "I don't know, just seemed that I could. Weren't you singing?"

"Well, the Bruins are playing," Maggie said dryly and the others laughed.

Keela didn't get it.

"What brings you all the way across the sea?" Grace asked.

Keela bit her lip. "It's a long story."

"I'll order us another round, then." Fiona stood and flagged down the reluctant waitress.

"Are there more of you?" Keela asked.

"Nope," said Fiona. "You're looking at the entirety of Clan O'Reardon here in Boston. We get together as often as we can, try to stay in touch like good cousins should."

"But there are other banshees here, aye?"

Maggie made a face. "Yeah, but who wants to hang out with them? You looking to trade up or something?"

"No. Only curious. I've never been away from home. America is so big, I thought there'd be more of yourselves, is all."

"Geez, we're O'Reardons, not O'Neills!" Noreen laughed. "There just aren't that many O'Reardon folk, not compared to other families. They hardly need us five, really."

The others nodded.

When the pitcher of ice cold Guinness had arrived and been distributed, Fiona bade Keela to start talking.

"Do they really drink it warm in Ireland?" Noreen interrupted.

"No place that I've ever been."

"I want to hear about the important stuff. You two can discuss beer later," Fiona told her.

Noreen apologized and Keela took a gulp of her beer to drum up the nerve to tell the whole story.

She started with the Cliffs of Moher, tearfully reliving her precious and short-lived romance with Michael O'Neill. They sniffled along with her, grew indignant at her betrayal and voiced their own revenge plots, then fell silent as she relayed her binding to them.

"Damn," said Maggie. "An honest to goodness *geis*. Who even does that anymore?"

"The Matriarch of Clan O'Neill apparently," Fiona answered.

"So the song," Grace asked. "What did she call it?"

"*Oran na Céle*. It means 'Song of the Companion.'"

The others nodded. "And you haven't any idea where it might be?" Maggie asked.

"No." Keela shook her head. "Honestly, I was hoping yourselves might know. It's supposed to be here."

"Here in Boston?" Fiona sounded incredulous. Meanwhile Noreen and Maggie made playful fun of Keela's accent. "*I was hoping yourselves might know.*"

"You've never even heard of it, have you?" Keela looked to Fiona who shook her head.

"But you hadn't either, right? Sounds like an O'Neill thing."

"I think they might be sending you on a wild goose chase," Noreen said.

"Wild goose?"

"Putting you on," Grace explained. "Sending you off on an impossible quest."

"No, I think it's real," she told them. "I can't explain why, but something about the way Eimear O'Neill talked about it made me believe her."

"I know how we can find out," said a small voice. Eileen pulled the iPod buds out of her ears and twiddled them, nervously. She had been sitting against the wall and only half listening to the conversation, offering little to it. But her eyes grew fierce and sharp, glittering in the dim light. Very few of these American banshees could be much older than 300 years, still teenagers by Irish banshee standards, but Eileen seemed to really enjoy looking the part.

"And how's that?" Noreen crossed her arms and glared down at the slip of a girl beside her.

"We ask the oracle, the Fae of True Telling."

Fiona laughed, unkindly. "Sure, we just pop right on over to her super-secret location and have a chat, eh? This isn't a solstice or equinox when she could be petitioned. We'd have to track her down and by the time we'd found her, Keela here'd have her little ditty and be headed back to the motherland."

Eileen shook her head. "For fuck's sake, Fiona! She's just down the street!"

That silenced the whole table.

"She's *what*?" Fiona rose and leaned across the table, her long braid nearly falling into her pint. "How the hell do you know that?"

"I went with a Guardian once. He talked in his sleep."

The others stared, open-mouthed, incredulous.

Fiona laughed. "A Guardian went out with you?"

Eileen licked her tongue against her tiny, sharp teeth and said without any trace of shame, "He liked to be bitten."

"Can you tell me?" Keela said. "I mean about the oracle."

"I can do better. I can show you. Come on, it's not far from here." Eileen pushed out of the booth, elbowing her sisters and heading for the door.

Keela caught up to the diminutive banshee and followed her closely. But they didn't go far, just stepped outside and crossed the street to a glass-enclosed T station.

"We're taking the Red Line?" Fiona asked, still sounding doubtful.

"Sort of. Follow me."

Fiona looked skeptically at the other three banshees and they shared a shrug. Keela decisively walked after Eileen as she skipped down the stairs like an ordinary commuter.

Down in the station, Eileen boldly walked up to the futuristic-looking entry gates. She pulled a plastic card out of her jeans pocket and blew on it. "Watch this."

She swiped it across the little icon on the gate. The tinted plastic gates slid open with a whoosh, and Eileen ushered them all through, ignoring the beep of protest as she held the gates a little too long. But no one seemed to notice them, and Eileen led the way past white and red tiled pillars decorated with handmade plaques created by the neighborhood schoolchildren.

"Is this something that all of you can do?" Keela asked, indicating the trick with the card and the gate.

Fiona laughed. "Hell, I didn't even know Eileen could do that!"

"Went out with a Tommyknocker, too."

"Eileen!" Maggie looked entirely scandalized.

"What?" She shrugged. "There's a lot more to me than you people realize. Still waters run deep, you know."

"Deep and slutty," Noreen muttered.

Maggie punched her. "Lay off. Shall we name all *your* boyfriends?"

Keela watched their exchange but said nothing. She was far from prudish, but even among her sisters she would never have been so frank in discussing her dalliances.

The door lock to a service entrance had a dozen silver buttons on an impressive-looking mount attached to the door itself, but with a showy puff of breath, the mechanism clacked open for Eileen and she ducked inside.

No one said another word about her erstwhile lovers.

They went after her into an overbright corridor with a line of "CAUTION: WET FLOOR" signs and stained industrial rolling mop buckets against one wall and a series of OSHA regulations crudely taped to the other. They followed the hall as it took a hard right turn and descended a set of stairs, then Eileen began to count the doors they passed. Each one had one of those electronic lock boxes.

Here the overhead fluorescent lights were dimmer, and only every few were lit. It gave the corridor a sinister appearance. Like Keela's, the American banshees' hair shifted from black to silver as they moved from light to darkness.

Fiona and Grace brought up the rear and remained silent, while the other two — Maggie and Noreen — held onto one another and chattered nervously. Eileen opened another door and waited until they all caught up.

"Now you can't go blabbing this to everyfae, okay? Anlon trusted me with this, sort of. I mean he didn't cut my tongue out when he found out I knew, so I'll take that as trust."

The cobweb-coated hinges made some complaint

as Eileen pushed open the door and sought out the light switch. A single compact fluorescent bulb flared to life showing them a corridor with mismatched walls of bricks and cinderblock and cement patching. Eileen opened the dinged metal cabinet near the door and pulled out a three flashlights, giving one to Fiona, one to Keela, and keeping the other for herself. She ignored Maggie's protests and continued into the waiting darkness that hovered beyond the circle of the bulb's light.

The three beams swayed and sliced through the darkness of the narrow hall and all conversation, even the nervous chatter, ceased. Keela stayed behind Eileen, sweeping her beam along the uneven floor while Eileen aimed her light along the walls, searching. They frightened more than a few rats, but Maggie only screamed once.

The shape of the corridor changed at some point, Keela realized, into a tunnel with a rounded ceiling and walls. She shone her light down on a strangely shaped bit of floor just in time to not trip over the length of metal sitting just above the unevenly poured concrete. Another one lay parallel to it a few feet away. Tracks.

"Are we in a train tunnel?"

"Yeah," Eileen said. "This is part of an old line they stopped using forever ago, like the 1920s."

Keela decided not to challenge her new friend on the concept of "forever ago" being less than a century.

Eileen slowed to a stop, her flashlight beam dancing around the curved wall. "The door is not easy to find." She approached an alcove that had once been part of a ventilation shaft now sealed off, running her fingers along the grooves between the large bricks and grumbling beneath her breath. "Got it!"

Noreen came over to help Eileen pull while Keela held both flashlights. They could only slide their fingers so far between the bricks, and it took several tries to get the door to even budge. It was pure trust that there was even a door there to begin with.

Finally, after a growling, scraping sound, a vaguely door-shaped hunk of wall swung out of what looked like solid brick. Before them stretched a long, narrow passage carved into the bedrock and reinforced here and there with stonework. At intervals someone had hung fretted copper lanterns that cast fluttering shadows in the shapes of Celtic knotwork and strange beasts.

The other four banshees drew a collective breath. Even Keela stood amazed. Eileen grinned with fierce pride and beckoned over her shoulder without looking back. She stepped into the warmly lit opening and drew aside to let the others through. As she pushed the heavy masonry door shut behind them all, they remained still, eyes adjusting to the soft, golden light. They turned off their flashlights and left them there by the door at Eileen's instruction.

"Well?" Fiona prompted.

Eileen shrugged, looking a little helpless. "Anlon always met me here in the corridor. I have never been any farther."

"Here?" Noreen sounded incredulous.

"Sometimes we went out. Sometimes we stayed in. There's another little alcove just over there. It's cozy."

"*Anyway…*" Fiona interrupted her and looked at Keela. "What do you think we ought to do?"

"Well, there is only one way to go." Keela glanced down the hall, squinting to see past the last few lamps. "So, let's be off."

She turned and led them deeper into this secret space, finding at its end another door, this one broad and made of oak, and unlike the hidden masonry door, quite obvious. It had been set into the wall that sealed the tunnel.

"Do we knock?" Maggie whispered.

"Why not?" Fiona came forward and rapped loudly on the well-aged boards.

The moment of silence stretched taut before heavy treads came to a stop on the other side of the door.

"It can't really be this easy," Noreen said.

"Who dares disturb our peace?" The rough, male voice sounded more bewildered than threatening. But all the same, the five American banshees all looked at Keela, and Grace nudged her towards the door.

"I am Keela O'Reardon and I come to seek the counsel of the Fae of True Telling."

"The oracle only hears petitions at the Solstices and Equinoxes. Come back, then." The footsteps faded away.

"Nope," Noreen muttered. "Not gonna be that easy."

Track 3

Keela knocked on the door. There was no reply. She knocked again, louder. And again, no one answered. Letting her temper get the better of her, she pounded on the door hard enough to make the hinges creak and long enough that the footsteps on the other side sounded hurried and flustered.

A series of locks clattered and slid, and the door opened inward. Keela fell through, into the arms of a tall, sturdy gentleman. The yellow lantern-light gilded him, casting strange shadows into the folds of the grey cloak he wore draped carelessly across one shoulder. He smelled damp and loamy, like the inside of a barrow. A dozen or so flickering swirls of greenish-yellow light bobbed around him like soap bubbles. A few of them trickled out and floated around the women who stood awestruck before the door.

Keela righted herself and adjusted her own cloak, one similar in styling but made of a lighter weight lambswool. The will-o'-the-wisps surprised her, and she couldn't help but smile at them. She reached her hand out to touch one and it dipped, almost playfully, away then coyly returned to brush itself against her fingertips before winking out and reappearing a few feet away. The others flickered in a rhythmic fashion before coming to hover between Keela and the tall man in the doorway.

A surprised smile softened his sharp, angular features. "They like you."

Keela smiled and reached out for one of the wisps with awe. "I didn't expect to find meadow spirits underground in Boston."

"I didn't expect to find a passel of banshees at the door." He crossed his arms and sighed. "I suppose I had best ask you ladies in, hadn't I?"

"We're not about to leave," Fiona said, firmly.

"And we did come all this way just for this," Noreen added.

He turned to look at her, wry amusement crimping the edges of her grey eyes. "I don't think you came very far, my dear and local Lady O'Reardon. How many yards is the Cornerstone Pub from this very spot?"

Noreen bristled and Grace laid a hand on her forearm. "Too true," she said, setting her other hand on Keela's shoulder. "It's this one that wanted the audience and it's this one what came the long way."

"How far?" he asked.

"Ireland. This is dire, a man's life depends on it."

"A *mortal* man? You've come across the sea and sought us out to beseech the Oracle on behalf of a mortal?"

Keela pursed her lips, holding back a comment that, although would make her feel better, would not help the situation. "Aye. A mortal. And there's much more to it than that, which is no business of yours."

He bowed towards Keela. "Forgive me, Lady O'Reardon ap Erin. I am Molan MacLiath, Guardian of the Fae of True Telling."

He did not, however, say a single word about letting them inside.

The sweet, musty odor from his cloak — like it had been left damp for too long — was not altogether unpleasant, but it filled her with a sharp pang of homesickness. She swallowed it and smiled up at the guardian as sweetly as she could. "A pleasure, sir. Is this a convenient time for speaking to the oracle? It is a terribly important matter, I assure you."

He pressed his lips together. "Well, we can ask. But I make no promises. Not a single one."

"Of course," Keela said, gently, making every effort to remain calm.

The wisps encircled her, drawing her forward over the threshold. She stepped into what only could be described as a foyer nestled into a cavernous chamber that had once been a rail car station. The bobbing wisps scattered in her wake, rising and falling and tumbling to all sides. The entry hall made every attempt at being welcoming and warm, even though the banshees' steps echoed along with the formidable boom of the door closing and locking behind them all. Maggie whimpered once more and Eileen tried not to make too big a show of looking for her former lover.

Molan guided them into the main hall and past the vaulted ceilings tiled with elaborate mosaic Art Nouveau designs. Several rooms, only slightly smaller, lay situated off this central chamber: the remnants of old passenger platforms. In one of these parlors, one decorated in warm tones of sage and amber, Molan left the others.

"You must present yourself to the Fae of True Telling alone," he instructed.

"You mean right now?"

He tilted his head to one side, a slightly impish smile tugging at his lips. "Of course. You said it was terribly important and I would be happy to take you immediately. Isn't that what you want?"

She glanced back at the other O'Reardon banshees and hesitated. The exhaustion was finally catching up with her.

How long has it been since I've slept?

"Come on, I'll walk with you until we get to the sanctuary. We won't know if she'll hear you until we ask. Afterwards, regardless of what she decides, I can I offer you the gift of our hospitality. We so rarely have guests, this is a singular treat. Especially you, so recently come from Erin." He drew a deep breath and his voice dropped even lower in volume so that Keela could barely hear him. "So recently come that I can still smell the night air on you, the mist, and the fog." His own homesickness ached through every word and Keela's breath caught in her chest.

"Can you ever go back?" she whispered.

Molan's eyes widened and he turned away, as if he had not realized that he had spoken aloud. "No. I am sworn," he said.

Tears prickled Keela's eyelids. "And I am banished," she managed to choke out.

He stopped and turned to look her slowly up and down, as if seeing her for the first time. His grey gaze, at first unreadable, melted into a sad, sympathetic smile. "I see. I'm so sorry."

She thought he might say more, but instead he motioned her onwards.

At the far end of the grand, decaying hall, a very unobtrusive door waited. It would have once led to the maintenance area of the station. Molan took her down a small, winding stair and into another domed room. The green-gold spheres followed them, drifting down around them. As they descended, the dampness that seemed to breathe from his cloak reminded Keela of the heavy scent of fog at night over the meads. Realization dawned: he was a Grey Man, a fae of the fog with power over the weather, the master of the will-o'-the-wisps who often confounded travelers by drawing them off the road and into the bogs. Grey Men were of the land as much as banshees were of the blood of Ireland.

How much it must pain him to be severed from it, she thought. And wondered how he ever came to agree to this.

"Things were dire in 1847," he said. "I made my choice and, were I faced with it again, I wouldn't have made another. I have replayed that moment over and over for more than a century and I always end up here."

"Do you often read people's thoughts?"

He looked genuinely rebuked. "You weren't speaking?"

She shook her head. "I wouldn't have been so bold to have asked you. We've only just met!"

Molan blushed and it painted his pale cheeks with a nearly joyful color. "I'm…sorry. We don't get many visitors anymore, my lady O'Reardon."

"Please, call me Keela." She touched his hand. It was as cold as hers. "And please don't go troubling yourself about it."

At the bottom of the stairs another guardian stood before a set of double doors made to fit directly into the rounded shape of the old train tunnel. A faint tracery of old rails disappeared beneath the dark wood door panels. This guardian was also as pale as Molan was, but not nearly as tall; his body was lean and his whole manner was unearthly and unsettling, somewhat like a banshee but also very different.

Molan greeted him warmly. "Anlon, you might want to head upstairs. There is an old friend up there who has found her way back to you."

"Oh, is there?" Anlon's voice rustled like silk over dry leaves and his water-pale eyes darted up the spiral staircase. He glanced back at Keela and stretched his thin lips into a smile. "There's a banshee here, I see. I can only imagine it is one of her sisters that waits up there."

"Aye, it is. I am Keela O'Reardon. I believe it is Eileen with whom you are acquainted."

His words were as hushed as a graveyard whisper. "Is she well, my darling death-singer Eileen?"

"I couldn't imagine her any better."

"I will send Eamonn down to take my place. I trust you can handle the little crow, here, can't you, Molan?"

He bowed. "You can count on that."

As Anlon made his silent way up the stairwell, Molan turned his somber grey gaze on Keela. "Prepare yourself. You are from Ireland, but you have never seen any such as her. I can tell you to mind your manners and not to gawk, but it won't matter. She has that effect on most everybody. Just mind yourself and take care not to get lost. I cannot enter with you, but I will be just outside the door, here." He drew back the cloak, releasing a renewed aroma of fog and damp. From somewhere in the folds of his simple tunic he brought forth a round, flat stone, polished smooth by the sea. His smile was tinted with melancholy. "Here, little Irish sister, take this with you. It came from the place where the River Liffey spills into the Dublin Bay." He pressed the stone into her hand, his fingertips lingering a moment against her palm. "The oracle's name is Radha."

Molan opened the double doors just wide enough for Keela to slip through and shut them again the moment she cleared the threshold.

The small chamber had once been a part of the tunnel, but either nature or intention had sealed it only a few yards in. A single candle burned in an intricate glass lantern hung from the ceiling. The flame stood straight and nearly motionless in the room which was quiet as a crypt. Keela rubbed the stone between her thumb and forefinger. She could sense that she was not alone in that room and rubbed the stone faster.

A low hum rose up from the far side of the room, quickly filling it with a graceful reverberation that made the marrow in Keela's bones want to leap forth and dance with it. Instead, she sank to her knees, surprised to find the floor mostly covered in plush carpets and pillows. The candle above went out and Keela could feel the change in her hair and her eyes as the light subsided. She was aware of the subtle silver glow that emanated from her and pulled her cloak up to cover it, feeling intrusive and rude.

"Do not hide yourself from me." A voice that was not a voice lilted through the darkness. Keela knew the words, but couldn't tell whether they were spoken in Gaelic, English, or some other language entirely. "Stand up, I want to see you."

The words compelled her to move, rising on shaking legs until she stood her full height.

"Turn around."

Again, Keela did as she was bidden, moving in a slow circle.

"Why have you come?"

"I seek your counsel, oracle."

"It is neither the solstice nor the equinox. I do not give counsel at any other time," said the voice.

"Please? I have come so far and I need this knowledge so badly."

"Grief does not suit you, banshee. You sing the death. It is not yours to carry the grief."

"But I caused a death. Sort of."

"Your comb. Yes, I know. I can see it in a young man's hand. Not of your blood. But he smells of your sweat." A sigh. "You were wrong to have dallied with him. You have paid dearly."

"Can I undo it? Can I bring him back as Eimear O'Neill said?"

"You can."

"Really?" Hope leapt unexpectedly and the room glowed silver with it for an instant. And in that illumination,

Keela could see her companion dimly. A woman-shaped figure, uncommonly tall and willowy, sitting with legs drawn up demurely beneath her. "Do you know where I can find the *Oran na Céle*?"

"I do."

"Tell me, please!"

"No. I only give counsel at the solstices and equinoxes."

"Then, I have come for nothing, then?"

"Of course not," said the oracle. "I only *give* counsel at those times. All others, it must be paid for."

"Oh. I have nothing."

"Nothing?"

"I am banished, lady. I come to you bereft, with only the clothes on my back and nothing of value. Not my comb, not my power, not even my voice."

"I hear your voice perfectly well, presently," Radha said with what might have been a chuckle. "How can you say that you no longer possess it?"

Keela faltered, unsure of what to say.

"You have a voice, child, and I daresay you could even sing if it pleased you to do so. And I have decided that it would please me. Come here." Radha raised one long arm and made a beckoning gesture and Keela shuffled towards her, half of her own accord and half the oracle's command. The room grew slightly brighter as Radha's flesh began to glow as well.

Radha, Keela realized, was only vaguely woman-shaped. Her impossibly long limbs ended in hands and feet that looked like pale, smooth roots, her neck curved up from her sloping shoulders like a swan's with her strange, angular face perched atop it, eyes closed in serene contemplation. What Keela had thought might have been some kind of intricately draping robe was in fact Radha's hair grown long enough to wrap up in and still spread out like vines all around her. In the dark, it looked colorless and pale, as moonlight reflected on water.

As Keela drew near, Radha reached out for her and with a single, deft motion, cradled the banshee against her body. The flesh felt as hard and smooth as ivory and smelled gently of peat and incense.

"I would like a tale from you," the oracle said.

"I don't know any."

Radha scoffed. "Don't be ridiculous. You know the song, you were born knowing the song, the *Oran na Bean-Sidhe*. I would like to hear you sing it to me."

"Right here? Right now?"

"Yes."

"Like a performance?"

"A private one, yes."

Keela sat up straighter, pulling away from Radha's statue-like body. "Because you asked, lady."

Radha smiled and settled in to listen.

It was less like a song and more like a narrative set to a tune, a sort of specific cadence. Shivering, Keela began:

"Banshee, or *bean-sidhe*, meant 'woman of faerie.' The banshee were not ghosts as many claimed. They were likewise not vengeful spirits that took delight in the deaths of the families they watched. No, the banshee were fae through and through and carried out their duty out of love, deep and abiding," her voice faltered through the ballad, coming out flat with nerves. She soldiered on into the next section, "In the days of the Tuatha de Danann, there were already faeries in Ireland. Leprechauns and skeaghshee and merrows and the pookah, even the little sheerie bobbing and blinking along luring travelers into trouble. When the Tuatha were driven into the earthen mounds by the Milesians, they did not remove themselves from the living realm entirely. The people of Ireland called them *Aes Sidhe*: people of the mounds. Their descendants they called the *Daoine Sidhe*: the fair folk. These noble fae developed a court system by which the light and the dark — the seelie and the unseelie — shared the reign by dividing the year in half by the equinoxes. Their faerie processions can to this day, still be seen criss-crossing the Irish countryside at Beltane and on All Hallow's Eve and at a holidays in between.

"The banshee, courtiers and cousins to the Daoine Sidhe, stood apart from the courts and Wild Hunts and trooping of the fae knights. While there was many a dalliance between fae and mortal, it was the banshee who — as a people — gave their hearts and souls to humanity. "In the early days of Ireland, Aoibheall, a noble Daoine Sidhe of the Seelie Court, fell in love with a mortal man in the clan of O'Neill. The O'Neill family traced its roots back to A.D. 360 and bore in its lineage the blood of the

Kings of Tara and the High Kings of Ireland and more than a little faerie heritage as well.

"The agreement reached between the Sídhe and the ruling clans served them both well. The clans could claim and own the land upon which the mounds were located, and the Sídhe could claim tithe and protection from the clans. As well as the occasional sacrifice, mostly livestock but rumors held of the fae taking the seventh son of the seventh son and the like.

"The Lady Aoibheall and Donell O'Neill made a love-match, but it was to end in tragedy. Aoibheall had the gift of sight — not so great as Radha, the Fae of True Telling, as she was one of the Tuatha," Keela blushed and cast a glance at Radha, who only sat serenely listening as if she weren't being sung about to her very face.

"But it was sight enough to see the lines of Fate that ran their courses through the short human lives around her. Aoibheall saw Donell's death on the field of battle against the invading Norse and begged him with all of her seductive powers to stay at the hearth with her.

"'My dear lady, what would you make of me, a coward? A chieftain who would hide behind his lady's skirts rather than face the honorable death that waits him? No. I will not stay. I will fight' he said to her. 'But knowing that it is not my destiny to return to your loving arms, I would share what pleasure is left to us.'

"When he rose from her bed at dawn's break, he had resolved his fragile human heart to face his end with dignity. Aoibheall followed him into battle, hiding herself from mortal vision behind her faerie cloak, and when Donell fell — as she knew he would — she knelt at his side, cradling his head into her lap.

"The song that rose from her lips stilled the battle around them. She sang of a lover's grief of knowing that they would be parted, but not so soon. And in her keening, the warriors heard her heart break; not just break, but shatter into a thousand shards cutting her soul to ribbons. When she finally relinquished hold of her beloved's body, the tall, red-haired woman with a fierce color in her cheeks was gone, replaced with a wraith-like creature of silver hair and grey eyes and flesh the very pallor of the dead.

"Aoibheall fled the battlefield, fled her home, fled all she knew, only to return some months later — a ghastly aura about her — humming a similar heart-wrenching tune as she approached the bedside of Donell's father, Nial, there in the great clan hall in Ulster.

"She bowed obeisance to him, her eyes wet with tears and the terrible, beautiful song humming behind the words she spoke. 'My lord, your time is indeed near. As I loved your son, let me do what I can to ease your passing, I am our most humble servant.'

"'Faerie bitch' he spat through cracked lips with his weak, wheezing breath. 'You took my son from me.'

"'No, no, I loved him. I would have given anything for him. And when he died, he changed me. I am no longer Daoine Sídhe. My family has shunned me and the child I bore.'

"'Child?' Nial's shoulders shook with the effort of turning his head to look at her.

"Aoibheall pulled aside her cloak and showed him a swaddled babe resting in a sling tied across her shoulder. 'My daughter,' she brushed a lock of dark grey hair from the babe's brow. 'Although she is no blood of yours, I have called her Donella after your son.'

"'No blood of ours? She is not my granddaughter?'

"'No, sir. When I swallowed the grief and the pain of losing my beloved Donell, it became a life of its own and came to rest in my womb. No, she is no blood of yours, sir, but she is of your family, inexorably so.'

"'My time is short, what do you want?'

"'Who is your heir?'

"Nial's rheumy eyes darted to a stocky man near the door, his youthful faced balanced between wonder and a scowl. 'My nephew, Hugh.'

"Aoibheall rose and bowed before him. 'My lord, I offer you this. It is a promise as eternal as the Sídhe and sworn by the very blood in my veins, in my daughter's veins. I will sing your honored uncle to his rest, to ease his travel to the land of the dead. I will do this for him because of the love I bore his son, that love made manifest by the child who sleeps at my breast. And when that deed is done, I will swear myself to you, eternally, into your service.'

"'And when I die?'

"'I will be at your side. And the children of my blood will ever guard the gates between life and death, singing sweet warning into your souls when your time has come to die.'

"'If I am pleased with your voice, madam, I will consider your offer,' Hugh said, grimly.

"The relief that rose into her features almost made her lovely. Aoibheall returned to the patriarch's bed and, touching the old man's wrist, she began to sing. She could feel the staggering, slowing pulse of his heart and the shuddering breath rattling in his lungs. She sang of the honor of the great clan of O'Neill, she sang of a proud family with many strong sons among them, she sang of the bravery in which they faced death. And as the old man's breath began to fade, the baby girl awoke and tilted her tiny head towards the bed. Her cry echoed through her mother's, soaring through the thick stones as grey as her hair and eyes and into the star-sprinkled sky.

"Hugh sank to his knees and mopped the tears away from his cheeks with the sleeves of his shirt, so achingly exquisite was the song. The Daoine Sídhe of Ulster were drawn from their mounds to the clan hall, unable to resist the song of death Aoibheall wove for the erstwhile chieftain. Among them, few came forward into the hall and added their voices to hers. And as she had, they lost their beauty and their youth and their fiery red hair.

"Nial fought his death, but finally, he looked up into Aoibheall's grey eyes, as fathomless as the fog. 'You love....' He rasped.

"She nodded.

"He weakly touched her hand and reached out for the crying babe, his dry, gnarled fingers brushing her flesh that was not plump and pink but pale and stony. 'Love us,' he whispered with his final breath, 'always.'

"And so it was and ever shall be, banshee linked by sorrow, bound by blood to each of the great clans of Erin's isle. And so it happened that the O'Neill clan became bound to the lady of the sídhe, Aoibheall, the first banshee. In the years that followed, Aoibheall's daughters sang not only for the O'Neill's. The first families of Ireland soon gained their own bloodlines of banshee through alliances and through love. The O'Briens were the first, and the Kavanaghs and the Kennedys and the O'Reardons and O'Connors and O'Gradys soon followed. Many banshee chose to offer themselves to a clan or a particular family lineage.

"A banshee must follow her family wherever they may go, including America, Canada, and even as far as Australia, even if it means leaving her mother and sisters behind." There was usually a bit about the particular family that was doing the singing, but Keela left that part off.

With that monumental task behind her, she relaxed and found herself encircled in Radha's arms.

"*Bean-sidhe*, faerie daughter, your grief will consume you. Already it poisons your spirit." The oracle sighed. "Yes, you can do this thing, you can bring that human boy back to the living. But would you not like to stay here with me instead?"

Radha's eyes opened. Beneath those parchment lids hid the light of the noonday sun. It blinded Keela with intensity and she looked away. But strong, long-fingered hands turned her face back, tilting it towards the light.

"I will let you see him. Through me. Look, here."

Keela thought she would fall up into those limitless eyes, so bright and expansive were they. She held fast to the stone from the River Liffey and thought of Molan guarding the door. How could she alert him that she needed his help?

"You do not need Molan to help you. You must find the strength in yourself, or be lost. But you came this far on your own. I believe you must be strong, *Cadhla.*"

Keela tensed. She could hear in the slight difference in pronunciation that Radha had used her true name and her soul lit up, shining fiercely bright as Radha's terrible gaze.

She saw Michael O'Neill. His auburn hair and his green eyes. In his hand, he held her silver comb with its long, elegant teeth and circles and swirls decorating it. He gripped it almost desperately, as if knowing that it kept him close in spirit to her, his only salvation from a life lost forever in purgatory. She reached for him, but her hands passed right through.

"You cannot touch him, *Cadhla,* your power is broken."

"How do I get it back?"

"You must sing for it."

Keela nodded. "*Oran na Céle.*"

"Yes. The song of death's beautiful companion."

"But it's lost."

"It is here."

"In Boston?" Keela's hope flared, shimmering again.

Radha's smile was sad. "No. Not in this city. But in this land." She unwound one arm from around Keela's body and reached out to touch the wall of the chamber. "West. It went west."

"How far west?"

Radha turned her gaze towards that wall and she squinted, as if she could see through the very rock. "Listen," her voice was hushed and her other arm pressed Keela close. "Do you hear it? When you found your American sisters, you heard their song, heard it in the music of this place. There are other banshees here, but you could hear the song of your own."

"Yes."

"Listen now, faerie daughter, this is the song of all banshees, the song taught to the very first of your kind. It was a song to seduce death, to lull it into submission, to rend holes in the veil that separates the worlds. It was meant only to ensure the safe passage of a human soul from the living realm to that of the dead. But Eimear O'Neill is correct, it can be made to work in reverse."

"Who taught it to us?"

"I did."

"Couldn't you just teach it again? To me, right now?"

Radha laughed and rocked Keela firmly. "Clever. But, no. It was crafted, it was given, it was gone from me. Handed to Eimear O'Neill as surely as Molan MacLiath handed you his river stone."

"Then how did she lose it?"

"She took a man to bed and he took it from her."

Keela couldn't help her gasp of shock. High and mighty Eimear O'Neill had bedded the wrong man and lost the legacy of all banshees. She could hardly believe it.

"What you banshees sing now is a copy," Radha explained. "The original has great power, too much power. Eimear was wise not to teach the entire thing. It is difficult for one to hold it all."

"How did her lover?"

"He took it and shared it with his brothers. They carried it here to America. I felt it when it came and when it passed." She looked towards the same wall again. "West," she repeated. "It went west. It stopped and stayed in a place they named Music City. So many have gone looking for it. So many want the power for themselves. It draws them all, inexorably, whether they realize it or not."

"There's a place called Music City?"

Radha nodded. "The map says Nashville."

"Nashville!" It came out as a squeak. There wasn't a man or woman in Ireland who didn't love Nashville, or so it seemed. Of course it would be there. That is where the Irish music had ended up when it came to the States, trading the dulcimer for the steel guitar and the pennywhistle for the harmonica and the fiddle for…well the fiddle stayed just about the same.

Radha nodded once more. "It is a place built on music, fed by music. That is where you must go if you are to find the song."

"And then I can save Michael."

"You can, or you may lose everything."

She didn't like the sound of that. "I have to try."

The oracle's smile lit the room. "Of course you do. "

"You have been kind, my lady. Thank you."

Radha's aura blazed. "You have put yourself in debt to me."

"I know. I probably shouldn't have done it."

"Do not be led astray. Your destiny is your own and no one else's. Let no one tell you otherwise."

"Yes, my lady," Keela said.

"Very good. I am sorry to see you go. You will come back again."

"Of course I will, if I am able."

"That was not a request. You *will* come back again, *Cadhla*."

The slight tug on her soul itched deep inside. "Yes, my lady," she repeated.

"Go, now. Reclaim your birthright and your honor."

"And my love?"

"Yes," the oracle said, and almost as an afterthought added, "That, also."

Keela stood, careful not to tread on Radha's hair, and pressed a kiss to the oracle's broad, high cheek. It, too, felt like ivory. She found her cloak on the floor where it had fallen and bundled it into her arms. "Good-bye, for now, my lady."

There was no reply. The light of a single candle barely illuminated the room, casting everything outside of its feeble circle in complete darkness. Keela backed up until she felt the doorframe behind her. She knocked quietly and collapsed into Molan's arms as he let her out of the presence chamber.

Molan carried her up the stairs and back to the room where her American counterparts waited. Eileen had her hand on Anlon's knee. After a cup of tea and a tray of sweets, Keela felt strong enough to relay a little of what had happened below.

"Music City," Keela said. "That's where she told me it was. Nashville, Tennessee."

"Are you going to go find it, then?" Fiona asked. Keela noted the singular. She hadn't thought any of her Boston banshees would be interested in going with her, but she had held onto a thin thread of hope they might offer.

"Yes," Keela said. "I'm going." *Alone,* she thought wistfully, and immediately caught Molan glancing her way.

"How do you plan on getting there," Grace asked.

"I don't suppose America has trods, does it?"

"Those fae paths?" asked Maggie.

"The same."

The banshees conferred with Anlon and Molan a moment before reaching the consensus that while there were indeed magical pathways that connected various parts of North America, none of them functioned the way that a trod did by opening a direct course from point A to point B.

"I guess you'll have to take the bus," Noreen suggested, sarcastically.

Keela frowned. Getting around had not been part of her plan. She could fly, she supposed. But it was a terribly long way and she wasn't sure how she'd manage to not get lost in this strange land. "Aye, I guess I will."

They bid Keela a bittersweet farewell, leaving her in the capable hands of the guardians.

Grace hugged her tightly. "I hope to see you again, dear sister." She kissed Keela on both cheeks before retreating to Fiona's side. Keela envied them; no mortal man would ever cost them dearly.

They pooled their money and left her with what they hoped was enough for bus fare. And then the good-byes were over and they were gone.

"I forgot to give you back your stone, Molan," Keela said as he settled her into another one of the parlors off the main hall. The couch there opened up into a bed. It smelled musty and the sheets were covered in dust.

He did his best to shake them out and fetch her a blanket or two.

"Keep it," he said.

"No. I couldn't! A Grey Man is sworn to the land."

"Not this one, remember," his smile was sad. "Keep

it as a token to remember what you're working for."

"As if I could forget."

"It'll help ground you. I think you need that."

Keela sighed and ran her fingers through her unbound hair, now black in the light.

"Would you like me to brush and braid it?"

"No!" She'd answered too quickly and he retreated a step. "I'm sorry. I meant only…"

"No, no, that was out of line. I apologize." He bowed. "Keep the stone, Keela. I insist."

"All right." She turned it over in her hands, enjoying the weight and texture of it. "Thank you."

Molan was taken aback. "You're making a habit of getting indebted, Keela O'Reardon. You can't just go thanking fae like that." His somber face was transformed by his smile. "But I release you. I shan't hold you to any debt to me. Ever."

She smiled back. "I don't know what I was thinking… Goodnight, Molan."

"Goodnight."

The lights were dimmed until only a small lantern far across the room gleamed under a shuttered cover. Its glow did not reach Keela's bed and her hair shone in silver waves across her pillow. She toyed with it and thought about Michael.

Tomorrow, it truly begins. Next stop, Nashville.

Track 4

It was a twenty-seven hour bus ride from Boston to Nashville. Keela could have traveled another way, but the bus was easy, the bus was cheap, the bus let her sit curled up in the back corner for hours on end watching the scenery swiftly pass, alone with her thoughts.

When the sun ebbed away, sliding below the horizon ahead of them, she pulled up the hood of her grey cloak, covering her face and her hair. A lock of silver peeked out from beyond the hood's woolen edge, turning black beneath the occasional streetlight. She fiddled with the stone Molan had given her, running her finger across its long side, turning it over, and doing it again. So much had happened in such a short time. It felt good to just sit and think.

Michael was likely terrified, wherever he was. And the longer she took to find the song, the worse it would be for him. Time had no meaning on the other side, that much she knew. But the transition to coming back to the living realm, that would be the problem. He would live out the rest of his days shadow-touched, and the longer he stayed the stronger that pull on his soul would be. She nearly dropped the rock.

Wrapping her fingers around it, she brought it to her chest, enjoying the solidness of it. If she closed her eyes, she could hear the soft mumble of the Liffey as it poured into the Irish Sea. It was just the reminder she needed. Molan's gentle presence came along with it, cool and somber and smelling ever-so-slightly of damp wool. She wondered if she'd ever see him again, him or the raucous bunch of Boston O'Reardons. There was something about their candor that she really enjoyed.

If she failed, they would welcome her, she knew. They would take her into their little American clan and Eileen would teach her to pick locks and Fiona would explain hockey and all in all it wouldn't be a bad life, really. Except for Michael.

The weight of what she was doing hit her hard, then. Sure, she could go off and live in America and pretend it was what she wanted all along, but he would never be free. He would be trapped in that place between worlds forever, where he could never live and would never die. She shivered.

"Michael," she whispered. "I'm coming."

She dozed in snatches, jolted awake by dreams that were all too real then settling back to let the vibration and sway to the bus rock her to sleep once again. The sun rose behind her and chased her down the highway, beating her to Nashville.

As soon as the doors of the bus opened, she heard the music. It wasn't even a weekend, but live music from a dozen or more sources echoed through the brick alleys, rising and falling with thumping drumbeats, the poignant drawl of an acoustic guitar, and now and again an exuberant whoop followed by muffled applause. Keela stepped down onto the pavement on uncertain legs and began to make her shaky way into the heart of Music City.

A vibration across her skin made all of the hairs on her arm stand on end. It was the feeling of stepping into a faerie circle, or into a graveyard. This place held power.

But not faerie power. She sensed no other banshees here and the threads of bloodlines felt dimmed and scattered. Too many generations stretched between these folks and their forebears, too much mingling to call any one clan to them. Keela felt a moment's pang of sympathy and longing for these displaced kin.

The humming welled up from the very ground

beneath her feet and permeated the air all around her. It wove in and out of the music that spilled from the open doors of the bars and drifted through the buskers on the sidewalks. The oracle had been dead on: the song was here. *Somewhere.* The different strains of melody and rhythm blended into a sensory overload that made her feel drunker than whiskey. She sat down on some white stone steps and despaired of ever being able to sort out the source of this whirlwind of energy.

Glancing behind her, she saw she had settled herself on the wide stairs leading to a courtyard beside an ornate marble building that looked like a concert hall. A statue of a woman in a diaphanous gown that cleaved to every dip and curve stood as a silent and gentle guard over the place. In the courtyard, Keela marveled at the architecture and the sense of peace it evoked. But even here, the serenity was tempered by that undeniable surge of strength beneath it. It made her head spin.

Two women seated by a reflecting pool exchanged a few quick words then rose, as if they might approach her. Keela retreated a step, resting her hand on the gate. The sharp sting of iron surprised her and she hissed through her teeth, rubbing her fingers together. Avoiding more contact, she ducked through the wrought iron gates and made her way quickly past the fountain of two twining bodies rising up out of a spray of water; the woman blew a horn, the man strummed a lyre. She was in no mood to be social, not until she got her bearings.

Nearly stumbling, she headed towards where the lights of the bars hovered like strange neon angels over the street. "Viva Nashvegas — Eat More Rhinestones" proclaimed chalk graffiti scrawled on the sidewalk. She wondered if any banshee had ever been here before. On Broadway, all Keela heard was country. Covers of the classics sung strong by fresh voices: Willie, Patsy, Hank, Dolly. She had to admit, seeing Nashville had been a secret dream of hers ever since the night she'd heard the house band play Johnny Cash's "Folsom Prison Blues" in the basement bar at the Stag's Head Pub in Dublin.

Broadway ended at the river, and Keela had paused to listen at every door from Tootsie's to the Hard Rock Café. At Second Avenue, different music drifted on the river's wind: rock and Celtic and even hip-hop, though much less of it live, except for the Celtic. Mulligan's simple façade was dominated by an Irish flag and an old-fashioned pub sign. There were ghosts here, unhappy spirits fortunately mollified by good music. The tiny stage at the rear of the dining room exploded with energy as the patrons banged ashtrays and beer mugs on the battered tables as they sang along. Keela rocked backwards on her heels, drinking it all in. Here were her people. Here was her music.

But she could sense, even in the country music, the hint of Irish roots. Not just the *Oran na Céle*, but something simpler, more basic. It made her curious. She leaned against the building, listening to the beat thrumming into her bones. There under the neon lights, she felt like an ordinary girl, one of dozens who came to the city every day in search of impossible dreams.

Inside Mulligan's the mood changed, the banging stopped and the raucous crowd quieted and leaned forward to listen. She recognized the song at once and began to sing along, her voice carrying over the amplified canned ambiance music and the karaoke coming from two doors down. The voice of the banshee, while often steeped with terror, could also be haunting, even sweet. It depended on her mood and on the situation. "Black Velvet Band" was one of her favorite songs and it definitely called for haunting and sweet rather than fear-inducing.

A handful of change clattered to her feet.

"You should put out a hat or somethin', missy, you're really good" said a middle-aged man in a straw cowboy hat as he passed by. His boots were new and gleaming and he limped in them just a little.

Tourist, she thought, despite herself.

Smiling, she turned back towards Broadway, passing the bar with the karaoke stage in the front window. "Buck Wild Saloon" read the sign with its curling, faux-Western font. It was not the type of place Keela would ever decide she needed to visit, but the allure of singing was just too strong.

Inside, the place looked like the set of an old movie, with knotty pine plank flooring and wood-trimmed everything. The clientele did not look like they belonged to a vintage western, however. Short shorts, short skirts, and skimpy tops abounded on the women, and the men dressed in everything from super baggy pants to skinny jeans. Keela nearly turned around and left when the karaoke host called her out.

"Hey little goth girl, you come here to sing?" He said into the microphone. He wore an odd combination of baggy carpenter's jeans over snakeskin boots, and a cowboy hat with a matching hatband. His oversized shirt with red embroidered roses and fringe at the yoke and sleeves looked like it might have once belonged to a rodeo star, and he wore it half buttoned over a t-shirt printed with $100 bills all over it. He looked like the world's only country-western rapper.

Keela nodded, unsure of what else to do.

"Who wants to hear the goth girl sing?"

A drunken cheer went up from the crowd of twenty-somethings. Keela couldn't imagine, looking at the throng of scantily clad women and the men who ogled them, what this place looked like on the weekends.

"Well git on up here!" The host reached down to haul her onto the stage. His black-painted fingernails just confused Keela even more. "So what's yer name?"

"Keela."

The host whistled. "Say that again?"

"*Keela,*" she repeated directly into the microphone.

"And, *Keela,*" he mimicked her accent badly. "I'd say you aren't from around here, amirite?" He laughed and dramatically indicated her wool dress and cloak, sticking out his tongue and making gagging noises. "We almost called the cops, you know. Homeless people aren't allowed in here."

"That's actually happened to me once before. In Boston."

The bar's patrons barked with laughter as if she'd told a terribly clever joke.

"Well, I can see why. Where you from with that pretty little accent anyway?"

"Ireland."

"Then why ain't you next door, sugar?"

Keela shrugged. "I don't know. I wanted to sing."

"Of course you did." The host put his arm around Keela's shoulders. He smelled like sweat and beer. "Because we have the *best damn karaoke* in Nashville!"

He held up his mic and the crowd screamed, chanting something that might have been his name and might have been the bar's name, or might have been some of each delivered in a drunken blur.

"Let's show these cowboys and cowgirls how they do it in Ireland. I've got an old-fashioned Irish song right here for ya."

"You do?"

"Hells to the yeah. Would you like to sing it? Would ya?"

"Yes, please. That would be lovely and very good of you."

The small flatscreen at the edge of the stage flickered to life and the host handed Keela another microphone. Within moments, the screen told her the song was "Tell Me Ma."

The song started up and for a terrifying moment, she could not recognize it. She had thought it might sound off, a little canned and synthesized, but not like this. Not *techno*.

The host nodded encouragingly, pointing to the video screen where the words swept by nearly too quick to read. Keela faltered through the first few lines, struggling to catch up to a much faster beat than she'd expected. At the break between the opening chorus and the first verse, she closed her eyes, ignoring the damned video monitor and just listened for the thread of music. It was there like shining silver ribbon twining through the current of the crazed notes and their maddening beat. She sucked in a quick breath and caught the chorus as it repeated, hitting each word now. With growing confidence, she opened her eyes and watched the crowd bob to the song.

"I'll tell me ma when I go home, the boys won't leave the girls alone. They pulled my hair, they stole my comb, but that's all right 'til I go home." She stumbled on the phrase *stole my comb* but plowed on ahead, a smile widening across her own face. "She is handsome, she is pretty, she is the belle of Belfast City! She goes courtin', a one, two, three," punctuated with three stomps with the heel of her black laced-up boot. "Please won't you tell me who is she?"

The bar's easily-impressed patrons cheered mightily; Keela could feel their energy in heat and chills across her entire body that filled the bleak void within her with light, albeit temporarily. And then Keela did something that surprised even herself. At the long musical break in the middle of the song, she danced.

She had never been much of a dancer, but she knew of no man or woman with Irish blood who could bear to sit still when a really good song played. She hopped and kicked as if she knew what she was doing and the drunken crowd couldn't care less if she did; they just cheered all the louder. The embers within her soul flared brightly, sending shivery sparks throughout her body. It was good. It was better than good. It was as if nothing had ever happened and she was goofing off in a Dublin bar with her kin, or a pub in Galway with Michael.

It was almost as if she could see him in the crowd, laughing at her antics, his green eyes merry and those damned adorable crow's feet crimping the edges of his eyes. Too soon, the song ended and Keela bowed, then curtsied and jumped down from the small elevated stage.

The host held his hands over his head and clapped in large, slow, exaggerated movements.

"*Daaaaaaaaaaaaaaaaammmmmmmmnnnnnnnnnnnnnnnnn,*" he drawled into the mic. "You're comin' up here for another one, don't you go anywhere."

Keela wove through the crowd, aiming for the relatively quiet bar to take a seat. She was giddy and a little bit dizzy. She felt so good, so good that she didn't even mind the idiotic host's demands for her to sing again. She climbed onto a studded leather barstool and the weight came crashing back. The reprieve had been only temporary.

The attention now focusing on someone else took Keela's elation away, returning the cold, dark edges of the *geis* to her soul. It amazed her how quickly her emptiness had come to feel normal. She hungered for that sensation of wholeness again, the warmth and the light.

She ordered a whiskey.

"Catholic or Protestant?" the bartender asked with a wink. He had a kind face with a neatly trimmed goatee that showed a few threads of grey amid the brown that matched his hair and eyes.

"Pardon?"

"Jamison or Bushmill's."

"Tully?"

He shook his head. "Nope, we don't carry Tullamore Dew. How about Jack?"

Keela shrugged. Jack Daniels was wildly popular in Ireland, although she had never tried it. "Sure, why not?"

"Rocks?"

"Neat."

"You're just full of surprises, little lady."

"I'll take that as a compliment," she said.

He nodded and put the tumbler on the bar, watching as she took a sip. The whiskey tasted sharp, a harsher heat than what she was used to. She grimaced and the bartender laughed, not unkindly. "We make it strong here in Tennessee," he told her.

"Indeed." She braved another swallow, draining most of the contents. "Good stuff, though. Fiery."

The bartender poured her another. "This one will go down better. This Jack is the Gentleman. A more sophisticated blend."

Keela agreed, nodding warmly after a taste. "This is very good. Tastes more like home."

"Liquid courage, either way."

"Yes, true."

"You were great. Didn't even need to hear you with music, I can hear it in the way you speak. You're a born singer. Just don't forget to breathe."

"Is everyone here a musician?"

"This is Nashville, ma'am."

Keela laughed, releasing a small measure of her tension. "And how about you?"

He laughed. "Guitarist, I must confess. And I do a little songwriting on the side."

"Anything I might have heard?"

"Unless you are familiar with Mullet Chop? Or maybe Bad Road?"

"I'm sorry, but no."

The bartender shrugged. "Don't sweat it; there are a lot of fish in this here sea." He leaned over, giving her a flirtatious smile. "Are you looking for work? You'll be a lock, little lady, as soon as someone hears that *gahr-geous* little brogue of yours," he imitated her, playfully.

"You do a fair impression!"

"Just recalling my dear ol' gran. She was a battleaxe

of a woman from County Clare."

"Lovely!" Keela could not help but peek at him through the many cracks and fissures in the veil that separated not only humanity from faerie, but life from death. She was relieved to find that she could still do it. He bore the mark of an old Irish family on his soul — a beacon to any banshee, but especially bright to any who served that bloodline.

He was also dying.

Keela didn't dare breathe a word of it to him. Instead, she smiled and said, "The O'Brien's are a good lot from Ennis. I know them well. You look like you could be of their stock."

"Well guessed, little lady." He sketched a bow. "James O'Brien, a pleasure to meet you." He put out his hand, the fingertips callused from years of strumming.

"Keela O'Reardon." She returned the gesture, delicately setting her palm against his, unsure of how he would react to her touch.

He pulled back, almost instinctively, and blushed deeply. "My apologies! But a shiver just ran down my spine like I just had a goose walk over my grave."

Keela waved off a repeat attempt to shake hands. "Perhaps you've got a poltergeist in here." She wriggled her fingers in the air around her head, laughing, but the shadow of illness that hung over him dampened her spirits a bit.

There was no binding on him to accompany that familial mark, which meant no guide to sing him sweetly to the grave, no guardian to lament his passing. That was a pity. He seemed such a kind man who would truly appreciate such a tradition. She wished she could call on one of her cousins to tend to him, but she knew her voice would not be heard. She would dare to poach him for herself, this lonely Irishman in a banshee-less town, but her voice would not open the gates of the netherworld any longer, unless she found the song and restored Michael.

And then… and then she would have the wrath of the O'Briens upon her, on top of the wrath of the O'Neills. She didn't know if this stranger was worth that risk, but she could hardly bear the thought of anyone dying alone.

"Are you all right, Miss Keela?"

She blinked, lost in her reverie. James smiled at her.

"That's better. Don't know where you got off to, dearie, but I'm glad you're back." He glanced past her and nodded. "And I'm not the only one."

Keela turned and the karaoke host was curling is finger at her. "Git on up here, little goth girl!"

Sighing, she went.

But once onstage, she made a silly and rash decision. She waved off the microphone and turned the video screen away. Fixing her gaze on James, the bartender, Keela began to sing.

Since she had no real power anymore, she figured that it couldn't hurt. And someone needed to lament him, this kind soul. And so she sang for his death too soon to come.

Although she had no ability to open the gates between the realms, she was still a banshee, and the fun-loving young things in the bar all stopped their conversations and turned to look. They came down from the upper floors, scantily-clad girls wrapping their arms around them as if to ward off a sudden chill.

Keela sang a *sean-nós*, an unaccompanied traditional song. She sang out in a language older than Gaelic and to a tune older than written music. She ignored their stares and their stupefied open-mouthed gazing. She looked at James. He had fallen still, but his eyes were sharp and canny. He knew what she was, and he realized what she knew.

There was no other sound in the bar. Even the karaoke host sat silently while she sang on, daring any other banshee to appear and reprimand her. She actually hoped one might appear, for the sake of the stranger who had shown her kindness.

But no one came.

The song wound down and James looked away, dabbing at the corners of his eyes with his thumb. The bar's patrons stood there, transfixed, long after quiet had settled as an unattended bass line thumped from the dance floor upstairs.

The karaoke host moved first, putting a trembling hand around his rhinestone-studded microphone. "Well, then," was all he said.

Keela bolted. She wanted very much to go ask James about the songwriting thing, thinking he might have a clue about where she could start the search for her own song, but the cold in the air and the dazed, glazed looks on the faces of the crowd told her she had gone too far.

She was off the stage and out the door before anyone moved. Out of the corner of her eye, she caught sight of James watching her go. He nodded a brief goodbye as Keela fled.

She hadn't paid for the whiskey.

Track 5

Keela found the old City Cemetery surprisingly cozy. Pale springtime moonlight made the old granite tombstones gleam, and the fat leaves of the magnolia tree were velvety underneath. Dressed in her crow form, Keela lounged in the broad branches and spent a long time thinking, enjoying the quiet of the place. Even with the freight trains that wrapped around the property's edge, it was a peaceful place, often visited even if just by one or two people at a time. The monuments ranged from simple headstones bearing names and dates to columns and mausoleums with much more flourish. It had a bit of an old-world feeling to it, this burial ground which housed a cross-section of Nashville's people. She liked it.

Keela spent a few days there, listening to a rather constant current of tourists, students, historians, photographers, and troublemakers who made for a good deal of entertainment.

She flitted between two of the property's largest magnolia trees. The taller one hung its branches down low over an assortment of plots near the intersection of Gulley and Elm, while the wider sat on the aptly named Magnolia Avenue and twined its massive roots around a handful of markers, including the tiniest white granite headstone she had ever seen. Someone's baby, no doubt.

The ghosts here were shy, for the most part. Keela explored the cemetery as much on two legs as she did on the wing. Only a few spirits ventured out very often, and while they were terribly polite, making small talk and calling her "ma'am," none of them really wanted to have more than the most casual of chats. She might have found it distressing if it were not entirely uniform across the whole lot of them. One of the newer burials, a certain stately matron named Bessie Davis interred on Poplar Avenue in 1979, informed her with a gentle chiding that this was the manner of Southerners and she'd have to hang about a lot longer before anyone would deign to talk to her about anything of substance or import.

Keela didn't walk Nashville's streets again right away, preferring to take an aerial view on crow's wings. She circled Broadway, soaring over old brick buildings and sleek, new construction. It seemed like this city was ever changing, and she wondered if she left and came back in a year's time, would she even recognize it.

She traced the river up to the north end of town and southeast to the big, fancy hotel just listening to the sounds of the city. Everywhere music flowed. In bars, restaurants, street corners, in the airport, in the mall, in hotel lobbies, on the riverboats that wandered up and down the Cumberland — anywhere that a live band could assemble where people might hear, they played. And where there weren't live bands, cleverly hidden speakers played a soundtrack that matched the part of town. Classical near the symphony hall, country near the Hall of Fame, and a little bit of everything up by the capitol. Music was quite literally everywhere.

Other music, embedded so deep in the fabric of the city itself that present mortal inhabitants could only read it on the big historical marker signs, sang the history of Nashville. Strains penned by an Irishman, part military march and part lamentation, followed the path of Civil War battles right through the center of town. Echoes of the Fisk Jubilee Singers, who had performed in England for Queen Victoria in 1874, rooted the chord that resolved in Nashville making "Music City" its official nickname in 1950. Keela chased a line that harmonized with the music that permeated Belfast; unheard music tied the sister cities together. She ignored the Dorian strains and lyre from a park west of downtown. Music City was also "The Athens of the South," but that would not help her find the missing *Oran na Céle.*

It was an amazing place, this Nashville, but all the delightful trivia got her no closer to finding the song. After a week on her own, she decided to enlist a little help. Bracing herself for the reception, she walked back to Second Avenue and into the Buck Wild Saloon. It was early yet, hardly five o'clock, and the karaoke hadn't started.

James idled behind the bar, playing with his phone.

"I owe you for t'other night," Keela said.

His head came up at once and he grinned. "Well look who it is! Been wondering if you'd come back for a repeat performance. You made quite a stir, little lady!"

She shrugged, not sure what she ought to say. "I'll pay you for the Jack." She reached into the inner pocket of her cloak where a small stash of faerie gold lay hidden.

James shook his head. "No need. Just come and sing another night and we'll be square."

"I'd rather at Mulligan's."

"Wouldn't we all?" He laughed. "But the owner's band has a lock on the stage, you know."

"Oh."

James tilted his head, making a great show of thinking very hard. "How about this, then? There's another Irish pub in town."

"There is?"

"Actually," he counted on his fingers, "there are three others. But I know the owner of McNamara's. He used to play at Mulligan's. He's a buddy of mine from high school. I pick up a couple of weeknights over there backing up Nosey Flynn. They'd love to have a female vocalist, especially one of your particular talents. You'll love the place. It used to be a funeral home many years ago."

Keela smiled. That was his way of letting her know he knew, she surmised. "That sounds lovely, James."

"Tomorrow, then? Seven o'clock."

"What about the whiskey?"

"Come and sing for us at McNamara's and I'd be happy to buy you all the shots you can drink. Here, there, or otherwise."

Keela winked. "Be careful with that promise. I can

drink an awful lot."

"I don't doubt it." He held out his hand to her but Keela only bowed instead of touching him.

"Tomorrow, then. I'll be seeing yourself at seven."

"Fantastic. And Keela? Don't change. You rock the faerie look far too well, little lady."

There's a reason for that. But all she said was, "Of course."

She left the Buck Wild Saloon fairly confident she'd never have to go inside again. But instead of heading over to Mulligan's, Keela wandered past the bar to Broadway. It looked different in the daylight, with business people heading home and a lot fewer tourists clogging up the sidewalks. She turned up Fifth Avenue and stopped in front of the Ryman Auditorium. Actually, it was the back now. It had been the front, one of the historical markers had said, until renovations in 1994 had given the place a lobby and requisite gift shop on the Fourth Avenue side.

The original brick and masonry façade, untouched since the place was built in 1892, still loomed so tall over Fifth that Keela had to cross over to the opposite sidewalk to get a good look at it without craning her neck. The building resonated, as if a silent concert were being played there every minute of every day. She came back to it, drawn inexorably, and sat down on the broad front steps with her head resting against the old wooden doors, just being there with the old place for a long time, its reverberations whispering to her. She couldn't make out what they were, these quiet confessions, but something about the building wormed its way into her heart.

The Mother Church of Country Music, the historical marker proclaimed, formerly the Union Tabernacle Church. Steeped with history, melodies, and ghosts.

She decided to come back and take the tour. But before then, she had some traditional Irish music to bone up on. Keela hummed her way through every song she knew between Wednesday night and Thursday, scrolling through countless lyrics in her head. Every song came with easily two or three or more variations on the words.

She had no idea why it made her nervous, but she feared letting James down. He'd been kind, and he'd covered her whiskey. And she wanted the applause. She wanted the feeling of wholeness and of power, the feeling of being herself once more.

So she took herself over to Donelson, a suburban area southeast of downtown, fluttering into the trees between the parking lot and the culvert. She stepped out into the light, glad she had her cloak to ward off the slight chill that permeated the spring evening.

Her hair was braided down her back, her dress and cloak shaken out, so she felt at least presentable. Inside, she found the pub surprisingly home-like, down to the basket of cut peat sitting by the fireplace. The trinkets and knick-knacks lining the walls had all come from Ireland, as had the jolly woman behind the hostess stand — Belfast, by her accent — who escorted Keela to the long room at the other side of the building, chattering charmingly all the way.

"James, you've found yourself a delightful young lass. I hope we can keep her." The hostess deposited Keela at the foot of a small, low stage already set with a guitar, mandolin, bodhrán drum, and fiddle.

"No one here plays pipes?" Keela teased.

James smiled and shrugged. "Come back another night and I'll make sure we've got an uilleann player, how about that?"

"Sounds like a deal to me."

"Let me introduce you to the others." He took her around the gathering of musicians. Not a proper band, she was told, but very much in the tradition of Ireland where folks just got together and played for the week or the night and enjoyed themselves. Lisa the fiddler, was the youngest of the group, petite and beautiful with long reddish-brown hair. Joseph played flute and mandolin, while his brother David played the bodhrán. James sang and played guitar, mandolin, banjo, and just about every stringed instrument known to man.

The band warmed up with easy pieces everyone knew, mostly lighthearted reels that didn't need vocals, to get them in sync. Keela sat at a table to the immediate left of the stage and fidgeted with the pint of Guinness that James ordered for her.

They called her up a few minutes later, a light sheen of sweat already showing on their faces and exhilaration in their eyes. It was palpable, the joy of it, and Keela drank it in.

"We'll probably do this one again later in the night, but it's a good one to start off with." James strummed a chord on his guitar, grinning. "As I was goin' over, the Cork and Kerry mountains," he sang out, starting the beloved old standard "Whiskey in the Jar."

Keela chimed in on the chorus, adding an alto undertone to his strong baritone, sneaking harmony in here and there.

As it neared seven, the pub filled up with the usual weeknight dinner rush. But the rush never ended. No one was leaving, Keela realized during their first set break. She sat at the table with the others, watching them eat steak fries smothered in shepherd's pie filling and topped with cheese, a concoction called "Irish Nachos." She nursed another Guinness and scanned the crowd. She caught sight of a pair of familiar faces but couldn't place the two women. Their frank, dark-eyed stares were off-putting, and Keela went back to her beer.

They opened the next set with "No, Nay, Never" and Keela gave herself over to a soaring interplay around and through the chorus that was far too high-class for the drinking song, but that the audience adored. The two women stood out sharply, not just because of their burnished bronze complexions and limitless eyes so dark Keela couldn't discern the pupil from the iris, nor because of their aloof, almost regal bearing. What set them apart was the fact that neither one of them was smiling. They exchanged the odd glance between them, in a manner that gave away their close kinship — cousins at least, if not sisters — and maintained a pair of matching serious expressions that cast a cold shiver down Keela's spine.

She decided to ignore them, shutting them out of the room before her so that she might drink in the adoration of the crowd. And adoring they were. She didn't know if it was the chemistry of the band or the interest of the audience or just the flow of alcohol that made it so much more powerful than it had been at karaoke, but whatever it was, Keela had never felt so very alive in her whole existence, nor so very drunk.

They came round again to "Whiskey in the Jar" and started putting in some slower tunes as well. James eyed her meaningfully as they came to the next set break. He took her aside with a barely suppressed smile.

"This'll be our last set for the evening, coming up. I want you to do what you did at Buck Wild." He touched her shoulder lightly, drawing his hand back almost immediately.

Keela nodded and drank her third pint of the night.

When they reconvened, the band began with "Black Velvet Band" and the night went solidly into melancholy from that point on. "The Fields of Athenry" was followed by "The Hills of Connemara" then "Danny Boy." At that point, James motioned Keela to step up and sing on her own.

She sang the song she'd done at karaoke. It fit the heady melancholy that pervaded the room now. From behind her, the fiddler struck up, soft and lilting, following her voice, anticipating where the melody would lead. David, the bodhrán drummer tapped out a bit of a dirge beat beneath that and it seemed that the darkness fell a little heavier in the pub. Tears, which had been gathering here and there, now flowed freely amid the patrons. Even the dark-eyed sisters looked choked up.

It was different than it had been in the other bar. Last night, there had been defiance in her song, a desire to shake those hedonistic hipsters out of their well-maintained comfort zones, a desperate need to connect to that part of her soul aching and lonely and confused. Tonight was different. Tonight, she knew what she was capable of doing, capable of making them feel. She crafted each phrase carefully, lingering here, caressing there, drawing out notes and rests with a purpose. She played the crowd, reading their energies and sending back to them the thing they most craved: the balm to soothe a loss, just the thing to heighten the nostalgia, a bit of commiseration for the wallowing. The Guinness could not hold a candle to this intoxication. Keela swayed on her feet feeling the emotions of the people around her, feeling it and feeding off of it. When once she would have felt emptied as she sang, hollowed out of energy and emotion, tonight she was filled to bursting and trembling with it.

And when she let the last, wavering note fade into silence, no one moved or spoke. Tears moistened her own cheeks, from melancholy, from homesickness, and from the sheer force of being overwhelmed by the attention and affection of this crowd.

Smiling, Keela dabbed her eyes with the edge of her cloak and began the darkly humorous "Isn't It Grand, Boys?" which sang about death and mourning in bold, unprettied ways. She segued this into the very peaceful and soothing "Parting Glass." And when she ended the song, "Goodnight and joy be with you all," the stage lights went dark and the applause went on a long, long time.

Track 6

Keela sang there again on Friday and Saturday nights. During the day, she hadn't the energy for much more than catching up on rest nuzzled against the fuzzy undersides of the magnolia leaves as a crow in the cemetery. On Sunday, she wandered the gravestones, wrapped in her cloak against the lingering morning chill.

She'd been there for about a week, and some of the inhabitants of the graveyard were starting to warm up to her, but they still mostly kept to themselves. These ghosts there were not going to be much help in her search for the song. None of them she had met so far knew anything about the music or musicians of nineteenth-century Nashville. So many of them were faded spirits, so old they had forgotten why they stayed. Keela introduced herself to a man named Elias, buried in 1846, about a dozen times. He had no ability to remember her from one meeting to the next. One young woman, who died in 1960 and whose name was missing along with the top half of her headstone, sighed dreamily at Keela and started in on stories about sneaking out Saturday nights to the Opry at the Ryman.

It was still early in the day and the sign on the Ryman building had proclaimed that tours ran daily. That must include Sundays, Keela reasoned. Ducking behind the tall Baxter monument, she became a crow and flapped up Fourth Avenue and touched down in the alley between the Ryman and the bank of honky-tonk bars that faced Broadway where she found a recessed, arched doorway in which to change back. The after-church crowd was already gathering in the large lobby, still dressed up from whatever services they'd just left. Ireland's after-church culture was nothing compared to what Nashville seemed to have. She slipped into their midst and drew the hood of her cloak up over her head. Closing her eyes a moment, she breathed out a shadow that shielded her from human gaze and moved with the group past the ticket windows and beyond the bronze statue of Minnie Pearl and Roy Acuff into the performance space.

The back corner was sectioned off for a short film about the building and the Opry. A smiling young woman with "Cathe" printed on her nametag gave them the requisite pleasantries and instructions. Keela pulled back the hood and tried not to look too out of place in her cloak and gown. She slid into an empty pew, marveling that the Ryman's seating still looked like that of a church.

"These are the original solid oak pews from 1892 when the building was first opened as a church, although some seating was removed during the 1993 renovation to make room for a proper stage with a proscenium wall and unobstructed seating," Cathe informed them cheerfully. "Can anyone guess what they did with the old pews?"

A few of the ladies in the row ahead suggested a charity auction or a church donation. Keela drummed her fingers on the seat beside her and immediately knew. The smooth, dense wood had an almost melodic reverberation.

"Guitars," she said, surprising herself that it was out loud. She blushed and wished she hadn't opened her mouth.

Cathe's smile blossomed into a wider grin. "Exactly! Was that a guess or did you read that somewhere?"

"Neither," Keela said. "Well, it was a bit of a guess, an educated one. This is Music City, is it not?" She thumped the seat, loudly this time. "And this has a gorgeous sound. It only makes sense."

"Are you a musician?"

"Aye."

"That was a silly question, wasn't it?" Cathe winked.

Keela laughed. "'Twould seem there are a lot of musically inclined folk in this town."

"And where did you travel from?"

"Ireland."

The expected reaction of the church ladies, the oohs and aahs and questions about this grandmother's birthplace and that great-uncle's relatives, made Keela really wish she'd kept her mouth shut. But still, she smiled and was as polite as she could be, given she didn't really know a whole lot about people who weren't O'Reardons and had never been to Cork. They finally left her alone and ambled out of the pews to look at the exhibits.

Keela sighed, perturbed that she'd missed half the movie.

"It's on repeat," Cathe said. "You just sit there as long as you'd like and watch it again, okay?"

Keela nodded with a smile and Cathe nearly touched her shoulder, then thought better of it and went to direct the church ladies to the self-guided portion of the tour.

The movie started over again, although there was no one but Keela there to watch it. The montages of the old Opry clips charmed her, but it was the music in part of one of the scenes that caught her attention. A fiddle solo played in the background for part of the interview with Marty Stuart. Keela sat up at once, feeling a tingle of something familiar in that snippet of melody. She searched frantically for Cathe, finally waving her down from across the auditorium.

"Did you have a question?"

"That song," Keela pointed at the movie screen. "How do I find out about it?"

"What song?"

"I don't know. It was playing when they interviewed that fellow, the one with the big hair and the guitar."

Cathe laughed. "You'll have to be more specific."

"Stuart. When they were interviewing himself, there was a fiddle playing in the background. Do you know anything about it?"

Cathe raised a finely shaped eyebrow and lifted her shoulders in a shrug. "Um, no. I've never given much thought to the background music, really."

"Is there anyone who might know?"

"I can bring you the DVD case, but if it ain't mentioned on there, and I doubt it would be, then you're out of luck." And indeed, there was no mention of any of the background music, simply a list of copyright holders and dates under the standard "used with permission" statement. "Sorry."

"It's all right," Keela said, feeling suddenly deflated.

"Is it a song you like?"

"One I used to know. A long time ago. Been trying to track it down." It was best to tell lies that were closest to the truth.

"And not one you can just look up online, is it?"

"I'm afraid not."

"Well, good luck finding it."

Keela nodded. "I get the feeling it was played here once upon a time."

"Ma'am, every song ever written I think has been played here at some time or another."

She smiled and nodded once more before excusing herself to take a look around. This place was literally steeped in music; she could taste it in the air and hear it humming in the walls, the floor, the pews, in everything.

But what stood out, though, beyond the history, the melodies, the personalities, the voices, was the presence of magic. Not all of it faerie magic, either. Also, there were ghosts. Several of them. It was enough to make Keela's head spin.

She sat down again next to a little one-room recording studio that had once been the ticket booth. Cathe was telling the church ladies all about how they could record their own song right here for just a small fee and capture a part of the history to keep forever. Keela tuned it out and slipped out into the hallway that had once served as the lobby. Signs pointed her upstairs to the Fifth Avenue vestibule exhibit space, showcasing the history of famous acts that had played there.

The quiet space ran along the entirety of the Fifth Avenue side, with tall windows that let in the light and gave views of the roofs of the bars on Broadway and the construction a few blocks farther south. No one was there when Keela came up, and she strolled the narrow space looking at the timeline and at the old advertisements, the reproduction Opry scripts, and many photographs and promotional posters. Several Irish groups had been there over time: singers, dancers, fiddlers, and more. Many of them were clustered around the early 1900s, when the church already doubled as a performance space. Any one of these bands could be the one she sought, the one that brought the song here. But not only was this ancient history in this town, most of the photographs weren't even identified aside from basic inscriptions like, "Irish immigrant band from Co. Wicklow, played the Ryman Auditorium in 1902."

Keela bit back a wave of overwhelming hopelessness. The song had been here, had been played here, she knew it, *she knew it*, but now it was buried like a needle in a haystack beneath a century and more of other songs, other magic, other powers. The echo of the *Oran na Céle* lingered, taunting her with its proximity yet remaining so completely out of reach.

"Buck up, girlie, all ain't lost." A crisp-voiced older women came up the steps. Her white hair was pinned back in a bun and her dress, while clean and pressed, did not look like the Sunday-service type of attire. She came up only to Keela's chin, but she seemed a whole lot taller than that. She looked Keela up and down appraisingly. "You come a long way looking for something."

"Aye, yes, ma'am." Keela bobbed her head, feeling the strength of this woman's authority.

The woman looked across the images on the wall. "We love the Irish here, and the Irish love us in return. Don't you, girlie?"

"I have to say I'm passing fond of country music, yes."

The woman looked at the wall again and nodded, her face growing solemn. "Something happened here. One of these bands," she pointed a wizened finger at the collection of Irishmen and women smiling in grainy black and white. "I can't tell you which, but I've been waiting for the day someone finally got over here to look into it."

"What happened?"

Her gaze went somewhere far away, looking into memory. "They closed their set with this song, sounded like every damn jig I ever heard and yet none of them at the same time. It was happy, but sad, had a fast beat but slow notes." She shook her head as if to clear it. "It was early on. 1904. When I first got here. Nothing was the same after that."

"How so?"

The woman blinked slowly, as if trying to collect and pin down the right words to describe it. She pursed her lips several times before finally speaking. "Every song ever played here after that night sounded better than it ever had before, better than it would sound anywhere else. I can't tell you why or how, but that's the solemn truth so help me, Jesus." She grabbed Keela's sleeve. "Look."

There were quotes posted along the timeline. "The best sound in town…maybe in the US!" was attributed to Chet Akins. Vince Gill's quote read, "The most amazing place I've ever sung in." Coldplay proclaimed it, "The greatest theatre in the world!" They went on and on, each describing something singularly awesome about the Ryman Auditorium.

"Everyone has always thought it was something the Captain had done, something with the acoustics — he was a very particular man, you must realize, and he did build the place with beautiful acoustics — but I know the truth. I was there that night. It was the song." She nodded emphatically. "It was the song."

"I need to find it."

The woman laughed. "I can't help you there except to say, honey, you're *in* it."

And then she was gone.

Keela blinked at the suddenness of her departure, her disappearance really.

Honey, you're in *it*, what was left of it, anyway. The song had been in this place, of that much Keela was absolutely certain. And it lingered here, like a ghost, haunting the auditorium still. But she did not think she could extract what was here and return it to Ireland.

She moved again, wandering the timeline, looking at the faces of the performers frozen in time, each reveling in the perfect execution of their craft. The song had power indeed, even a century and more later, Keela could feel the strength in its reverberations.

At the far end of the timeline was a little area, a little shrine almost, dedicated to the Ryman's most beloved, most respected, most influential manager, a little woman named Lula C. Naff, known as L.C. She used to stand up in this vestibule and count the heads of the people waiting to come in for the show and compare it to the take at the ticket window. She was a music lover and shrewd businesswoman and credited for saving the Ryman from the wrecking ball more than once. She was rumored to haunt the auditorium.

She was pictured as an older lady, white hair in a neat bun, wearing a freshly pressed dress and a no-nonsense attitude.

"*It was the song,*" echoed L.C.'s voice.

"It was the song," Keela agreed. Yet she was still no closer to finding it.

Track 7

Keela slept in the eaves of the Ryman as a crow for
two nights, listening to tourists and concerts. Under every
note of music, she could hear the steady thrum of the *Oran
na Céle*, as if it had entwined itself into every song played
inside that hallowed auditorium. It lingered, its presence
potent and delightful, but it was not there. This new puzzle
drove Keela to sleepless distraction. When she finally did
doze off, it was only to dream of Michael playing it on his
fiddle and dancing deeper and deeper into the underworld,
whence neither he nor it would ever emerge again.

She went back to McNamara's on Thursday and
sang with the band. There was no uilieann player, but Keela
didn't care. James and the others, they had a good chemistry
and Keela only added to it. It was a good feeling being in an
ensemble, being part of a performance that didn't require
anyone to die. If she weren't careful, she could get used to
such a thing.

The dark-eyed sisters did not return that night, and
for that, Keela was grateful. Something about their scrutiny
unnerved her, all the more because, if she was correct in her
recollections, they were the pair she had encountered in the
courtyard of the symphony hall her first night in Nashville.
She had felt something from them, then, something that

made them stand out in her memory, something that made them stand out in a crowd of energetic pub-goers, and it was something besides luminous dark eyes and perfect skin. She just couldn't put her finger on it and decided to stop trying until she had a better reason to do so.

Friday at the pub, however, another singular woman came in to listen. The crowds had been increasing each night, adding to the energy and to the delight. The woman sauntered in wearing a tight-fitting skirt suit made in sea-green silk and just sat down at a vacant seat at a table as if she belonged there. No one already at the table seemed to mind, or even notice, and it struck Keela as strange. This woman was tall and curvaceous, with stormy blue-violet eyes and a deep tan. Her jet black hair was held in a bun by an ivory hairpin that dangled a half dozen or so aqua-colored freshwater pearls. She smiled at Keela with perfect white teeth. She was the most remarkable woman Keela had ever seen, yet her presence went so unremarked that it made her immediately suspicious.

Keela stumbled more than once during the set, forgetting a word or flubbing a note. The woman in the audience watched and smiled. It was harder to blot her out of the room; she seemed to be trying to invade Keela's attention, all the while hiding from everyone else.

They had just finished their set — the applause was still going — when the overly beautiful woman approached Keela.

"So, you're the one folks have been talking about, hmm?" Her eyes flickered over Keela's body, a disapproving squint speaking volumes. "Well, at least you can sing. My card." She flicked a pearlescent card out of her tiny purse and held it between her index and middle fingers.

Gingerly, Keela took it, fingering the expensive paper a moment before focusing on what the card said: *Ottilie Moisés ~ Vox Beata Records.* "What does this mean?"

"Mean?" Ottilie laughed. "Aren't you just the prettiest little thing, all naïve and stuff! It means I want to hear you sing. In my studio. It's a personal invitation. Those don't just come along every day, you know."

Keela frowned. "Why?"

Ottilie fluttered her long eyelashes. "Why, what?"

Everyone was paying attention now, like she'd

flipped a switch. Keela's skin began to crawl under the curious gazes of the crowd.

"Would you like to sit down?" Keela pointed at the little table to the side of the stage where she shared drinks with the band. It would make her feel more comfortable, she realized, and so did Ottilie.

Ottilie smiled, a charming but manipulative one. "Yes, let's." She turned away from Keela's favorite table and took a seat at the bar.

She nearly turned away, turned and walked right out of the pub and changed into a bird to fly home to her quiet cemetery when Ottilie's gaze caught hers and Keela saw the raw adoration in it. An unexpectedly unguarded moment from this otherwise polished woman, she looked toward Keela with so much yearning it sent a thrill of excitement through her.

So she went over to the bar and climbed somewhat gracefully onto a stool with her cloak folded across her knees. The bartender slid over a perfectly settled pint of Guinness. He must have poured it midway through her last song. He was good that way, and she really liked it here.

"I represent one of the finest record labels in town for truly gifted singers. We're not talking songwriters, guitar players, or chart-topping pop wannabes. I mean *singers*, bona fide talent. I only want the very best. And darling, I want you."

Keela took a long drink of her beer, pretending to consider what she had just heard. "But what does that mean, really?"

"It means, my dear, that I want to make you very famous and us both very rich."

"Ah. That's very kind of you, but I'm afraid I'm not interested." Keela saluted her with a tip of her pint. "Good night to you, madame." She slid down off the barstool and joined the others at their customary table.

"Did you really just brush off a record producer, Miss Keela?" James looked halfway between terrified and amused.

Keela shrugged. "That's not what I'm here for. And I can't afford to be pulled too far off my path."

"What are you here for?"

"I'm looking for a song. It was once played at the

Ryman."

"Oh," he said, stifling a laugh. "That narrows it right down."

She smiled and nodded. "That it does. It's an Irish song, it was played by a traveling band in 1904."

"The band was from Ireland?"

"Aye."

"Hmmm," James ran a finger along the stubble on his chin. "You might want to try the Country Music Hall of Fame. They have a surprising amount of information on the roots of country and bluegrass, which goes right back to Ireland, you know!" He made to poke her playfully but stopped short of actually touching her.

She smelled death on him again and her heart clenched. She turned away.

"Keela? You okay?"

"Of course," she swallowed her sorrow. "And yourself? Been feeling a'right?"

His smile twisted into something resembling a smirk and he laughed. "We were talking about you, Keela. Do you know the name of the band?"

"No. Names weren't listed with the pictures and L.C. didn't seem to remember anything specific about them."

"L.C.? At the Ryman? You've been talking to ghosts, I see."

Keela nearly dropped her beer.

James clucked his tongue. "No worries," he said gently. "I believe in 'em too, I just can't see 'em."

She smiled and hid her furious blush behind drinking more stout.

"Check out the Hall of Fame, they might have more information for you."

"That's a wonderful suggestion, I'll do that." Keela rose. "I'll see you tomorrow night."

"Let me walk you out."

"That's not necessary."

James smiled and followed her through the bar, confidently walking her past Ottilie's shrewd gaze. "I know it's not, but I feel like a jerk every time I let you walk out this door alone." He held the front door open for her.

Keela was grateful for the well-lit parking lot, it kept her hair black. She worried, though, that James might be falling for her as they lingered on the steps that led down from the pub's entrance to the parking area.

"Where do you go when you leave here?" James asked.

"Home. The only one I've got at the moment, but it suffices."

He nodded. "And you're safe there?"

"Oh, yes! Safe as houses." She resisted the urge to touch him for comfort, knowing that the gesture might be misconstrued and would certainly not be comforting in the least.

"Good," he said looking only marginally relieved. "Don't be afraid to ask any of us in the band for help, okay?"

"Of course."

He walked away then, without a backward glance. She was grateful as she stepped into the dark shadows of the woods that ringed the parking lot. Her hair fell silvery over her shoulders and her skin glowed softly. The transformation from woman to crow came easier in the darkness. Within moments, Keela was stretching her wings over Donelson, following the river towards downtown.

Something was amiss in the cemetery when she landed atop the bricks of the big monument standing alone at the corner of Rock and Oak Avenues. From there, through the branches of the budding trees, she could see a small car with the dome light on parked in front of the information building. Someone sat inside, and someone else paced around the small paved area with a flashlight.

Keela flapped to the nearest magnolia, already thick with leaves, where she could observe them without being seen. She peered down and recognized the sisters. These two were not mortal, that much she could ascertain from the look of their souls. Not mortal and not bearing a single drop of Irish blood. Although knowing what they were not was helpful, it brought her no closer to figuring out what they were or what they wanted with her.

After maybe an hour or so passed, they finally started their car and slowly drove out of the graveyard with their headlights dark until they had turned onto Fourth Avenue. She followed on the wing, pacing them as they jogged eastward through the narrow, often one-way streets that criss-crossed this old, industrial part of town until they came upon Hermitage Avenue and crossed the river into East Nashville.

Keela had not yet been into East Nashville, but found it a confusing, amazing, beautiful mess of gentrification and poverty. She tailed the car through a few confounding intersections and finally up a quiet, narrow street that led into a park. The sisters pulled into the gravel driveway of the last house before the park's entrance.

Keela perched in the tree that overhung the driveway, her feet nervously clenching and unclenching the branch and digging her talons into the bark.

The driver was the taller of the two, but not by much. Her hair was tucked into a knit hat while her companion's was coiled tightly into a bun. That sister paused and glanced up into the tree a moment. Keela froze. But the driver was in mid-conversation and brought her sister's attention back to the frustration at finding nothing at the graveyard.

"All the signs are there, you know?" She gestured with her keys. "She's Irish, she's hanging out in the old cemetery-"

"You *think* she's hiding there, Teri."

Teri shook her head, knocking her cap a little askew. "It's more than a hunch, Polly. Couldn't you sense it when we were there? I can smell music and I'm telling you our little friend was there and recently too."

"She was probably still at McNamara's. I told you we should have checked there."

"What's to check?" Teri crammed her key into the lock, turning first the deadbolt then moving onto the doorknob. She lowered her voice and drew her sister in beside her. "We know what she is, we just need to find out why she's here."

"I think we know why she's here," Polly said, voice equally soft, nearly too quiet for Keela to hear. "What we need to do is find out what her intentions are and how much she knows."

Polly had the more somber face. A well-defined nose and sharp jawline made her look perpetually melancholy. Teri had similar eyes to her sister, large and angled slightly downwards at the outside corners, but something about her more heart-shaped face gave her a dreamy instead of sad expression.

They exchanged a nod and went into the peculiar little cottage with an expansive main room with a double-sided hearth rising up through the center. Large windows filled every exterior wall, and it did not have the look of a residential building at all, regardless of the cozy furnishings and rugs inside. It looked like it had once been a train station, especially the way the covered porch stretched across the entire front of the house with wide steps that matched the porch's width and sturdy benches set between the windows.

Keela fluttered down to one of these benches and tried to listen at the window. Inside, Polly went into the tiny, open kitchen and put a copper kettle on the stove and took two tea bags out of a small wooden chest. Teri hung their coats beside the front door on a beautiful antique coat tree. She paused, her attention caught by Keela's window. Keela froze, willing herself not to be seen.

"That all depends on if we're right in our first guess," Teri said, settling into a well-loved velvet sofa. She tugged a chenille throw over her lap as Polly poured the tea and liberally added honey from a clay jar.

"What else would she be but a banshee, Teri?" Polly brought over two large mugs incised with a Greek key design around the rims.

Taking off her hat, Teri took one of the mugs and sipped at it gingerly. She toyed with a lock of dark hair with her free hand and stared out into nothing. "I don't know," she answered, at length. "I don't know what else she could be. I've never met a banshee in person, so I can't make a comparison. But I know that song is here and that it came from Ireland. Chances are really good that's what she's here about."

"We can't let her find it."

"I know."

Keela made a sound. Had she been wearing her woman's form, it might have been a gasp or a yelp, but in her crow's form it came out as a squawk. And altogether too loud.

Teri was on her feet at once, mug still in hand. "Did you hear that?"

Polly nodded and set down her tea. "I did."

They both went for the door and Keela bolted, taking

flight in an entirely unstealthy manner and leaving more than a few feathers behind. But the darkness was kind and she vanished from their sight in seconds.

"This gets weirder every minute," Polly grumbled.

"What do you think it was?" Teri bent down and picked up one of the fallen feathers, spinning it between her calloused fingertips. "Or who?"

"Can banshees turn into crows?"

"I don't know. But I mean to find out. We may have been on the right track after all."

Polly laughed, which looked out of place amid her lachrymose features. "And finding a single bird in the whole of Nashville will be somehow easier than tracking down a strange Irish girl?"

"Oh, shut up."

"I know, I know, you can't think when I'm right."

They went back inside and Keela made for the cemetery. She would be safe there, at least for one more night.

Track 8

Ottilie was at McNamara's again on Saturday. Keela almost refused to sing. Seeing her distress, Ottilie came over, this time wearing tight fitting jeans and a dark teal t-shirt with fluttery silk sleeves, along with a smile.

"I came on too strong last night," she said. "Most newbies I meet really respond to that. I should have known you were different."

Keela, still wary, smiled in return. "Don't worry yourself about it."

Ottilie retreated to the bar and listened to their set. In the break, she came around to the band's table, her smile softer and more genuine than it had seemed last night.

"What brings you to Nashville?"

Keela looked up from her Guinness and paused, unsure of how to answer. She shrugged, feigning a playfulness she didn't feel. "Seemed like the best place to land given my circumstances."

"And what circumstances were those?"

"She's on the hunt for a special song," James supplied. "One that's going to knock everyone's socks off!"

"A song?" The excitement jumped in Ottilie's eyes like blue-violet flames.

Keela waved her hand, "It's nothing. Just a hobby,

really." She wished she hadn't mentioned a thing to James. She hadn't even told him half of the truth, not even half of half, but here he was trying to be charming and helpful.

"I know many songs, have access to some great old ones as well. What kind of song are you looking for? Something to showcase your range? Or maybe something to touch the heart? You name it, I've got it."

It was on the tip of Keela's tongue to blurt out "*Oran na Céle*," but she didn't. Instead she said, "It's an old Irish song, came here in the nineteenth century, was played at the Ryman a time or two in the early 1900s." It was what she'd told James. She wondered if it might spark something in Ottilie. James hadn't been any help in the matter.

"There's an Irish song you don't know?" Her manner was teasing but her eyes were more calculating. She was sounding Keela out.

"Lots of them, actually. Many came over here to the States during the famine and when the family back home died, the legacy of the songs in Ireland died, too," she lied. Well, only a little. Keela was sure that might have happened a time or two, maybe, but she wanted to sound out Ottilie a bit as well.

"So, you're collecting." Ottilie nodded, as if making a mental note. "From your specific genealogy or just lost Irish songs in general? Or is this one song special?"

There was something in her tone that but Keela on edge. Something about the way she said the word "genealogy." Keela could almost hear the quotes around it, as if Ottilie was using a deliberate euphemism.

"It's a particular song I'd love to find. It was very precious to a cousin of sorts, or so the story goes. But really, I'd be happy to uncover any lost musical treasure," Keela said.

James and the fiddler, Lisa, applauded at that. Ottilie nodded, the wheels in her mind obviously turning.

"I think I can help you," she said, softly.

Keela laughed and Ottilie touched the back of her hand. She did not pull back.

"I have access to archives and resources that ordinary folks don't. I would be happy to help you find what you're looking for."

Keela wasn't sure what was more stunning, that this

woman was practically holding her hand or that she was trying to say she could possibly find the song. "You'd… what?"

"Your song. I'm sure it's in a musty old archive someplace in town. Nearly every song is, I imagine. Besides, you obviously have fun performing. I'm sure we can work out a little trade, hmm? I give you access to my sources, you give me some demo tracks. Win-win." Ottilie gave her hand a friendly squeeze and let go, as if she felt nothing out of the ordinary.

Keela sat back in her chair, her mind buzzing with too many possibilities.

"Will you come over on Monday in the morning? I'll pull out my old nineteenth century song books and we can start there. You'll adore my music library, I just know you will!" Ottilie manifested another business card, this one from a pants pocket, Keela thought, judging from the slight curve in the paper.

What harm could it do to browse the woman's library, she wondered. And if Ottilie had an interest in nineteenth- and twentieth-century Irish music, it might actually be to some benefit.

"Monday, it is," Keela said slipped the card into the inside pocket of her cloak alongside the stone from the Liffey.

The smile that spread across Ottilie's face was more than pleased. It was victorious.

What unease Keela might have felt evaporated the moment she stepped back on stage. Lisa, a beautiful girl with amber hair that reached to the back of her knees, stepped out first with a long mournful fiddle solo. The audience settled in, ready for one of Keela's sweet, chilling dirges. They exchanged a glance and then Lisa leapt into the frenzied fiddling of "Lannigan's Ball" and Keela spat out the tricky, fast lyrics with obvious glee.

Ottilie sat in the audience and just grinned, watching her. The crowd sang along when they could, often left behind by the fast tempo of the song as they clanked their pint glasses on the tables to the beat. This set was rousing, energetic, and left Keela breathless and dizzy. She danced. More than once.

When the night finally rolled to a raucous close,

Keela was nowhere near sleepy. She said her good-byes in the parking lot, leaving James until last as usual. He turned and walked purposefully away, leaving her alone to slip into the trees and transform.

She stretched her wings feeling the wind under them; it felt like rain was coming. She circled and perched atop McNamara's, watching the last of the cars pull out and head on towards whatever destinations awaited them.

Ottilie had left without incident, happy with Keela's promise to come to her studio on Monday. She wanted very much to follow James home, to speak to him directly — banshee to Irishman — about his impending death, too near now to be ignored any longer. But she hesitated, afraid of yet another transgression that would bar her from her home and her family forever. She thought instead about the sisters and their strange little train-station cottage.

The mugs.

The mugs were decorated with a Greek design. There was a big Greek temple in town.

She startled herself from her perch, soaring out towards downtown. Gliding westward, she saw the temple rising out of the well-tended trees of Centennial Park, glowing like some gilded relic. It was a replica of the Parthenon in Athens, Greece.

The park was empty that late at night, save for a few discreetly parked cars with indiscreetly fogged windows. Vanderbilt University was just across the street, after all. Keela ignored the wooded side streets that snaked through the east side of the park and fluttered down to land on one of the large banks of lights illuminating the structure. The building itself could not tell the difference between night and day, so brightly it was illuminated at all hours. It only knew there were lonely times, but that at some point, all the lovely people came back to it.

She landed at the foot of the large steps at the front of the building, becoming a woman in the blink of an eye. Keela approached it, reverently. The force of its presence echoed through the realms of the physical, as well as the spiritual. It was a holy place, in truth and on many levels. The aura of it gathered around its edges, but also glowed from within. She gingerly set foot onto the first of many tall, deep steps, marveling at the multitude of little golden rocks pressed into the concrete. Built with an awkward proportion, Keela heaved her foot up onto the second step and found herself regarding the tiny stones again. And again at the third. Pausing mid-stride, she realized the unusual height of the stair treads caused her to rock far forward in order to make the next step. With each step she took, she was all but genuflecting before the great bronze doors that guarded the inner sanctuary and the great replica statue of Athena.

Clever, she thought to herself with a smile.

As she finally gained the main level after the arduous climb, she marveled at the stillness. The pillars ran along the long sides of the rectangular structure with a fairly wide path between them and the building's wall. She strolled along the southern arcade, where the lights of West End Avenue played peek-a-boo with her from behind the pillars. In the dark behind each one, she could feel the subtle shift as her hair and eyes gleamed silver for a pace before emerging into the light once more.

She had nearly completed a circuit of the building when something disturbed the quiet. Had Keela been any ordinary human, she might not have noticed a stirring of air and the near-silent beat of wings in the direction of the wide front platform. A Great Horned Owl perched on the railing that set off the entrance to the ticket lobby on the lower level of the temple. The mantle of divinity lay heavy on the bird.

It stared, unblinking, with its wide yellow eyes. The fathomless irises expanded and contracted as it tilted its head first one way, then the other. The owl's speckled throat fluttered as it *churred* at her — in greeting or warning, Keela could not tell. She bowed her head and curtsied, drawing her skirt wide beneath her cloak. The owl clucked and Keela rose, fancying that she could understand the creature. They stood a moment in tense silence before the owl, apparently satisfied with its scrutiny, launched itself from the railing in a barely audible rush of wing beats and disappeared over the roof of the Parthenon. Keela watched it go and felt — not welcomed, no — but tolerated.

When she turned back towards the building, she wasn't alone.

The sisters waited there, watching her.

"She summoned you, did she not?" Keela nodded to the place where the owl had just been.

Teri, the taller of the two, nodded. "When the lady summons, we listen. She doesn't do it often, so it must have been important."

Polly nodded, her frown deepening. "And as we can see, it apparently was. We've been looking for you, you know."

"Aye. And I haven't exactly been hiding. Been at the pub three nights a week for two weeks."

"We've been hoping to speak to you in *private*," Polly said.

Keela glanced around the open, empty park. "And do yourselves suppose this is private enough for a chat?"

"Come inside," Teri put her hand on the enormous handle of the great bronze door.

"You're joking!"

With a curving of her brow and a smirk, Teri pushed the door open. "You're obviously new here."

It was like going into a barrow, yet entirely not. The large central chamber was lit with torches, and the slightly sunken floor shimmered with something liquid and slightly viscous — it might have been oil of some kind. Reflected in that gleaming surface was the blazing form of Athena, splendid in golden robes and a spear held comfortably, but ably, in one hand while a dancing goddess in miniature perched on the other. Keela knew just enough Greek mythology to reckon the smaller figure was supposed to be Nike, the goddess of victory. The great statue at the end of the hall seemed to breathe while it watched them, although that could have been a trick of the ever-shifting pool that threw reflections of firelight and gold throughout the room to dazzle the eyes.

Her companions had changed as well, betraying their nature as goddesses. Their dusky skin glowed with a serene inner light and their ordinary enough clothes had been transformed into white lambswool gowns that sparkled diamond-bright.

She knew herself to be changed as well, her hair cascading silver down her back and her eyes gone glowing red as embers. They faced each other in their true forms and waited for someone to speak.

Teri broke the silence, stepping forward in her wrapped dress, the hems embroidered with thread of gold in that famous key pattern. "I am Euterpe, Muse of Music. This is my sister, Polyhymnia, Muse of Voice. You are intruding here, faerie."

Keela straightened, drawing herself up to her full height, feeling her bones elongate just slightly as she did. "And I am Keela O'Reardon," she replied. "I have not violated anyone's sovereignty here or anywhere."

"You are here to steal," Polyhymnia said, her perpetually sad eyes, even more morose and dramatic here in this place, narrowed unbecomingly.

"Steal? You are quite mistaken. What I am looking for belongs to me, to my family. I am here only to reclaim what is rightfully ours."

Euterpe smiled unkindly. "As these humans are fond of saying, 'possession is nine-tenths of the law.' Where have your people been for the last hundred and a half years?"

"Yourselves are quibbling over a century or two? Ladies, please, we're *immortal*."

That silenced them at least for a moment. Euterpe finally spoke, "I am here, bound by promise to guard that what you seek."

"Then we are going to have a problem with one another. For I am here, bound by promise to take back my birthright." Keela folded her arms and looked each of the sisters in the eye.

"I don't like that we should be enemies," Euterpe said.

"Alas, we are at cross-purposes," Keela replied.

"We can make it so you never leave this place," Polyhymnia warned. "We take our duty quite seriously."

"I do not doubt it." Keela reached into the inner pocket of her cloak and retrieved the stone from the Liffey, keeping it squeezed tightly in her hand. "But you won't be wanting to take that route, I promise you. This place might have been tied to the Greeks a long time ago, but there's a fair bit of Irish here now. I don't have goddesses at my beck, but I've got enough to see me through. So don't be casting your threats at me, thinking I'm going to turn tail and run. You don't know banshees very well."

She could see her reflection out of the corner of her eye in the oil. And she could feel how she looked, the very image of a harbinger of death. Bony, angular, pale, with greying flesh and sharply pointed teeth, with gnarled fingers and hair that wrapped her ethereal body like a shroud. Her voice, which she could make honey-sweet and full of comfort, howled and growled like the wind in a thunderstorm full of warning and danger. Her eyes — usually dark, depthless, and mysterious — burned ferociously now the color of blood, raw and radiant, daring even these goddesses assembled here to look into them and not tremble, not fear death just a little bit.

This was the power Keela kept tamped down inside of her, lest it overwhelm her, this is what the loss of her comb had taken away, what her exile had stolen. But not here. Here she could tap into the primal, elemental forces that ran through the city, ran through this shrine, here she could unhinge herself from the mortal form she wore about on the earth. Here she could show them what she truly was and what power was at *her* beck.

And she could see that they were at least a little bit daunted by her true nature.

"Oh, my. Is that what you are?" Euterpe whispered.

"I am," Keela said and drew a quick, deep breath before she lost the courage to do so then let out a shrill keening shriek that reverberated along the chamber's stone walls, doubling back on itself as the echoes wrapped around one another like writhing serpents. The great statue of Athena stood silent, but the muses each retreated a half step under the onslaught of that wail. Keela stretched one finger towards them and with far more bravado than she felt said, "Stay out of my way."

She turned on her heel and her cloak fluttered out behind her, tattered and smelling like the grave. Focusing on the set of bronze doors, she tapped the considerable reservoirs of power here and bid them open for her. They did, flinging inward on their well-tended hinges with a tremendous force. The boom of them hitting their stoppers echoed through the park, sending birds scattering from the trees. A car alarm blared from somewhere nearby.

Keela was only two steps over the threshold when she transformed herself into a crow and soared away, heart pounding with thrilled terror. She didn't want to make enemies here, but some things were worth the trouble.

Track 9

In the afterglow of her snarky victory at the Parthenon, Keela returned to the City Cemetery after all. She wouldn't be bullied away from this little bit of home she had wrought for herself. She spent most of Sunday alternating between bird and human forms and wandering the graveyard part preening, part patrolling in case either of the muses decided to come have another word with her. They didn't show up.

She did encounter, however, a musician buried there: Ella Sheppard Moore. A former slave, Ella became an accomplished pianist and wound up being the accompanist for the Fisk Jubilee singers. She was there when Queen Victoria made the quip about Nashville being a "musical city." But she didn't know anything about the *Oran na Céle*.

"Try the churches," Ella suggested. They strolled along Cedar Avenue. "This town was built for music. It always has been. And the churches is where the talent went."

"Did traveling musicians ever play churches? Or was it just religious music?"

"All the time," Ella smiled wistfully, gazing into the pale blue sky with its littering of clouds. The wind blew a little warm now and again, piling the clouds into enormous castle shapes. "Once services were done, many people played there. It was what we had. Have you been to the Ryman? It was once a church, you know."

Keela nodded. "Aye, I took the tour the other day."

"They were built for sound, from the preachers to the choirs to the soloists, each church, from its very foundations, was made to celebrate the music played there."

"So, what you're saying is that the churches were designed to make music sound better? Like a symphony hall or theatre might be today?" It was an interesting thought, and it made sense, seeing as how most churches were doubling as concert spaces.

"Yes, that's the way they were designed."

Keela wondered if any church had been designed to hold the *Oran na Céle*.

"How many churches are there in Nashville?"

Ella counted in her head a minute. "Well, I'd say there are about twenty or thirty…"

"Churches?"

"Denominations."

"Oh." The momentary giddiness of being able to spend an afternoon peeking at a few dozen buildings evaporated.

"But not that many remain from the time you're asking after."

"Oh," Keela's hopes sank further. There was a good chance, then, if a building had been erected to hold her song, it was long gone by now.

Ella frowned. "I'm sorry I couldn't be more help."

"You've been wonderful," Keela assured her.

"I'd love to hear you sing, you know."

"And I'd love to hear you play."

"That's a little harder, not many pianos in cemeteries."

Keela laughed. "'Tis true. Maybe I'll work out a way to find you one. While I'm on the subject of impossible tasks."

Ella stretched out her hands with her long and widely spaced fingers, a piano player's hands to be sure. "I miss the feel of the keys."

"I'll bet they miss yourself playing them, too."

They parted ways and Keela went out on crow's wings to listen to the churches downtown. Ella was correct in the sheer number of types of churches. In Ireland, there were Catholic ones and not much else. Even in Northern Ireland where Protestantism held sway, there were not nearly so many sects. It seemed that every block boasted some different kind of Christianity. Keela had never bothered with any religion at all to begin with, so the whole thing struck her as strange and rather definitively American.

But one thing was certain: the old churches did seem to be built for celebrating the human voice. She visited the oldest one in town, a Catholic church now dwarfed by the enormous downtown buildings around it. The resonances there were rich and deep. Hand-laid plaster over old-growth wooden beams made for beautiful acoustics. It was also pleasantly haunted, this church. Saint Mary of the Seven Sorrows had once been the city's cathedral, which Keela found a bit boggling as it was so tiny. She was no stranger to tiny churches, but when she heard "cathedral," a pleasant little Greek-revival-influenced building hardly larger than a chapel was the last thing that came to mind. It was a beauty, but it did not hold her song.

The Downtown Presbyterian Church was another story entirely. Built in the 1850s to replace a structure that had burned, this church was more Egyptian temple than Christian worship center. It also had a rich history of non-churchy goings-on, having been a hospital, a hostel, and an emergency shelter many times in its existence. It was also a favorite place for performances. That was enough to pique Keela's interest in it.

Pillars shaped like lotus plants flanked a large pipe organ with a trompe l'oeil painting of more pillars stretching into the distance, and nearly every surface within was trimmed in gold leaf or faux faience. For such a poshly decorated building, it had a bit of a lonely feel, even just after Sunday services. The musty odor of a damp basement drifted up from the floor, not quite the pleasant sort of damp that Molan smelled like, but just the funk of an old building in a high-moisture environment. For sure there was no resonance of the song here. It was one more disappointment.

Tomorrow, she thought. *Tomorrow I will find out something in those archives.*

Keela sat awake with anticipation most of the night. Early the next day, she shook out her dress and her cloak once again and braided her hair neatly down her back. She hoped it would all stay so neat when she came out of her crow form. It usually did, but she was nervous today.

The address on the card read 1013 16th Avenue South, AKA "Music Square East." This was the beating heart of Nashville's recording industry, nestled in a handful of blocks between collegiate suburbia and the fringes of downtown. It wasn't much to look at, really.

Vox Beata Records, however, was definitely a sight to see. The purple brick Victorian was a novel choice for a record label's headquarters and the building stood out from its eclectic peers on the block, mostly lower profile bungalow-style houses and 1920s-era cottages with a handful of taller buildings thrown in for good measure. Its immediate neighbors were a very rustic log cabin and an ultra-modern office building hidden mostly behind shrubbery and crepe myrtle.

Keela hesitated on the manicured lawn, worrying at the corner of the business card that had already started to grow ragged and a little dirty from handling. It carried all of her desperate dreams. It might enable her to find the song.

Her encounter with the muses last night emboldened her. What had she to fear from a mortal record producer? She walked straight up the path and onto the porch. There was a quaint twist-bell done in bronze set into the door just below the large stained glass window. She gave it a couple of turns, listening to the chiming it made.

As the chimes faded into silence, the door opened. The man there smiled pleasantly. He was tall, well-built, and handsome; his dark complexion offered striking contrast to his jewel-green eyes.

"Good morning. I have an appointment." Keela bobbed her head to him as she came into the opulent parlor. He said nothing. It rattled her nerves.

A thickly woven carpet covered the glossy hardwood floor, muffling their steps, and a charming arrangement of chairs and knick-knacks gave it an air of a hotel lobby. He shut the door behind them and bowed. He extended his right arm, then brought it in a sweeping gesture towards his torso. Next, he moved his hand across his chest, making a pinching motion with his fingers, then pantomimed shrugging off a coat.

"My cloak? I appreciate the offer, but no, I'll keep hold of it."

He nodded and started away, out of the parlor.

"Begging your pardon," Keela hurried to catch up. "But you can indeed hear me?"

Glancing back, he nodded.

"Aye," was all she said, keeping to herself her thoughts about how a man with no voice might be of use at a record label.

The house was a good deal longer that it appeared from the front walk. A long, narrow conference room on the right side of the house looked to have originally been a formal dining room; ivy threatened the edges of series of tall windows on the outside wall. To their left, a recording studio paneled in rich, dark wood and topped with elegant moldings even had sound dampeners to match the regal furnishings, themselves wrapped in thick brocades that matched the carpets strewn across the floor.

"This is such a delightful work space," Keela marveled, and her guide beamed.

On both sides of the main hall, small offices with large windows and antique furnishings overlooked the flower gardens alongside the building.

As they approached the first closed door Keela had yet seen, her escort raised his hand. She stopped and waited as he opened the door just enough for him to slip through. Keela paced a bit, nerves gnawing at her insides again, and looked at the photographs on the wall, each hung in an identical gilt frame as its neighbor and each had been signed with a flourish using a gold marker.

The black and white photographs were also identically emblazoned in the lower right corners with the Vox Beata logo: an Art Nouveau-inspired image of a woman with an open mouth and what looked like a jewel emerging from it. Keela guessed that these must be Ottilie's clients. They were each intimidatingly lovely, with smiling faces that belied a certain ferocity of ambition within.

She had actually turned and made a half dozen steps back toward the front door when she heard Ottilie's silken voice call her name.

"Keela, so glad you could make it." Ottilie swung the office door open and beckoned. She wore a variation of the suit she'd worn to McNamara's: a short skirt and snugly fitted jacket made of subtly shimmering silk in deep teal.

"Please, come in."

She did not see her handsome guide as she entered.

Ottilie noticed. "I've sent Cayden to bring some refreshments. I haven't had my breakfast and I think so much clearer when there's coffee involved."

"Cayden, the young man who showed me in?"

"The same. He's my right-hand-man, or I suppose in my case, *left*-hand-man," she chuckled to herself. "I don't know what I would do without him."

"He is quite a gentleman." Keela glanced around, eager to make small talk that did not include the sweet and silent Cayden. There was something in Ottilie's tone that implied an intimacy that Keela did not wish to hear.

This office, smaller and situated in the rear of the house, had a much cozier feel than the others. Scattered on the large oak desk were trade magazines as well as *The Scene* and *The City Paper*, the free weekly papers that circulated around Nashville. There was an order and focus to the abundance of knick-knacks and trinkets, mostly shells and stones and bottles — some clear, some colorful — all intricately wrapped in copper, gold, and silver wire strung with beads. Among the wall full of artistic photographs of bodies of water — streams, beaches, lakes, and ponds — were several that raised a bittersweet reminder of home.

Behind her, Ottilie sighed with a similar sense of longing. "As you can see, I'm a waterbaby living in a land-locked state."

"You have a lovely office," Keela said.

"Thank you. It's my sanctuary. Come, sit down. Let's talk about you for a bit, shall we?"

Keela sat in one of the plush, curved chairs opposite the desk. "Where do you keep your archives?"

"On the second floor. There's a whole library up there plus a rehearsal room and another recording studio." Ottilie smiled. "You'd like to see it, now, wouldn't you?"

"If you wouldn't mind."

"Only if you sing a little, just for me, after you've had your look."

"Aye. I'll do it."

"Good!" Ottilie hopped up from her chair. "Follow me. We'll take the back stairs. They're right here." She opened her office door and turned into a narrower corridor than the main hall. "Cayden, we'll be taking our breakfast upstairs!"

Keela followed, eager to see this music library for herself. The upstairs was far less opulent than the first floor, but no less elegant with hardwood floors, intricate molding, hand-stamped wallpaper, lace curtains, and Edwardian furnishings.

They came into an informal lounge area with a camel back sofa and a very incongruous vending machine sitting side-by-side in front of a flatscreen TV on a credenza strewn with magazines and flyers. An empty Coke Zero can sat on the side table beside the TV's remote.

"This *is* a working studio," Ottilie said by way of apology, snagging the Coke can and tossing it into a blue recycling bin.

A short hall opened into a sparsely furnished room that took up the entire width of the building, with a few chairs and music stands clustered in one corner along with a grand piano and an enormous armoire that she guessed held more instruments. The other recording studio took up the far side of this room with walls lined with old books for sound-proofing. This studio was much larger than the other downstairs, she could see where the glass walls could slide open to roll in the piano. Keela thought a small orchestra could squeeze in there.

But Ottilie simply pointed out the studio's existence and moved into the real prize: the mahogany-paneled room at the front of the house. Built-in shelves lined the two side walls and along the half-wall where the more formal front staircase ended. A large round sofa, the kind usually seen in posh libraries, sat in the center of the room. A row of waist-high wooden filing cabinets ran along on one side of the room with a row of tables and chairs along the other.

Keela gaped at the sheer magnitude of music collected in this room. Sheet music, vinyl records, bound volumes, and more were all collected here.

"It's categorized by date, more than style. The early stuff is all standards, folk music, spirituals, and the like." Ottilie pointed at a section of shelving closed off with slightly frosted glass doors. "They aren't locked. Neither are these." She rolled open a drawer and ran a fingertip gently across the filing tabs. "Here you'll find loose sheets, notes, letters, and ephemera. Most likely you'll find what you're looking for in here. Much of this stuff is archival items never published." She patted the top of the second cabinet. "Mid-nineteenth century starts here and goes on for about four or five drawers, the timeline continues down through the twenty-first century about halfway through the last cabinet, the rest of it isn't filled yet. This first one is seventeenth and eighteenth century, or at least copies of such. I have a few originals in the horizontal files upstairs."

"Upstairs? There's more?"

"The attic. Where I keep my Victrola and the truly rare valuables, musically speaking of course."

Keela chewed the inside of her cheek, wondering whether her song might be up there instead. "Can I see that some time?"

"Maybe." Ottilie shut the drawer. "Depends how much I like your voice."

"That's fair, I suppose."

A bell rang from the lounge. "That's Cayden with our breakfast. The books will still be here when we're through, let's go have a bite shall we?"

Cayden had not only brought up the breakfast tray but also an iron garden table with a round, pierce-work top. Keela hesitated. No fae liked the touch of iron of any sort.

"Sit, my dear. How do you take your coffee?"

"Black," Keela answered, settling herself gingerly onto the wrought iron stool that accompanied the table. She could feel the ache of the iron through her cloak.

Her wariness of Ottilie immediately increased. That table had to have been a real pain to bring up to the second floor. Ottilie knew, or at the very least suspected, what Keela was and was sounding her out some more.

The silence hung there between the three of them. Keela sipped at her coffee while Ottilie watched her. Cayden hovered near the stairs and watched them both.

"What is your schedule like today?" Keela asked. "I hate to impose on your time if you have other clients."

"I cleared the morning just for you. And after I hear you sing a little for me, you're welcomed to stay up here reading as long as you'd like." Ottilie smiled and took a drink of her milky-sweet coffee. "We can do that now. Go downstairs to the little studio. It's set up for solo voice." She lifted a pastry and bit into it, golden flakes raining down onto her perfect lapels. She chewed, half-closing her eyes and took another drink of coffee before licking her fingertips clean. "You should have some, these are divine. They come from a great little place in East Nashville called Sweet 16th."

"I've already eaten," Keela lied. She never ate. Well, she ate rarely and only specific foods at specific times, neither of which was here and now.

Ottilie pursed her lips a moment, pastry crumbs clinging to her sparkling lipstick. "You're really missing out. Just a taste?"

"I'll pass. But you are very kind to offer."

"This one is made with guava and goat cheese. Can you believe it? I've never tasted anything so divine!" She all but pressed the danish into Keela's mouth.

Keela sat straighter, putting herself just out of Ottilie's reach. "Really, no."

This too, was a test. Keela glanced at Cayden, but he remained impassive, observing but not reacting.

She drained the last of her coffee and set the mug down, carefully not touching the table with her wrist. "As soon as you're done eating, we should go down to the studio."

That did it. Ottilie put down her half-eaten pastry and dabbed her fingertips on one of the crisp napkins. "Why wait?" She was brushing past Cayden in an instant, leading the way back down to the ground floor.

Out of the frying pan, into the fire, Keela thought.

Track 10

*O*ttilie closed the studio door behind them, and it felt for an instant like the sealing of a crypt, so quiet was the room. Plush carpets overlapped one another, their fringes flirting and tangling along the strange angles they formed across the small room. Ottilie went into the booth and shut herself in there with a barely audible click of the door. She set headphones over her ears carefully so as not to muss her perfect hair.

Keela nearly ran.

This woman was dangerous.

But a single thought stayed her feet: the music archives upstairs. "Michael," she whispered, breath-soft, like a prayer. The shame then caught her, how long had it been since she had thought of him? Days, at least.

"I'm ready when you are, my dear," Ottilie said, her voice coming through the little speaker mounted on the wall above the plate-glass window of the recording booth. "You warm up and I'll do a little sound check."

Unsure of what she ought to do, Keela hummed and sang a few awkward scales.

Frowning, Ottilie leaned over the speaker. "Why don't we just start, then. This is going to be a rough cut anyway."

Keela sang. She wanted to be timid about it, but her shame and her anger at herself caught her off guard and the song came out fiercely. It was a banshee song, nothing fancy, just a simple lament that could be sung a variety of different ways. It covered her fear nicely and she enjoyed seeing the momentary confusion on Ottilie's face. She didn't know what the woman had been expecting, but whatever it was that song hadn't been it. She sang on, soaring towards the high notes and crashing down to the low with the terrible force of her abilities. Even Ottilie's calculated mask couldn't hide her awe.

Michael, Michael… Keela thought and she touched the stone that Molan had given her in her pocket. She remembered the muses and the temple and her display of power to them. Her confidence rose. She thought of the nights at McNamara's, of the faces in the crowd smiling or weeping by the power of her voice alone.

It was intoxicating.

By the time she had finished her song, Ottilie was on her feet, hands pressed to the glass. There was a look of wonder on her face, wonder and longing. It was the most honest thing Keela had yet seen from her, and they passed several long moments just watching one another. Ottilie snapped back to herself first, her smiling mask declaring that she was once again in control of her emotions.

"Well, if that don't just beat all," she said.

"That's good, right?"

"Darling, you have no idea, do you?"

Keela shook her head, smiling despite herself. "When it comes to performance quality, no, not really." She stepped away from the microphone and edged around the music stand. "I'll be upstairs," she said.

"Don't you dare leave before you come say goodbye to me."

"I won't." Keela escaped from the studio before Ottilie could step out of the booth, dashing up the back stairs.

The dry, warm scent of old paper and leather underscored by the acrid tang of ink settled her nerves. She pulled open the first drawer of nineteenth century archives and began to go through them, page by page. She stood at the cabinet until her knees started to ache, then moved to the reading table, and finally brought stacks of paper with her to the couch. No one bothered her while she sat up there reading until dusk.

She noticed the coming night only when a stray shimmer of silver hair fell across the page she was reading. Looking up, she saw that it was full dark in the library. Keela immediately went to go find a light to turn on. It wasn't that she couldn't see any longer — in fact her vision was far better at night than during the day — but she feared Cayden or Ottilie coming upon her in this mode, with lambent silver hair and inhuman eyes.

The bronze and crystal chandelier came to sparking life at the touch of a button. She'd been at this for hours, she realized, and had nary a clue to go on. Of course, she was only through the first drawer. There were so many more to search. The items were catalogued by date and date alone, so she sifted through German and Spanish documents, Negro Spirituals, and pulp sheet music sold on street corners for a penny. Every now and again did she find something Irish, but it was simply a country ditty or folk song that had no tie to the song she sought. She didn't know if she could take six more drawers of this. Eight if she wanted to push through until 1910, to make sure she covered the time period that she knew the song was played at the Ryman.

She thought perhaps she might jump to 1904, just to see what was there then backtrack or move forward if she found anything worthy.

But not tonight. Tonight she wanted nothing more than to settle into her favorite magnolia, the one where the roots and wrapped around a handful of graves, and just sleep until she felt like waking. Between the searching and the singing for Ottilie, Keela was utterly wiped out.

She nearly sneaked down the front steps and let herself out the door when she remembered that she had told Ottilie she'd say goodbye before leaving. It wasn't exactly a promise, but she wanted to keep things civil between them. Ottilie was not to be trusted nor trifled with, but she also had something Keela wanted, or at least Ottilie seemed pretty confident that she did. Keela wasn't willing to rule out the possibility that this strange woman, who was indeed much more than she seemed, had somehow come into the possession of the *Oran na Céle.*

So she went down the back stairs, holding a smile on her lips. "I'm taking m'self home," she announced at Ottilie's door.

"So soon? You can't be done already, can you?"

"Aye, for the night. I'm getting cross-eyed up there, time to take a rest."

"Then you're planning on coming back, then?"

Keela nodded. "So long as it's all right with yourself, I thought I might, yes."

"Excellent. You're going to have to sing for me again."

"I am?"

Ottilie's smile was sharp and Keela wasn't too sure she liked what lay beneath it. "Just earning your keep, is all. We can't keep that light of yours under a bushel, can we?"

"I suppose not…"

"Keela, your voice is singular, it's amazing, it's awe-inspiring and you weren't even trying. What I could do with a woman of your abilities… Will you come again tomorrow?"

"I'll think on it."

"Please? If not tomorrow, sometime this week. *Any* time. My door, and my library, is always open to you."

Keela thought of the archives just above her head. "Aye, all right. Tomorrow, and later on in the week as well."

Ottilie clapped her hands and jumped to her feet. She rushed to give Keela a hug. "Let me work my magic on you, Keela, and yours is a voice that will go down in history."

Ottilie walked Keela to the door, chattering brightly about all the possibilities that lay ahead. Keela politely told her goodnight and walked a good block and a half away before ducking into some shrubbery to transform. A heavy fog was rolling in off the river when she finally perched in the cemetery for the night. She closed her eyes and let exhaustion claim her.

When morning came, she went back to Vox Beata Records through the clinging mists that blanketed the city. Cayden came to the door, his face solemn.

"Good morning," Keela said with more cheer than she felt. "Is your mistress in?"

Cayden shook his head. He glanced furtively down the street before drawing Keela in by the sleeve and shutting the door behind her. His green eyes widened and he pointed at her throat and shook his head.

"Don't speak?" she asked.

He shook his head again, frustration darkening his cheeks. This time after he pointed he opened his mouth and mimed something coming out of it.

"Don't *sing*."

He nodded, relief clear on his face.

"Why not?"

At this, he pressed his lips together and sighed through his nose. His hand rolled in the air and he shook his head, closing his eyes briefly, as if in defeat.

"There's too much to tell," Keela guessed.

He nodded again, a sad smile tugging at his lips.

"Can you write it down for me?"

The very notion seemed to frighten him and Keela backpedaled on the suggestion immediately.

"Your concern is noted, I'll put her off for today if I can. Would that make you happy?"

He nodded and pointed up the front steps. He put his finger to his lips and went, "Shhh."

Keela went up quietly and sat herself down in front of the drawer for 1904.

Of course, not a whole lot of note happened in 1904. The Irish band that had played the song at the Ryman hadn't even been remembered at the auditorium and certainly no mention of them was made in any periodicals or other primary sources Keela found in the drawer. The only glimmer of hope was a bundle of sheet music bound with twine that was labeled "Traveling Irish Players."

But before she could even untie the string, Cayden was tugging at her sleeve. He took the bundle from her and tucked it back into the drawer before firmly tugging the shoulders of her dress and nearly pushing her towards the stairs, he was following so close. She heard a car door slam at the rear of the building. Cayden opened the front door, his body so tense Keela thought he would surely burst at any moment, and nudged her through it. He shook off the shiver and hustled her along the porch until he reached the ornate mailbox on the front of the building. He quickly gathered the mail and, giving her a significant look, ducked back inside and firmly shut the door behind him.

What Ottilie would think when she was found out to be a no-show for the day, Keela didn't know. She decided to make herself scarce, taking crow's wings back towards downtown. Instead of heading back to her magnolia, she touched down on Second Avenue and sought out James at Buck Wild. The fog was quite heavy this close to the river.

"Well hello there!" James slid his phone into his pocket and gave Keela a warm grin. "If it isn't my favorite vocalist! You know, I was just thinking about you."

"Were you, now?" Feeling more at ease, Keela took a seat at the bar. As usual, the place was nearly deserted at this time of day. She had no idea why it even stayed open.

Noticing her scrutiny of the place, James laughed. "They pull in a good lunch crowd, makes it worth keeping the doors open all day." He put down a glass in front of her and poured a finger's width of Jameson into it. "I have a proposition for you."

"So it would seem. Buttering me up with the good stuff straight away." She lifted the glass and nodded at him over the rim before taking a sip.

"A friend of mine's birthday is this week. She wants to have a little shindig at McNamara's and was wondering if we'd come in and play. And if you, specifically you, would sing."

"Sure. When?"

He hesitated. "Tonight. I know it's short notice…"

Keela waved off his concern. "Don't be worrying yourself, tonight is fine."

"Really?"

"Aye. Really."

"Awesome. Thanks! I'll call Teri and let her know, she's gonna be thrilled."

A quiver of apprehension went through her. "Teri?"

"Yeah, she's a dear friend. Lives over in East Nashville with her sister, Polly. I wouldn't be half the musician I am today if it weren't for the two of them. Although," he laughed at himself, "I guess that's not saying much. But she has been such an inspiration to me that I couldn't say no to a little favor like this. I'm excited you're game for it, too." His smile widened. "I can't wait to introduce you to them. They've been in the pub before and heard you. They were *really* impressed."

Keela nodded, the apprehension had built to full-on fear. But she had faced them before and come out of it unscathed. She saw no reason to be afraid, and yet her belly churned with nerves. So she changed the subject. "That's quite a fog we're having, isn't it?"

James looked past her out the large front window. "Happens in the spring and the fall around here. Weather changing, hot and cold fronts colliding. Just wait 'til one of the big thunderstorms pop up. Southern springtime thunderstorms are the stuff of legend, I tell you."

"We don't have those in Ireland."

"Then you, little lady, are in for a treat. Given the way this fog is rolling in, I'd say we're likely in for a doozy of a storm in the next twenty-four hours."

"Lovely." Keela thought of her cemetery home and tried to work out which crypt would offer the most shelter from the rain.

She sat with James for a little while longer, until the lunch crowd began to roll in: a few tourists, but mostly businesspeople from the surrounding buildings. Mostly young, mostly affluent, they almost seemed like they simply changed their clothes and came back in for karaoke, which, for all she knew, was exactly what happened. She made her goodbyes to James between drink orders and slipped back outside.

Clouds were rolling in from the west, blanketing the sky in silvery heaps with occasional splotches of dark grey. Although it was still pleasantly warm, the wind carried a bite of cold, as if winter was not quite through with Nashville just yet.

She fretted about the thunderstorm because it took her mind off of the bundle of papers she hadn't gotten to investigate and the bad case of nerves she had about singing tonight.

Track 11

As it turned out, she shouldn't have been nervous about McNamara's.

Teri and Polly were waiting in the music room when she arrived, chatting with James. Two of the long tables had been decorated with flowers and balloons and hand-lettered signs that said "Reserved" in beautiful cursive.

"…appreciate it, given that it was last minute!" Teri was saying to James.

Keela joined the conversation already in progress. "It wasn't a bother at all. Any friend of James is a friend of mine." She stood beside him, staring defiantly at the two muses.

"Teri, Polly, this is Keela. I know you're acquainted with her voice, but here she is in person."

Keela put out her hand and smiled. "Well met, ladies."

The exchange between the two sisters was hardly more than a quick glance, but Keela noticed it just the same. Teri took her hand in a hearty shake and Keela clasped hers tightly, daring her to flinch or draw away. To her credit, she did not and neither did Polly. Although there was a brief and surreptitious wiggling of fingers afterwards, the kind one might do to dispel pins-and-needles.

Keela could not hide a satisfied smile.

"What's your fancy for the evening, then, birthday girl?" Keela asked. "Is today your actual date of birth?"

"Nope," Teri answered. "But we all have kinda agreed that this is the day we celebrate it. And really, as for the music, I'm going to leave that to the experts." She nodded at Keela and James.

"You're not the expert?" Keela did not have to feign her surprise at the muse's statement.

"Honey, it's my birthday today. I'm off the clock."

"Well, all right then." *And I suppose that means you won't be bothering myself now, doesn't it?*

Teri raised an eyebrow, acknowledging the unspoken comment made in her direction. Keela could have sworn she was answered with, *Not today, anyway.*

James moved towards the stage where Lisa, their favorite fiddler, was getting her gear in order. They wanted to already be playing as people arrived.

Polly wandered off towards the front door to greet their guests, leaving Teri and Keela standing near the bar without a whole lot to say to one another.

"Nice trick you pulled the other night," Teri said, at length.

"'Twas hardly a *trick*."

The muse chuckled. "I'd like to see you do that now, then."

"Can't here and you know it."

"Do I? You assume I know an awful lot about your kind."

"I have no idea what you know and what you don't," Keela said, tartly. "But I meant what I said about finishing my quest."

"And I meant what I said about stopping you."

"Is that why you were wanting me here to sing tonight? To warn me off of finding the song again?"

"Nope."

Keela raised an eyebrow in disbelief.

"Believe it or not, you little goth fairy princess, you're actually a damn good singer and I am in the unique position to appreciate that better than most. And it's my birthday and I want the best. So here you are."

"Aye. So here I am."

Another moment of tense, uncomfortable silence passed before Teri turned away and went to sit down. Keela watched her go then proceeded to the stage.

The music was just starting, something instrumental to get everyone warmed up. Keela hummed along. They weren't through the first piece before guests started arriving. It was obvious that these were not the average McNamara's crowd. Not to disparage the Donelson residents in any way, but these folks had a definite East Nashville feeling about them: artsy, intellectual, individualistic, and certainly more grounded than hipsters — although there was quite a bit of overlap in fashion sense there. Vintage New Look dresses and cats-eye glasses with rhinestones, skinny jeans paired with kitschy aprons or bowling shirts, floor-length gypsy skirts and hand-knit scarves, a range of haircuts and colors, and more tattoos than Keela had ever seen in one place. It almost seemed like college night in Temple Bar in Dublin. They sat and settled, murmuring over their beers — more Guinness than Pabst Blue Ribbon, thank goodness.

But as soon as Keela opened her mouth to sing, they all fell silent and turned to listen. It was early yet, far ahead of the usual dinner rush, and there was no one else in the pub besides these bohemians. Something about them, their intensity and appreciation, made Keela's head spin. They knew, she realized, they had been told about her. They had come with expectations and admiration already. Whatever Teri had told them, it must have been grand, for they sat mesmerized as Keela went into her first song.

Her skin tingled pleasantly as her audience, which grew by slow but steady numbers for the next hour, sat raptly. This was a new sensation, a new high almost. Sure, people had come to hear her before, but not like this. And not people like this, not people who knew music, knew art. By the third number, Keela was positively giddy.

They took their first break early on, while the birthday guests nibbled on appetizers and the usual dinner crowd started to trickle in. Keela could hardly stand still.

"You're quite the hummingbird tonight." James smiled when he said it, but Keela noticed his face seemed thinner, his eyes shadowed. It stopped her in mid-fidget and made her wonder how she had not noticed it at Buck Wild. He'd been better rested then, she realized, that had been much earlier in the day.

"How're you feeling?"

He seemed taken aback by her question, the flush rising in his cheeks told her what she needed to know: he was feeling poorly and trying to hide it and she had seen through his bluff. But he smiled again, tilting his head as if her question had been nothing more than a curious *non sequitur*. "I'm fine, why do you ask?"

"I'm jumpy as all-get-out, wondering if it was just myself," Keela answered as if she had seen nothing amiss in her friend.

His relieved smile did nothing to soothe her worry. "It's always like this when Teri's around. She's got a marvelous energy, doesn't she?"

"Energy, aye." Although Keela wouldn't quite agree to it being *marvelous*. "Should we go back up now?"

"Now? It's hardly been five minutes! You are jumpy, aren't you? How's about you go do a solo a cappella, but nothing dreary, okay? This is a happy occasion, so let's keep it light."

"Aye. I've got one." Keela left him at their favorite table beside the stage, feeling unsettled. She stepped up near the microphone, not really needing it, especially if she was singing alone with no accompaniment. "If 'twould be all right with yourselves, I thought I might do a little bit on my own."

A small round of polite, appreciative applause answered her then died down as the party-goers and regular dinner guests returned their full attention to her.

"This is called '*Puirt à Beul*,' it's a traditional unaccompanied song, the name is Gaelic for 'mouth-music,' meaning you don't need anything but your own voice. There's actually lots of different kinds, but this set of verses is the usual one." She drew a deep breath and quickly dove into the song before she thought too much about the repetitive, folksy lyrics about milking sheep, dancing, and girls with red hair. "*Tha bainn' ag na caoraich uile, tha bainn' ag na caoraich uile, tha bainn' ag na caoraich uile, 's e cho sleamhain ris an im.*"

The first part of the song was lyrical, a lilting melody that let the voice rise and fall smoothly through the Gaelic words, the sweetness of the tune at delightful odds with some of the rough sounding pronunciations. It seemed so odd to be singing about sheep's udders with such reverence. She wondered if she had been a mortal girl in Ireland, if the song's lyrics would resonate with her on a more profound level. She wondered if she had been a mortal girl in Ireland, if she would have been married to Michael by now.

Michael.

The intense surge of emotion about him caught Keela off guard. She kept singing, having moved onto the faster portion talking about the old women of the town and how they danced. This rhythm bounced joyfully, like a reel itself, with a cadence of words to match. The people at the tables tapped their feet. Keela closed her eyes a moment and she could swear there was dancing.

She heard Michael's voice, or thought she did. He liked this piece, its changing moods and tricky words. He often sang it to her in a thrilling baritone, and she always dreamed of singing along with him. It had pained her so much to keep silent while he sang the words she knew so well, but not tonight.

Something was in the air at McNamara's — the energy from the crowd, the phase of the moon, the alignment of the stars, Keela couldn't say. All she knew was that Michael's voice was there and it was as real as anything.

He came in, just as he was supposed to in this section, on the line about "yellow-haired William's old woman," *"sheatadh cailleach Uilleam Bhuidhe."* And they flirted and played with one another, passing the verses back and forth between them, twining in and around each other's words.

The final segment was the fastest, about wanting to dance with Allan, *"Thoir a nall Ailean thugam, Ailean thugam, Ailean thugam."* By this time, Keela had forgotten all about the pub and the people, she was lost in the world of the song with Michael. They could have been anywhere, any time that wasn't here in this place of loneliness and longing, separated from all that they both had ever known. Singing that song with him was sweeter than making love.

The folks at the pub that night all assumed that it had been James singing from the table beside the stage. Keela couldn't tell them if they were right or wrong. The song ended abruptly on the third repeat of the stanza about Allan, and Keela found herself standing alone on the tiny stage at McNamara's with tears on her cheeks and applause in her ears.

She had never felt so conflicted.

She had also never felt so radiant, so alive, so free.

The part of her that wanted to run away from the stage, cut through the kitchen and fly away to her quiet sanctuary of graves and ghosts was immediately overwhelmed by this sensation of power. Banshees never performed for an audience; their voices were for the dead and the mourning, no one else. But that had been taken from her. The specifics, but not the voice. She'd used it a hundred times before tonight, yet tonight felt different. It felt real, it felt right. For just a moment, she held the music within her as she always had, as was her birthright. She contained that power and she touched, however briefly, however softly, the other side and she had sung with Michael.

Keela quivered at the thought of what the "*Oran na Céle*" could accomplish if a mere *puirt à beul* could do this.

James and Lisa came up behind her, instruments in hand, ready to continue. The energy in the room was palpable now and everyone was getting drunk on it. This was going to be a very long, very awesome night.

"One of these days," James whispered in Keela's ear, "you're going to have to tell me exactly how you did that."

"I could tell you now, but you'd never believe me."

"That sounds like a bet."

"We'll talk after," Keela assured him, unwilling to slow the momentum.

They didn't take another break for the rest of the night. Not until closing when the owners shooed everyone out into the rainy night with the old saying, "Y'all don't have to go home but ya can't stay here!"

Teri, Polly, and a small knot of evidently very close friends stood in the parking lot and begged Keela and James to come out to karaoke with them. As the high of the performance faded and the damp and chill set in, Keela saw James's face turn from beaming to sunken in a matter of minutes. He was polite but firm to the muses, rubbing his calloused fingers and complaining of stiffness and ache. He playfully chastised Keela for never slowing down or stopping to rest, promising to make her tell him that secret of hers some time later. And finally waved cheerily from his car as he headed out for home.

That left Keela with the muses and their friends and a tough decision. In the end, she opted to go back home. There was too much to think about and being in the presence of the sisters unnerved her still.

They were kind, however, bestowing kisses on each of her cheeks and ample gratitude for her time and talent. They wished her goodnight and went to their cars to strike off for further adventures downtown.

Keela pulled up the hood of her cloak and watched them go.

When she arrived at her favorite perch, she fussed and fretted and dodged raindrops. Just when she thought she found a cozy canopy of leaves, water wormed its way down onto her head, her back, under her wings. Still, it was warmer there than in one of the concrete nooks of the crypts, so she fluffed out her feathers as best she could, tucked her head under her wing and tried to sleep.

She roused at every car, every sound. Long hours later, the sky brightened a little and Keela took off for Music Row having hardly slept but feeling refreshed and energetic. She was waiting on the front step of Vox Beata when Cayden showed up for work an hour later.

"Don't try and convince me otherwise," she told him as she headed directly for the stairs to the library. "I'm going to find that song and I'll sing for her every bloody day if I need to."

He said nothing, of course, but his gaze held a great deal of disappointment. And something else that perplexed her: fear. For whatever reason, the very thought of Keela singing for Ottilie struck terror into him the likes of which Keela had only seen other banshees accomplish. It was strange and she wasn't sure how to broach the subject with him.

But she put all that out of her mind as she hung her damp cloak over one of the study chairs and pulled out the tied sheaf of nineteenth century Irish sheet music. Carefully, she pulled loose the twine bow and lifted the first page off the stack.

Track 12

It didn't seem like late afternoon, so dark and dreary was the day. The storm lingered with intermittent rain and growling thunder. Keela found it strangely comforting.

She paged through the stack of brittle papers, carefully laying aside what she didn't think was important. That was the hardest part. Handwritten notes had been scrawled in the margins of most of the sheet music, but the shorthand used wasn't anything she could read. And even if she could make out the cramped or uneven writing, there was no context for many of the comments.

Some were obvious: "Ask M about the banjo" and "popular with ladies" and "First fast, then slow." Those types of things made sense. But the purposes of other notes were forever lost to time. "Eggs stand on end at solstices," was written in pretty cursive on the edge of a folk song about fishing. Another piece of sheet music said "I need some tea" across the back, and her favorite strange comment was "What should I do about the anvil?" put in between lines of music, as if it were a suggestion of lyrics or some kind of musical notation.

It was maddening.

Closing her eyes, Keela rubbed her temples, trying to

convince herself that no secret code had been placed here for her to follow. Eggs, tea, anvils — just strange things people thought to use the nearest piece of paper to jot down.

She didn't even hear Ottilie come upstairs. The scent of her perfume, water lilies, caught her attention. Keela looked up to find her standing near the far end of the study tables. Her posture thoughtful, almost relaxed. She wore wide-legged trousers in vivid blue silk and a matching jacket with a billowy scarf-like collar. Chips of sea glass strung on nearly invisible wires gleamed around her neck and dangled from her ears.

"The whole town is talking about you, Keela." Her words had a strange ring to them, a strange weight. It took Keela a moment to recognize Ottilie's actual voice and inflection, lacking the upbeat Southern charm she usually layered on.

"What *whole* town? How's that even possible?"

Ottilie laughed a little. "Okay, point. But what I mean is, everyone that matters is talking about you."

"Why?"

"*Why*? If that wasn't you singing last night, then I think I might have the wrong girl in my library right now."

Keela actually blushed. "Oh," was all she said.

"Oh, indeed." Ottilie swept into the chair beside her. "*Oh*. They say it was James singing with you, but I know James O'Brien and I know his voice and from what the folks there describe, he didn't sing a note. I would love to ask you how you did it — whatever it was you did — but I'm not going to. First, because I know you wouldn't tell me the truth anyway, and second, because I don't really care how you did it. I just want to know if you could do it again."

"I don't know. And that's the honest truth of it. I mean I know how I did it, sort of. But I don't know if I could do it again."

Ottilie glanced around the library, making sure no one else was up there with them. "Banshee," she said conspiratorially. "I figured it out. Not that you were really hiding it."

Keela felt as if the floor dropped out from under her. But, keeping her composure, she leveled a cool gaze at Ottilie. "Iron table, offering food, you weren't hiding that you were trying to figure me out, either."

The other woman just looked back at her, eyes calculating, mouth giving nothing away. "Fair enough," she said, finally. "Now we're even."

"I wouldn't say that, exactly."

"I suppose not," Ottilie answered with a coy little smile. "Have you found anything of interest here?"

Keela shrugged and allowed her to change the subject. She remained wary, however. "Of interest, aye. Of particular relevance to what I'm looking for, I don't think so. But I'm not sure."

"Come sing a little. It'll clear your head."

"I want to finish this bundle." Keela indicated the fan of papers laid out in a slightly less than chaotic manner that made perfect sense to her.

"Come back up here in fifteen minutes with fresh eyes." Ottilie rose and nodded towards the back stairs. "After talking with people about you all damned morning, I want to hear for myself this 'pooch bell' thing you sang last night."

"*Puirt à beul*," Keela corrected her. "'*Poorsht a bee-ul.*' And it's nothing but a diddling little folk tune, that same thing won't happen again, I assure you."

"That's not what I'm after. I just want to hear it. Everyone said it was fantastic before an invisible man started harmonizing with you."

Keela followed her, a little reluctant to leave her research but thrilled with the unexpected opportunity to sing again. Ottilie still made her nervous, but she was correct. A little music would set her right again.

They went back to the small studio downstairs. This time, however, Ottilie did not sequester herself in the sound booth. She set everything up then came out into the room with Keela. "I'd like to have the full, live banshee experience."

"Don't be tossing that word around like it's nothing. I don't appreciate it." It was on the tip of Keela's tongue to threaten to leave and never sing for her again, but she knew it was a lie. And so would Ottilie.

"Trust me, I'm the very soul of discretion when there are mundanes about!"

Keela didn't trust her, but the woman couldn't very well have gotten this wealthy and influential shooting her mouth off inappropriately, so she let the matter go. For the time being.

"If you're going to stay out here with me, I'm not going to use the mic."

Ottilie got comfortable in one of the chairs she brought in from the sound booth. "Quit stalling and sing, damn it."

"I'm not stalling." But she was thinking of Cayden's desperate fear. She hadn't seen him since she had arrived hours ago and wondered where he might be. He was usually hovering at Ottilie's elbow. Keela shook her head and took a deep breath, followed by another.

That the traditional *puirt à beul* had that gentle lead in, she was grateful; for it saved her from a lengthy warm up. Really, today it saved her from any warm up at all. She languidly sang about the sheep's udders being full of milk and was ready for the sprightly verses about dancing that pretty much dominated the remainder of the song. While she did not quite put her whole self into the singing, that delicious feeling of light and wholeness crept up on her.

Keela remembered that first night singing karaoke at Buck Wild, only a few short weeks ago, yet it seemed like a lifetime. She had felt that first surge of power return to her soul, to eclipse the emptiness with the adoration of the audience. She opened herself up, letting the notes she sang pour everything out of her — all the hurt, all the betrayal, all the loneliness — and then refill her soul with happiness and light and love. Nashville had a magic to it, the kind that could take a broken heart and heal it with music.

She had felt that again at Teri's party, like it was a new thing, that dazzling rush of *yes, this is why you were born: to sing*. And even now, but in smaller measure, the joy in the singing was there, the relief of the process itself, as if the breath which carried the tune took away every little burden. It felt good. Really, really good.

She watched Ottilie as she sang, watched the admiration blossom across her beautiful face creating a radiance unmatched by all the makeup she wore. Again came that longing gaze. It was a hungry look and one that disturbed her a little. She figured Ottilie was seeing dollar signs streaming from Keela's mouth.

Ottilie had told her that her voice could make history.

Halfway through the song, a few unfamiliar faces appeared at the studio windows. They were all young and attractive, like Cayden, and Keela couldn't tell if they were employees or clients. But they all stood silently and unobtrusively at the large window in the hall and disappeared right as Keela finished. But while they were there — rapt and awed every last one — they fed that sensation of light and power. And even though they left, they did not take that feeling with them. Keela thought she could wrap herself up in it and keep warm forever.

Ottilie jumped up, clapping, as the song ended, her grin strangely genuine. "It's amazing isn't it? What might seem so basic, so banal can really hide such magic? I love it. I think that's what we'll start with. Ten tracks. A mix of Irish folk music and some old standards, you'd knock 'em dead with 'Smoke Gets in Your Eyes,' and maybe a contemporary bluegrass tune to round it out. Keela O'Reardon's *Timeless Beauty*." She nodded and paced the few steps between her chair and the door and back again. "Yes, that's perfect. We'll start it with 'Danny Boy' and end it with 'Amazing Grace.'" She punched a button on the sleek intercom box on the wall beside the door. "Cayden, meet me in my office, pronto!"

Keela watched her, confused. "What are you talking about?"

"Your debut album, of course. It's perfect. The old-timers and hipsters will be all over it and who in between doesn't love the classics?" She stabbed at the intercom button again. "And get Monica on the phone!" Turning back to Keela she said, "She's my arrangement expert. We'll meet with her in person next week to go over the particulars of each song."

Her words washed over Keela without quite sinking in.

"You're not listening!" Ottilie snapped her fingers in front of her face and Keela nearly got a teal-lacquered fingernail in the eye. "We need to talk image here, too!" She went back to the intercom, "Kristy, too! She's my stylist."

Keela nodded, her mind still far away. *Something so basic, so banal can hide such magic,* she thought. *I'm trying too hard, I'm looking in the wrong places...*

Ottilie had her by the arm and was hustling her down the short hall back to her office, still talking. Cayden was there, looking grave. He pointed calmly to the blinking line one, pointed to the still dark line two and touched his wrist, making a single circle over it with his index finger.

Ottilie sighed. "Well, I guess I should be done with Monica by the time Kristy calls back."

Cayden nodded and turned to leave, casting one last glance at Keela with pleading eyes.

"So you need me for this?" Keela asked Ottilie.

She frowned. "I suppose not." Her face changed, a sly smile tugging up one corner of her mouth. "You want to get back upstairs, don't you?"

"I'd like to finish what I had started reading through this morning."

"I'll be calling you when I need you. Don't go anywhere without telling me."

Keela shrugged. "I'm fairly certain I'll be up there for a while."

She escaped to the hall but found it empty. A brief peek into the kitchen didn't reveal Cayden, and he wasn't upstairs, either. Keela went back to her stack of papers. She turned over the top sheet, one she was very certain she had already set aside, and saw a post-it note written in small, neat handwriting.

You are in danger, leave Vox Beata

No one could have left that note but Cayden, but he was nowhere in sight. She folded the little square of paper and slipped it into the pocket of her cloak, still hanging on the back of the chair and still damp. It was going to be a long night in the graveyard with a still-wet cloak.

She paged through the sheet music, no longer scrying the notes in the margins of the sheet music for clues. What she was looking for was not necessarily going to be written down. But she read over the last few items in the sheaf, not feeling she was on the right track, any longer. The wind went out of her sails a bit. Cayden's warning gnawed at her, and she wanted nothing more than to go home or, even better, go back to McNamara's and sing.

She picked up her cloak and went to drop the retied bundle back into the drawer. Underneath where it had sat was a folded Hatch Show print. She could see the shamrocks pressed through to the other side. Curious, she lifted it up and opened it. It advertised a weekend of Irish music with "real immigrants!" and it had taken place in March 1904.

Keela ran her fingers over the depressions made by the letterpress, her mind wandering. This weekend had likely been when the traveling band had played that song. A song they knew by heart, committed to memory because the *Oran na Céle* wasn't a song that had ever been written down. Not by the time it was lost by the banshee and not when it was brought to the States and certainly not after. This would be a different world had that song been printed and published, even in the small scale that many of these pieces were. She refolded the poster along its original creases and put it back into the drawer, just behind the bundle where she'd found it. The drawer closed with an almost ominous click. What she sought wasn't there. Maybe, *maybe* upstairs with Ottilie's rare papers, there might be *something*. But not here.

She went down the back stairs, pausing in front of Ottilie's office door to wave before leaving. But Ottilie was fast, hopping up to stop her.

"You don't write any of this stuff yourself, do you?"

"By 'this stuff,' do you mean the music?"

"Yes, of course!"

Keela shook her head. "It's all…traditional."

Ottilie leaned back through the door and shouted at her desk phone. "No, she doesn't, so the Bluebird Café is right out."

"Got it," came the crisp reply. "We'll work on the Grand Ole Opry then. They're always open to a new voice now and again."

Keela backed into the hall. "I'll be going now."

Ottilie grabbed her sleeve. "When do you sing next at the pub?"

"Thursday. Day after tomorrow."

"Perfect. I'll have Kristy here tomorrow. We need to do something about this." She indicated Keela's dress and cloak with an expression just short of disgust.

"I haven't anything else. I never have."

"That's the problem! And that's for me to worry about, darlin'. Where are you staying, by the way? Some dark, terrible place, no doubt."

"Yourself would probably think it terrible, yes."

"Perhaps. But we have to get you into better digs

if this is going to work. People like to know where their favorite stars live. It just wouldn't do to tell them you lived under a bridge downtown."

"I hardly live under a bridge!" Keela snapped.

"Just don't tell me you sleep in a cemetery."

"All right, I won't."

"You've got to be kidding me!"

Keela shrugged, "You just told me not to tell you."

"Girl, you are a hot mess!"

"I don't even know what that means."

Ottilie put her hands on Keela's shoulders and smiled. "It means don't you worry your pretty little head about a thing and let Ottilie Moisés take care of it all." Ottilie's grin widened she ran a fingertip down Keela's throat. "Especially that magic voice of yours."

Track 13

Thursday night at McNamara's came as a blessed relief. Keela had spent half of Tuesday and all of Wednesday with Ottilie and her minions. She'd sung innumerable scales for Monica, a slender, elegant platinum blonde with a list of credits longer than her shoulder-brushing feathered earrings, until the arranger had a good feel for the "tone and color" of her voice. Next she met with the petite and bubbly stylist, Kristy, whose personal fashion sense terrified Keela but who made tasteful, sound clothing decisions when needed.

Keela found herself standing in a cozy, one-bedroom, furnished apartment across the street from Vox Beata Records with piles of shopping bags spreading across the living room floor and heaped on the sage green couch. Kristy had covered every little detail in her buying excursion: skirts, pants, blouses, shirts, underwear, socks, night clothes, shoes, and accessories. It was exhausting just looking at all of it. In her entire life Keela had only ever worn one green wool gown and one grey wool cloak. But now she had eight pairs of jeans all in slightly different variations of texture, fit, and cut. It made her head spin.

Ottilie and Kristy set about filling Keela's closet and dresser, giving her instructions on what to pair with what and how to wash it all. In the end, Kristy wrote out a list of basics and Ottilie promised to send a housekeeper in once a week to deal with the laundry.

But before she had been allowed to leave for the pub on Thursday, the bouncy ash blonde returned to help Keela dress.

"I'm going to go sing, same as I have for weeks now. They know what I look like and what I wear."

"See, there's where you've got to change your thinking," Kristy said, pulling out a pair of dark-washed denim jeans and laying them on the bed. "You can't make a name for yourself if you don't have the image to go with it. Now, I respect that you like simplicity. So here's what I've got for you." She pointed at a selection of blouses in the closet. They were nearly all dark colors: black, blue, green, red. "I'm keeping it simple for you, girl, keeping your homespun vibe, too. See? Lots of linen, cotton, raw silk. Ottilie wants to glam you up, babe, but that is not your thing, I can see that. I'm keeping it more folksy, keeping it more *country*, as they say around here."

"I appreciate that."

"Since it's still raining and cold, let's do you something layered. How do you like this?" She took out a simple jersey knit shirt with a deep, rounded neckline in charcoal grey and then took out a long vest with a high collar in a chunky knit that made a pretty fan pattern going from teal to brown in a soft ombre pattern. Next came some simple, low-heeled black boots. "You like? We can pull your hair back in a loose braid and you'll be rocking the modern gypsy look with style!"

Keela nodded. "I do like it, I suppose. But will you be here every night to help me?"

Kristy's lopsided smile opened into a laugh. "Honey, so long as Miss Ottilie pays me, I'll be waiting here to help you get your jammies on if you want me to."

"Oh, no. I think I can manage that, myself!"

"I'm just joshin' ya. But here's the thing, you need help, you just text me and if I can't swing by, I'll give you a few outfit ideas to work from, how's that sound? After while, you'll get the hang of it, I promise."

Keela nodded again, overwhelmed. Kristy brought her the cell phone Ottilie had left for her use and placed it in

Keela's hand.

"All our numbers are in here already. You just scroll on through and see, you can select 'call' or 'text,' it's that easy."

"Aye."

"Okay. Now what jewelry do you want to wear tonight?" Kristy brought over a glass-topped hinged box. "Again, kept it simple. Some Celtic, naturally, but also pearls, because they're classic, and a few Art Nouveau things. Stylish stuff. Noticed your ears weren't pierced so you've got necklaces and bracelets only."

Without waiting for Keela's approval, Kristy took out a narrow silver chain and a round Claddaugh pendant with a tiny heart-shaped green stone sparkling between the clasped hands.

"Here, let's ease you into this." She put the necklace on Keela and continued talking about color story and textures.

But Keela was lost, staring at the necklace. She had never owned one, herself. Claddaughs were for mortals — mortal *tourists* — who came to Galway on romantic excursions. She figured someone in Ireland probably actually wore one, but she'd never met them. But the hands of friendship, the heart of love and crown of loyalty glimmered just below her collarbone, like any lovestruck lass in Galway. Had she been mortal, she thought again, she might indeed have been married to Michael by now. And he probably would have bought her one. Michael always thought of himself as a romantic. She touched it gingerly, as if it might evaporate, but the coolness of the silver felt so very real beneath her fingertips. Absently, she reached back for her silver comb, but it wasn't there.

She found Kristy standing aside, a patient smile on her face. "Are you back from Planet Keela?"

"Aye." Keela blushed. "Brings back memories, this pendant."

"I figured it might. But that's good. We want to use that! You need to make a connection with your clothing."

"I already had one."

"Yes, but you can't go to every event, every interview, every photoshoot in the *same green dress*. And who wears a cloak everyday anymore? Trust me, Keela, this is not a judgment call on your taste, but the public isn't going to understand it. Hell, I don't understand it."

"It would take too long to explain."

"I bet it would," Kristy said with sincerity, and a definite note that said she wasn't really interested in hearing it. "But what I want to know is: are you comfortable with these choices? Nothing too short? Or too tight? Not too revealing or too modest?"

"No. It all seems…serviceable. Comfortable, aye. I've just never gone about in anything else but my old dress."

"You're scared?"

"How do I know when I look good?"

Kristy laughed. "I'll tell you the secret. When you feel good, you look good."

"Then I'm doomed," Keela cried.

But she wasn't. She actually didn't feel too self-conscious by the time Cayden dropped her off in front of the pub at six.

She let Kristy leave before closing all the curtains and stepping out of her dress. She laid it lovingly out on the bed, the enchanted green wool still perfectly clean and fresh-looking despite the centuries of wear.

She was first going to tackle pants. She pulled on a pair of simple cotton undies and tried to ignore how strange and binding they felt on her body. There were bras in the selection Kristy had brought but Keela decided she wasn't feeling that daring yet, plus her bosom wasn't so large she'd ever felt the need to heave them up in any manner before. So she folded the colorful tangles of satin and lace and placed them back into the drawer.

As Keela stepped into the jeans, she felt an immediate dislike for the sensation of having her legs wrapped in the thick fabric, even if it was nicely flexible and hugged her slim hips fetchingly.

The shirt felt good against her skin, lightweight and soft, and the weight of the knit vest put her in the mind of her cloak. The socks, at least, were wool and the boots were not unlike her lace-up leather shoes. She braided her own hair loosely, just as Kristy had suggested, letting a few errant strands escape to frame her face and neck. She sprayed on some of the stuff from the aerosol can, watching the fine, perfumed mist settle over her head. Her hair felt sticky for a moment, then dried to a soft sheen that left her artfully arranged fallen strands perfectly in place.

If that wasn't sorcery, she didn't know what was.

Keela stood in front of the full-length mirror on the closet door and studied herself from every angle. She looked the same, yet so different. Never in her life had she worn pants or styled her hair. One part of her recoiled at the image in the mirror, but another part, a larger one, preened. Her slim figure was accentuated by the look of long legs and willowy arms. Her faerie proportions looked otherworldly in the best possible way, more like a fashion model, she realized, than an inhuman creature. Kristy was right, the clothes made her look good and that, in turn, made her feel good.

The sky had darkened just before sunset and it had actually grown warmer as night fell. By the time they got to Donelson, the heavy clouds had rolled low over downtown, obscuring the two tall spires of the AT&T building, known to locals as the "Batman Building."

She could even hear the thunder rumbling from inside during warmups.

James alone seemed happy about the impending thunderstorm. "See? I told you, these springtime storms are exciting!"

He was distracted enough that he didn't comment on her wardrobe change. In fact, nobody did. They all looked, some in pure shock and others simple curiosity, but no one said a single word.

The management convened an impromptu meeting with the staff to refresh their emergency procedures. Keela worried that the crowds would be thin on account of the weather and a bubbling well of anxiety opened up within her.

All dressed up and no one to sing for…

While the place was far from empty that night, it wasn't quite the raucous audience Keela had been craving. They had to play loud once the skies opened up to cover the noise of wind and rain and thunder. The occasional rattle of the doors and windows subdued everyone's mood even though the music was louder than ever.

During their long break, James sat down to his dinner but he seemed to have no energy to eat it. Keela came to sit beside him, cradling her Guinness as if it would give her strength. The dark streaks of death were far more prevalent now than they ever had been.

"How are ya tonight, James?"

He smiled, bluffing for all he was worth. "Damn sore throat. Can you solo the rest of the night? Happens every spring. Much as I love this season, it really messes with me."

"Aye," she said and sipped her beer. "I can do that."

"Thanks." He smiled and picked at his sweet potato fries, but didn't eat much. He was losing weight. It was becoming more obvious now, the slight hollowness in his cheeks and the more pronounced hang of his shirt.

"Not hungry?"

"Not tonight. You know how it is when you're sick. Nothing tastes good." He looked up at her, gazing for a long time. "Maybe you don't," he said, softly.

"No," Keela whispered just loud enough for him to hear her. "I don't know."

His smile was sad, suddenly. "That's what I was afraid of."

"You shouldn't be afraid. Not of me."

"No," he agreed, "not of you, Keela." He reached out and touched her hand and didn't flinch.

Her heart sank. It was a very bad sign when mortals didn't mind touching her. The mortals that could tolerate it and even like it, like Michael, were few and far between. When a human who had previously shunned physical contact with her suddenly seemed not bothered by it did not bode well for his health.

Forcing herself to be chipper, she said, "You'd better eat something, you're going to need your strength. I have a mind to sing 'Lannigan's Ball' tonight and you're going to need to keep up."

"Not tonight." James shook his head. "Tomorrow."

"Can we at least do 'South Australia'?"

He thought about it, seeming to gauge his own strength and stamina. "Yeah, I guess we could. We should work on some faster stuff, eh? Beat the funk this storm's trying to put everyone in."

"Aye. I'd like that."

"I'll muster my energy, then. To hell with this cold, right?"

Keela nodded. "To hell with it all."

James smiled. "You look nice. I admit I was shocked when you walked in wearing pants."

"I'm glad you like it. I thought yourself hadn't noticed, or didn't care for it."

"No, I am just wondering why the change?"

"You know that lady, Ottilie Moisés? She comes in here sometimes?"

"Yeah, the stylish broad. What's her label…oh, yes, Vox Beata. With the Art Nouveau logo."

"That's her."

"Don't tell me she's signed you!"

Keela blushed, suddenly self-conscious that he might think she was gloating. "Aye."

"No shit? Keela, that's awesome! What's the deal like?"

"Nothing official, yet. She got me a new wardrobe, set me up in an apartment, got me a cell phone." She wiggled it out of her pocket and slid it across the table to him. "Here, put your number in it."

He took and it deftly entered his name and contact details. "You'd best get something on paper, pronto, Keela. Just in case she decides to take all these 'gifts' out of your royalties and you end up owing *her* money!"

"Can she do that?"

"Sure, she can. Not saying she is, but I'm a little suspicious. You're too green to be handing all of this without an agent. I don't want you to be taken advantage of."

Keela laughed. "Don't worry. I haven't got anything for her to take."

"Just promise me you won't let her exploit you."

"Oh, James, I'll be fine!"

He caught her wrist, his grip suddenly strong, his face fraught with worry. "Promise!"

"I promise. I won't let her exploit me. Trust me, I want as much or more from her as she wants from me."

"Just be careful, okay? If something seems too good to be true, it probably is. That's why…"

"That's why you've never signed?"

"I did once. It didn't go well, let's just say."

Curious, Keela asked, "What happened?"

"Let's just say that bit about owing the label your

profits, well, I can speak from experience. And I don't know if I'll ever be financially solvent again."

"Oh, no! Is there anything I can do?"

"Nah. It was a long time ago, but credit takes a long time to rebuild. And anyway, really, what more could I want from life but having an easy dayjob that pays most the bills and getting to do what I love every night with my friends?"

Keela found herself smiling at that. Music and friendship, what more could anyone want, indeed.

James pushed his food around on his plate, ate another one of the mini corned beef sandwiches and stood up, wiping his hands on his jeans. "So, let's open up with 'South Australia' while I'm feeling up to it."

He played with as much heart as always, but he wasn't his usual self. He flubbed a few chords and got off beat a time or two, nothing the audience might have noticed, but they were mistakes he never made, and to Keela every single one was as loud and obvious as the thunderclaps outside. It also became obvious that it was going to be an early night.

They wound down with some slower tunes, things easier for James to keep up with. He pleaded his cold when the crowd cheered for a duet. Lisa sang with Keela, which was a nice change. Her sweet soprano was a bright counterpoint to Keela's darker and more powerful voice.

Patrons lingered, unwilling to head out into the storm, now blown up into quite a tempest. The owners finally came up on stage and announced they were stopping alcohol sales and closing early to make sure everyone got home safe. The crowd groaned and complained, but they began settling tabs and gathering belongings, making ready to head for home.

Keela was suddenly thankful she had a room with a ceiling and walls and a soft bed to climb into, but felt a little guilty for forsaking her beloved City Cemetery.

They got up to play the last round of songs while people began to trickle out into the pouring rain. Halfway through the "Mingulay Boat Song," the front doors blew open, drenching the foyer and lobby.

The man who walked in was tall and wrapped in a dark cloak, so soaked through with rain it looked black. Keela's voice fell silent as she recognized him, not by his face or bearing but by the strange, musty-sweet odor that swept with him. He was one of the last beings in the world she had ever expected to show up here in Nashville.

Standing in a spreading puddle of rain at the far side of the music room, Molan MacLiath, Guardian of the Fae of True Telling, lately of Boston, pulled back his hood and fixed his endless grey stare on Keela.

Track 14

"What are you doing here?" It came out harsh, accusatory. Keela winced as she said it, knowing it was the wrong thing to say but unsure what else would have sufficed.

His brows drew together into a stormy scowl. Lisa and James stood behind her, looking at each other, at Molan, and finally at Keela. She didn't have any words to explain what they were seeing.

Without turning, she said quickly, "Molan is a friend from home. In a roundabout way." She stepped down off the stage and crossed the nearly empty music room. She had forgotten how tall he was.

"What are you doing here?" Keela asked again, this time, in the tone of voice she had meant from the beginning: surprised and secretly a little pleased.

"I was worried," he said. "Whatever are you wearing? Where are your clothes?"

She blinked at him. "That's all you have to say? Yourself came all the way here and all you can say to me is *where are your clothes?*"

He glanced around the pub, uneasy. "We should speak outside."

"In the rain?"

"Don't worry about that." He turned and made his way back to the front door, clearly expecting her to follow.

Keela smiled back at James. "I'll call you later." She stepped out into the storm, surprised to find the front drive quiet and dry.

Molan waited at the bottom of the steps, in the parking lot. He paced between the sidewalk and the stairs, obviously agitated. When she arrived, he stopped and looked at her again, looked through her almost. "What happened last week?"

"What?"

"Last week. You held the stone I gave you and you called on it."

"I did no such — oh, that. I wasn't trying… I mean, it wasn't my intention… I was only looking for strength, and courage."

"What were you facing?" The concern in his eyes humbled her. He took a step forward and touched her upper arm gently.

"There are a good many powerful beings here, some more friendly and more helpful than others."

"So, I take it you ran into the less friendly, less helpful kind last week?"

"I had to let them know I was not to be trifled with."

Molan nodded. "Where is the stone now?"

"At the apartment, I suppose."

"You suppose?"

Keela's temper kindled. "Yes. I keep it in the inner pocket of my cloak, which is currently lying on my bed." She crossed her arms. "I had only thought yourself gave me that damned stone as a keepsake. For strength, you said. If I had known it was more like a leash I would have hurled it right back in your face!"

"It isn't!"

"Then why are you here, Molan?"

He pressed his lips together and shifted his weight, as if he might start pacing again. "You called on it. I felt that. Felt the echo only. It sounded like you were in trouble. And then, there was nothing. Just silence. I was…worried."

"What do you mean you felt it?"

He didn't meet her eyes. "You know what I am, sworn as I am to the land. I gave you a bit of that land to which I was once sworn. I feel you through it. Only shadows, echoes. Not a *leash*," he growled. "And you've not once put it down. Not once. So, I thought, maybe… But then you *did* put it down. After calling on it for a great deal of strength. So I worried. I heard nothing through the fog and I feared for you. And the Lady finally bade me go to you and see for myself."

"And what do you see, then?"

"I see you tarted up, for one thing, and far away from what you said you'd be doing, for another."

"*Tarted up?*"

He looked as if he might apologize, but then glowered back in the face of Keela's anger. "Yes. Tarted up. Look at you! For cryin' out fuck, Keela, you're a banshee. Where is your gown? Where is your cloak?"

"For cryin' out fuck, Molan, I'm in Nashville! How long did you expect me to go about looking like I wandered in off a plague ship?" She wasn't about to tell him that had he come a day sooner, she would have still been wearing her gown and cloak. Her ire at his judgment of her was too sharp. "And as for what I said I'd be doing, how do you know what I'm about? Have you been spying on me?"

"Enough to know you've got a record deal to go along with those tight jeans and you haven't found the *Oran na Céle* even though you're practically sitting on top of it!"

That gave her pause. "Does yourself know where it is? Can it possibly be that yourself has found it and you've come just to torment me about it?"

"No, that came out wrong! But really, haven't you been here long enough to have come across it by now? The Lady said it was a part of the fabric of the city itself. I mean how hard can that be?"

"You have no idea! *How hard can it be,* he says!" She threw up her arms and walked away. "I can't believe you would come here and say this to me. I can't believe you, *you* of all people, would be so heartless!"

"Keela, wait. This isn't at all what I wanted."

"Well, at least that's something! I'd be altogether upset if I knew yourself wanted to pick a fight with me!"

"I thought something had happened to you, something terrible."

"Maybe you should have asked your rock."

"I'm sorry. I shouldn't have come."

"I don't mind that you came," Keela said, seething. "But you could have kept your *opinions* to yourself."

"I thought we were friends."

"I hardly know you."

Angry, he snarled at her, "And how well did you know Michael?"

"Don't bring him into this!"

"He's the entire reason there is a 'this'!"

"Well and yourself had best be thankful since you never would have met me without him!" She was yelling now and had no idea why. Molan had unsettled her, had questioned what she was doing, and had made some pretty valid points, all told. And that only served to upset her. She was angry at herself, but it was far easier to be angry at him. "And you know what? Your stupid stone is going back to the river. You can talk to the Cumberland all you want about it!"

She turned away and ran a few steps across the mostly empty parking lot. Once she was a few yards away, she felt the rain again, tiny drops falling fast, feeling like needles on her skin. She leapt, transforming as she did, only to fall hard against the pavement in a tangle of wet clothes. Molan was beside her in an instant but she batted him away with her wings. The cell phone skittered out onto the asphalt and she snatched it up in her claws, holding it tightly to her belly in the hopes it would stay dry there. She flapped away from the pile of discarded garments and the Grey Man who stood beside them, watching her go. He didn't follow her, but the thunder had a particular sulky tone to it for the rest of the night.

Once back at her apartment, she realized she had her phone and nothing more. No keys, no money, no clothing. The building was small, only a dozen or so units and nearly all rented to some client of Ottilie's or another. Careful of the phone, Keela hopped up to the intercom console. It was a Thursday, it was late, it was raining. She had an idea.

She pressed button after button until someone answered. "Pizza," she said in a corvid squawk.

"I didn't order any," said the woman on the line and hung up.

She tried it again. This time a younger-sounding man answered.

"Pizza," Keela said.

"Finally!"

The outer door buzzed then clicked loudly, swinging open a little. It was enough for Keela, a goodly sized crow, to shoulder her way in. She had no idea how she was likely to get into her own apartment, but at least she was out of the rain.

She lighted on the large pipes in the emergency stairwell and took human form. She hesitated a moment before calling James. He picked up right away.

"You want to tell me why I found every last stitch of your clothing in the parking lot tonight, Keela?"

"No." She flushed, realizing that he was likely as worried as Molan had been, but he had no way to track her down to find out if she was all right. "If I gave you the address, do you think you'd be up to bringing them to me?"

There was a long pause on the line. Keela could hear him breathing and the sound of rain battering a car roof. "I shouldn't, but yeah, I can."

"Thank you," she whispered, guilt-ridden and sorrowful.

"I hadn't left McNamara's yet. Was just sitting here wondering if I should call the police. Lisa said she saw you arguing with that guy and then I found your clothes. Minus your phone, which worried me. Thought maybe he had stolen it and done something awful to you."

"For the *phone*?"

"Keela, you realize you have the brand new iPhone in a LifeProof case, right? Do you know how much money is sunk into that?"

"No," she answered slowly, thinking about how much money she might actually owe Ottilie if James was right.

"So you're okay, then?"

"Aye. Just naked and without my keys."

James laughed. "Let me guess, this is new for you? Living like a human?"

"Aye. Just hurry yourself over to Music Row before someone finds me and thinks the worst?" She told him the address and that she thought the main door to the building was still ajar.

"I'll be right there."

She sat on the chilly pipes, glad they weren't iron. There were too many people in town who knew her secret. James had figured her out, but his knowledge bothered her the least. He was an Irishman; he was entitled to know what she was. But the muses and the record executive, those were a different story. And she didn't like what either of those implied.

It took James longer to find parking than it did to drive to her apartment. Between the hour and the storm, the roads were quiet, if a little treacherous to navigate. When he came into the stairwell, he was soaking wet. Keela began to unfold herself from her perch but he shook his head and covered his eyes.

"There are some lines I don't wish to cross," he said. "Just tell me what apartment number is yours and I'll go unlock it for you."

"310," she answered and he nodded and went back into the hall.

He took a long time coming back, so long that Keela finally got tired of waiting and crept up the emergency stairs to her own floor. Her door was closed but unlocked and she passed no one in the hallway. Inside, her soggy garments had been hung in the shower to dry but there was no other sign of James. She pulled on the black satin robe that Kristy had left hanging on the hook in the bathroom and walked through the small apartment twice, checking everywhere a man could possibly hide but to no avail.

Her phone made a funny chiming sound and the screen told her that she had a new message. She touched the word "view" and it opened up into a text from James.

Sorry, couldn't stay. Home now, reply to let me know you're safe too.

"Reply" was a handy option at the bottom of the message screen and upon touching it, she was given a blank message already pre-set to send back to James with a selection of letters to touch in order to type out what she wanted.

Aye safe inside, was challenging enough so she touched "send" and waited.

Moments later the phone chimed again. *Good. I'll call you tomorrow, when you're dressed. :)*

Still wrapped in the bathrobe, Keela climbed into

bed. Her dress and cloak lay next to her, almost as if she was sharing the queen sized bed with another. And in some ways, she felt like that was a little bit true.

Although she was still angry with Molan, and with herself, she slipped her fingers into the pocket of the cloak and pulled out the stone from the Liffey. The weight of it in her hand, the texture and shape, all brought her unexpected comfort. The comfort she knew it brought Molan, however, was expected. He was one of many on this journey who wanted to help her, and she shouldn't have been so hurtful towards him. She rolled the oblong stone across her palm. In some ways he had been the most helpful, or at least the one who had been willing to give her the most.

Keela wrapped her fingers around the stone and brought her hand to her lips. "I'm sorry we fought," she whispered to it.

There came no reply. But that didn't stop her from sleeping with it clasped her hand all night long.

Track 15

Keela waited until quarter to noon before she gave in and called James. There was no answer so she left a message. Followed by a second one a half hour later.

By the time he called back, it was nearly one. "Hey there, Keela, sorry. I overslept and you caught me in the shower."

"I hope you didn't catch your death out there last night," she said, then regretted it.

After a pause, James laughed darkly. "It's too late for that, I'm afraid. I caught my death a while back."

Keela had no idea what to say to that.

"But, this isn't news to you, is it," he asked. "Tell me I'm right on that score."

"You are," she said.

"Good. That means that I'm not crazy."

"You aren't, I can verify that, myself."

He laughed again, sounding a little less bleak. "Well, now that we're all awake and the storm has cleared, you want to take a ride downtown? I'm betting you never have gotten around to visiting the Country Music Hall of Fame, have you?"

"Oh! No. I forgot."

"I figured as much, because if you'd'a went, I'm sure

I would have heard about it."

"Aye, I would have told yourself all about it."

"Then let me show you around the place. I'll be by to pick you up in fifteen minutes. You are dressed, right?"

"Aye, I'm dressed. And I mean to stay that way."

"You can explain the how and why of last night's escapade to me in the car."

"Aye, all right. You deserve to know."

She'd found a comfortable skirt, ankle length, in subtle tones of brown and green and wore it with a short-sleeved green sweater. It was almost too much, as the storm left a rather warm and humid day behind it. She found a brown purse that matched well enough and put in her keys, phone, and Molan's river stone.

James pulled up in a simple small car, cheerfully blue. With shadows under his eyes, he didn't look like he had slept well. "At least whoever they have picking your clothes knows what colors you like."

Keela opened the passenger door and climbed into the front seat. "She tells me she's a professional at this, although I can't imagine what that's like."

"People have all sorts of weird professions," James agreed. "And also, most people don't know how to dress themselves, so it makes sense. Especially in this town where image is everything."

"That's almost exactly what Kristy said! Kristy being the lass whose job it is to dress me."

"Well she done good. I like this better than the jeans last night."

"You're not the only one."

"Not a fan, eh?"

Keela blushed. "They chafe."

James laughed. "I'm sorry! But yeah, I can imagine. I mean if you weren't used to such a thing." He pressed his lips together in an effort to keep from laughing more. It made his goatee quiver.

"Go ahead, laugh all you like. 'Tis a pretty funny thing to hear a lady say."

He went to put the car in gear and hesitated. "Keela…"

"Ask whatever you'd like of me, James, you've earned the right."

"You're what I think you are, aren't you?"

"If you think I'm a banshee, then aye."

"Aye," he said, imitating her. "Did you come here for me?"

"No."

He put the car in drive and pulled out onto 16th Avenue. "I didn't think so."

"I'm sorry to disappoint you."

"You didn't." He smiled briefly over at her as he headed towards the roundabout. "But you know, don't you…"

"Aye, I do."

They came around the tall sculpture of stylized naked people dancing and James headed into downtown.

"Pancreatic cancer," he said. "They gave me three to six months to live."

"How long ago?"

He grinned. "About a year and a half now."

"Lucky bastard."

"Yeah, you could say that. It hasn't been without its troubles, but, for a cancer no one can do much of anything about, I'd say yeah, been pretty damn lucky." He came down Demonbreun Street, past the new convention center. "It's catching up with me, though."

Keela could only nod. "I know," she said softly.

"I was pretty sure you did. I was pretty sure you knew the day you met me."

"Aye."

"That was my first clue. I mean maybe not the very first. You're Irish, wearing something out of some fairy tale, and sang like nobody's business. Those were my first clues. Cold hands, pretty close second." He headed into the parking lot of a coin dealer and parked in a spot labeled "CUSTOMER PARKING ONLY — WE MEAN IT!!!"

"Um?"

"Don't worry about it." He waved through the door as they got out of the car. "I know the guy who owns this place. Used to play with his brother way back when."

"Ah."

"He's dead, too. Seems we all are going young."

"What took him?"

"Motorcycle accident."

The parking lot was on the corner of Fourth and Demonbreun, across the street from the Country Music Hall of Fame. James crossed north to the corner with the angel statue, at the back end of the symphony hall, before heading west.

"I want you to see the whole façade. It's awesome," he said.

And sure enough, the building was indeed grand from across the street. The curving roofline looked like a keyboard and the handrails for the front steps were shaped like treble clefs. Behind them in the park between the Bridgestone Arena and the Schermerhorn Symphony Hall, the rose bushes were just beginning to bud.

"In the summer, it's magnificent. There's roses here named after every major country star and all sorts of Nashville and Tennessee landmarks and such. This is one of my favorite places to come downtown."

"I've really enjoyed downtown Nashville," Keela said and she meant it.

They jaywalked across Demonbreun to the front of the museum. Inside, James flashed a plastic card from his wallet. "I'm a member," he said, "and I get a plus-one."

"That doesn't surprise me in the least."

He led them through the lobby and open-air café. A large, simple fountain cascaded down through the two-story space at a leisurely angle, emptying into a pool and stretched the length of the lobby.

"You'll get the significance of the fountain by the end of the tour," he explained. But for the moment, they went on past and towards the back of the building to the elevators where James showed his card again and they were escorted into one of the several wood-paneled elevator cars.

The doors closed and some kind of narration started up, but James spoke over it. "So, this song you've been looking for?"

"Haven't found it. I know what it's called and when it was played at the Ryman, but nothing else."

"They have archives here, I mean this whole place is archives. It'll be here, Keela."

"I'm afraid it isn't written down."

"It has to be."

She shook her head. "Most of our old songs aren't."

"No, your songs aren't. But our song, American songs I mean, those are. Last night, we sang the 'Mingulay Boat Song.'"

"Aye, we did. And?"

"You didn't recognize the tune?"

"The...tune?"

The elevator slowed and finally opened on the back side of the car. They were at the top of the building and the barriers were all glass, allowing them to see down several floors and across to the similarly glassed-in archives. Shelves of manila folders went on for what looked like an eternity. On other levels, she could see boxes of things, memorabilia and the like, stacked and stored in the climate controlled central chamber of the building. It was almost unsettling how much was held there, in view but out of reach.

"See, a lot of American folk songs are just rip-offs of European ones. I mean, really, even our national anthem is just a version of an old British song called 'To Anacreon in Heaven' and our unofficial anthem, 'My Country, 'Tis of Thee,' is sung to the tune of 'God Save the Queen.'"

"What are you saying?"

Just off the elevator was the beginning of a long series of alcoves and interactive displays, each one with a different snippet of history explaining the origin of country music and how it came to call Nashville home.

"I'm saying 'Danny Boy,' I'm saying 'The Star-Spangled Banner,' 'Mingulay Boat Song.'"

Keela caught his drift. "You're saying that the song I'm looking for, the *'Oran na Céle,'* might exist but as the tune to a different song!"

James put his finger on his nose. "Yes! I'm saying 'Londonderry Air,' 'To Anacreon in Heaven,' and *'Oran na Comhachaig.'* And once we find that, we should be able to trace it back to its origins."

Keela's mouth fell open. She had never considered such a possibility. "But...wouldn't they be calling up all sorts of trouble if they were singing it? It wouldn't be lost and mysterious, would it?"

"I'm telling you, I can hear 'God save the Queen' and after 'My Country, 'Tis of Thee' and not immediately realize they're the same damn song. I think if the lyrics and melody were divorced, it might fly under the radar. Especially if the tune got tweaked at all — the tempo, the phrasing, the chords, any of those things could've been altered just a little bit and it would become a whole new song. I mean, who gets the alphabet song mixed up with 'Twinkle, Twinkle Little Star'? They're the same exact tune but the phrasing is totally different so no one notices."

Keela stopped then. "Now wait, are you serious? 'Twinkle, Twinkle Little Star'?"

James smiled sideways at her. "Hum a few bars."

She did and then began to laugh. "Well, I'll be…"

"I think if we can uncover the melody, finding the complete song will be easier. Because right now, I'm willing to bet you don't even know what it sounds like, do you?"

"I have no idea."

"I think you're about to." His hopeful grin banished the shadows from his face, for a moment, anyway.

The very first installment was a curved wall covered in images of faded-out hand-written sheet music and old photographs of traveling musicians. The text told the story of the Irish roots of bluegrass and country. There was a picture of four brothers from Ireland that caught her attention. The caption beneath the image made a reference to a peculiar song they played that was said to be the root of nearly all country songs ever written.

Keela grabbed James's wrist. "Look!"

He read over her shoulder, but his smile told her he already knew this bit of trivia. "So the story goes," he said, jumping ahead to the center of the block of text on the wall, "a group of itinerant musicians from Ireland played a set that included one of the most amazing tunes ever heard and that tune was recreated and replayed over and over by everyone who heard it, until it became the backbone of just about every country song written today."

Keela read over each word again, James's paraphrased version was completely accurate, this one song was said to have been the very beginning of the entire music industry here in Nashville.

"This has to be it, James! But where can I find it?"

"Step inside."

On the inside of the curved wall, there were more pictures, more notes, another block of text, and a speaker cleverly hidden within the wall. A tinny recording of what sounded like a slow Irish song played. A pleasant-voiced female narrator said, "This brief excerpt is the only known recording of this song, played by audience demand at the closing of the St. Patrick's Day music extravaganza held at the Ryman in 1904. This tune was so popular that it is said it influenced everyone who heard it and that it's echo can be still felt today in modern country music."

She spoke over most of the song, but stopped for long enough to hear a few seconds of the lament. It was slow, but not heavy, it had a slightly hopeful angle to it. Keela cursed beneath her breath that she couldn't hear the lyrics.

"Do you think they have the base recording? Before they put the lass talking over it?"

"Somewhere, I'm sure. "

Keela waited until the recording started over again. "The original doesn't have music," she said. "It'd be a *sean-nós*, an unaccompanied style like I sang for you that first day at Buck Wild, do you remember?"

"That memory will keep me company in the grave," he told her with a melancholy smile.

She ignored his allusion to death, for the moment. "So they put it to music, the brothers, when they performed it." Keela paced the little curved cubicle. "But they must have sung it unaccompanied at some point. Else it wouldn't have made such an impression, right?"

James shrugged. "I don't know. If what they sang was anything like what you sang that day, it was bound to leave a mark. And a big one. The tune sounds a little like the traditional, 'Give Me Your Hand.'"

"Aye, it does. So the music, the melody *did* enter into both Irish music and country. Probably bluegrass, too."

"The signage here agrees with that assessment."

Keela touched the wall, as if she could reach into that invisible speaker and pluck out the song and call an end to her journey. "But where is it?"

"You got nothing from the Ryman?"

"I wouldn't say 'nothing,' but it was not an answer. Just a clue. Just *the* clue, that I was looking in the right place. That it had been here. That I was close."

James stood by her as they listened to the recording a third time. "Have you gone to the Opry?"

"Aye, I went on the Ryman tour and walked through the whole building."

"Not the Ryman. The *Opry*. Over at the Grand Ole Opry House, by Opryland, er what used to be Opryland. It's a mall now."

She frowned, "I suppose if yourself thinks we should…"

"Keela, I'm telling you. If the song wasn't at the Ryman, it's going to be at the Opry. Trust me." He pulled out his phone and his fingers danced over the screen. "They're playing tonight. Tickets available. Tickets… bought!"

"James!"

"What? Do you think I'm not going to want to be right there when you find it?"

"And what about our gig tonight at McNamara's?"

"They'll be fine. They have their own house band, you know."

"I thought that was us?"

"Nope, we've just been the extra-special special guests that keep showing up every week. Let me text Sean and tell him we're not going to be there tonight. I'll explain that it's really important. I'll tell him it's your birthday."

She had to smile at that. "You've been a dear friend, James. I don't know what I would have done without your good self."

"You'd have gotten here eventually. You're a pretty smart little lady." He pressed send and slipped his phone back into the holder on his belt then extended his arm. "What say we finish the tour, then we head over to Opry. We can grab some dinner at their Irish pub and head over to the show."

"They have a pub, too?"

"I told ya, being Irish is big business in this town nowadays."

"Apparently." But before Keela could walk away from the display, she stopped to look at the photograph of the four brothers. The tallest of them looked boldly into the camera with a smirk that seemed to brag of cheating death. If Keela had to pick which had been Eimear's lover, she'd have chosen him. He was handsome and dangerous, an intoxicating combination. "I would have loved to have met them. Even if just to find out how the hell they did it, how did they get that song away from the O'Neills?"

"Aren't the storybooks just filled of tales where the humans tricked the faeries?"

Keela laughed. "You know what, they are."

The rest of the Hall of Fame was a blur: Elvis's gold piano, a car decorated with guns, pieces from the set of *Hee-Haw*, dresses someone wore for some award, and walls covered with gold records. Keela's mind wandered to Ottilie and Vox Beata. Maybe when she got this *Oran na Céle* matter settled, maybe she really could make history and earn a spot on these walls. Something inside sprang to life, a tickle of excitement that flared into a sharp desire.

They finished up on the second level, passing through a circular room where the fountain began. Keela looked back at it as James hurried them towards the ramp back down to the lobby. There was a circle set into the floor of the round room but she didn't have a moment to go back and look at it.

They followed the quietly cascading water down to the large, shallow pool in the lobby. James told her it had to do with the ebb and flow of music, that every new voice adds to the whole just like a river adds to the sea.

"It's supposed to be poetic, I guess. It sure looks nice, though."

They passed up the gift shop and made their way back to the car, still happily parked over at Music City Coin with nary a parking ticket in sight.

As they got in and James started the car, he leaned over and grinned at Keela. "And I also know where to get free parking at Opry, too."

Track 16

The Gaylord Opryland area was huge. The Grand Ole Opry House itself was situated between an enormous hotel and the adjacent mall. James parked at the back side of the mall, near the movie theatre, and walked Keela through the paved pathways that led to the hotel.

"This was a theme park not too long ago. Used to come here all the time as a kid. See over there?" He pointed to some large rocks clustered around what looked like a dry riverbed. "That was a ride. That concrete canal was filled and you'd hop on this round raft and go sloshing over rapids and stuff. It was really cool. The Opry House was right in the middle of it, and it ran right up to the hotel."

They passed through what had once been some kind of turnstile situated next to a faux log cabin. It was both eerie and quaint that so much of the amusement park was still lingering there, like some kind of ruins of another time.

Keela laughed. "That's brilliant," she said, "all we have in Ireland are castles."

"Oh, only?"

"Aye, that and monasteries."

The path went under a covered walkway and then curved towards a large, round driveway. The hotel loomed large before them with tall white columns and copious windows. Magnolia and gingko trees dotted the garden beds that separated the sidewalk and the perimeter of the building.

"It's lovely!" Keela said.

"This is the *back*." James pressed a button on one of the columns and the doors opened into a low-ceilinged mini-lobby.

It seemed strange, Keela thought, to have such an unimpressive entryway after that grand façade. Then she stepped out into the Delta Atrium.

The glass roof soared over what looked like an entire village nestled within. All around them the hotel's interior walls looked like exterior ones, with wrought iron balconies and French doors that opened onto the enormous interior space. Full-sized palm trees grew along the paved walkways that were trimmed with ferns, lilies, hydrangeas, and orchids. The replica town square sat raised up on brick archways and elegant, airy bridges connected the various sections to one another. A wide, winding river encircled the marketplace like a moat, and from somewhere beyond, Keela could hear the whispering growl of a waterfall. A flat-bottomed boat cruised by, packed with people.

"…one hundred and fifty feet tall," the guide said, pointing to the ceiling. "And these waters we're sailing on came from all the bodies of water in America, sent here in Jack Daniels bottles."

Keela turned to James as the boat rumbled on out of range. "They did not!"

"They sure did, look." All along the water's edge, a long plaque had been erected listing the names of each river, stream, and lake that had donated water for the Gaylord's river. "There are even fish. Two of the catfish have gotten so big, they don't fit in the regular river anymore and hang out in the deeper waters where they store the boats at night."

"This has got to be the single most amazing thing I have ever seen."

James laughed. "Oh, honey, this is only the first room. Granted, it's the biggest, but it is still just one of the three atriums."

"Three?"

"Yeah, the Delta, the Cascades, and the Conservatory. You'll like that one best. Come on, let's stroll. The Irish pub is on the other side of the complex, so we might as well take the scenic route."

They wove through the little lanes of the central Delta shopping area, pausing to let Keela exclaim over this or that she spotted in the windows. They went back into the hotel proper, passing the large gift shop, and then into the second of the large atrium lobbies.

"The Cascades is actually the main hotel lobby, where the registration desks are. It gets its name from the big indoor waterfall, see?"

They came in above a sunken dining area that was more like a grotto. Tables were situated on islands surrounded by ponds filled with ferns, papyrus, and bromeliads. Dancing waters leapt from pool to pool in a charming display that delighted a knot of children who had wandered away from their tables. James waved to the bartender at the round bar, and Keela's heart raced for a moment with worry that James might stop and bid her rest on one of the tall, elegant bar stools in white wrought iron. He had marked her as banshee, but it did not necessarily follow that he knew all the aversions of the fae. The waterfall wasn't very large, but it was quite impressive for being indoors. The path curved behind the falling sheets of water then under a ledge draped with moss and orchids.

They walked down the other side and immediately up an escalator. "We can enter the Conservatory from the ground floor or the Skyway level. It's more impressive to see it from up here I think."

Another quick passage through an intersection of hotel corridors and they were in yet another world. The Delta Atrium had been bustling with tourists and jazz music, and the Cascades was marked by the chatter of splashing water, but the Conservatory was quiet. They emerged onto a walkway elevated over the trees and plants and ponds connected to one another by streams full of goldfish swimming about. The Skyway crisscrossed the Conservatory, giving a bird's-eye view of the restaurants and the secret little glens and grottos below. The black wrought iron railing curved with elegance that delighted the eye as well as kept a body from falling over the side. James leaned far over to point out this or that, but Keela kept her distance.

At the far side, James showed her down a stately set of stairs and into the tropical garden, eschewing the wide central path beneath the Skyway in favor of one of the side trails weaving through ponds and plants and little statues and even copses where pairs of lovers found a moment's privacy among the fragrant blossoms. Bromeliads, orchids, ivy, ferns, hostas, begonias, and more strange and wonderful flowering plants greeted them — and several photographers — at every turn.

"This is not a side of Nashville I had expected to see," Keela said.

"A good surprise, right?"

"Aye. It's gorgeous!" She turned and went around the next bend and found herself inside the domed gazebo covered in roses that she'd seen from above. "Ah! James!" But he wasn't behind her. She retraced her steps to find him on one of the benches along the way.

He looked pale, and a sheen of sweat shimmered on his forehead.

"James?"

"Heh, figured you'd come back for me. Not to worry, little lady, I just overdid it. Ain't as spry as I used to be and we've done a fair bit of walking today."

"Can I call anyone? To help us?"

"Oh, god, no. That's not necessary, I'll be fine. Just needed a breather."

She sat down beside him and tried not to peer between the cracks of the veil again. "Should we do this another time? Last night yourself was…"

He waved her off. "I'm *fine.*" He stood and stretched, shaking out his limbs like a boxer readying for the ring. "See? Fit as a fiddle. Let's go."

Meandering back through the conservatory and into the convention area of the hotel, the Magnolia lobby, they passed through a section devoted to Grand Ole Opry history.

"Are you excited?" James asked, nodding at the iconic red barn image.

"Aye, a little bit. It's never something I ever thought I'd do. Never thought I'd leave Ireland, really."

"Are you glad you have?"

She looked at the pictures of gentlemen in cowboy

hats and rhinestones and ladies in tight, spangly dresses gathered around the microphone. "Not glad of the reason, but I have to admit that I am enjoying the result."

"You could write, you know, Keela. Songs, I mean. I think there's enough there to fuel a dozen albums, easy."

She laughed and scoffed at him. "Now I know yourself is feverish, to suggest such a thing!"

He stopped and touched her shoulder. "I'm serious. You've got stories, I can tell. Good stories. Stories people want to hear, put to music."

"No one wants to hear it."

"You're wrong, little lady. Promise me you'll try. Maybe it doesn't work for you, but you've at least got to try. I don't know a record producer who doesn't want some original material from their clients at least once in a while. Makes for good marketing."

"If yourself thinks the good people of Nashville want to hear what I've got to say, then I'll give it a whirl."

"Not just the *good people of Nashville*," he said, playfully imitating her, "but the good people of the world."

They came to the section of restaurants and James pointed out Findley's Irish Pub. It was small, more like Mulligan's than McNamara's, but open and hospitable with a hardwood floor and a beautiful stained glass ceiling. A cluster of musicians played in the front corner of the place while the tourists and convention-goers mostly ignored them.

Keela didn't even have to ask, James secured them a table nearest to the foursome: a fiddler, a mandolin player, a bodhrán drummer, and a penny-whistle player.

"I'm still waiting for my uilleann pipes, by the way," she told him tartly as they were seated.

"Aw, hell, I promised you that, didn't I?" James pulled out his phone and tapped out a text. "Hopefully, Robert'll get back to me tonight and we can figure out a good time for him to come out to the pub and play. I'm sorry it slipped my mind."

"Yourself has had plenty else to worry about."

James's smile was a little self-deprecating. "Yeah."

He ordered shepherd's pie and enough Guinness to keep the both of them in full pints all evening. The band was good, if subdued. No one sang; they just played.

"Do you want to?" James whispered to her as the waitress cleared away the dishes and glasses.

"Sing?"

"Yeah."

"With them?"

"Yeah."

"Do you know them?"

"Um, I know the fiddle player, that's Paul. I think the tin whistle guy's name is Grant, but I'm not sure. I've played with so many people, it's hard to keep them all straight. But regardless, they'll let you if you ask. I've been here enough times to know that."

Temptation wrapped its silky fingers around Keela. The pull was strong, so very, very strong. "No," she said, against her own desires. "Not tonight."

"Color me surprised," he laughed. "Teri mentioned your drive to perform, so I'm amazed you're passing up any opportunity."

"Not tonight," she said again. "Too much like work."

"You're snowing me, now."

"It's time for the show almost, isn't it? Half-six, the house should be open."

James looked at his phone. "Geez, you're right." He waved for the check and sent the waitress away with a few bills, telling her to keep the change. "Let's get on gone, little lady!"

They completed the circuit of the hotel, coming upon an enormous grand staircase that brought them back down to the Delta Atrium where they had come in.

"It's not a long walk from here," he told her. "Just a little past where we parked, over by the mall. We'll get there in plenty of time." He was trying to hurry nonetheless and his breath was starting to sound a little ragged.

"Let's us rest a spell," Keela said, urging him towards one of the benches.

"We'll be sitting for a couple of hours in just a few minutes! I don't want to make us late."

"I'm far more worried about yourself!"

"OK, if it'll make you feel better, let me text you the confirmation number so you can go pick up your ticket. Leave mine at Will Call and I'll be right behind you." He forwarded her the email from his phone and it arrived at hers with a pretty chime.

"Thanks, but I'm not leaving yourself here, James. Come on, then." She put her arm around his waist and they walked on together past the Delta River.

James stumbled and she caught him, chiding him gently about having had too much beer. He laughed. They made it a few more steps towards the door when his knees gave out entirely and he fell, hard, to the concrete floor.

Keela yelped in surprise and dropped to her knees beside him. He braced himself with his hands, gasping for air.

"James!"

He began to tremble. He looked over at her, pain and fear blazing across his face. The cracks in the veil yawned wide and his death was so close on the other side that she could have reached out and touched it.

"James, no! No, not yet!"

"Go…to…the…Opry…"

"No, I can't!"

"Tickets…no refunds… You have to see." His face contorted and his arm strength flagged. "It's there…I just… know it. The floor…"

Suddenly, booted feet were rushing towards them. Someone lifted Keela by the shoulders and immediately pushed her away, harder than they meant to, she surmised. The paramedics crouched over him, checking this and that and speaking to one another in low, intense tones; they had James strapped to a stretcher within seconds of the serious convulsions starting.

Keela sat on the floor, watching the scene before her in horror. One of the medics approached as the others took her friend away.

"Are you his sister? Wife? Girlfriend?"

Keela shook her head. "Friend. We're just friends," she managed to say. "We play in a band together, at McNamara's."

"OK, we're taking him over to Summit. You can check in on him there."

She nodded.

"We're going to do everything we can for him. Do you know what might have caused this? Is he epileptic? Have any medical conditions that you know of?"

"Cancer," Keela replied, still staring at the backs of the paramedics as they pushed James towards the doors and the waiting ambulance beyond. "He hasn't been feeling well these last few days."

The medic nodded. "Any clue what kind of cancer?"

"Pancreas, he told me."

The medic nodded, although the slight tightening of his mouth spoke volumes. "Pretty advanced?"

"Aye," Keela said. "So I'm given to believe."

"Thank you, this helps a lot."

"His name is James O'Brien. And he's dear to me."

"James O'Brien, got it. We'll do what we can." The medic sprinted off after the rest of his crew. The doors slammed and the ambulance was underway, sirens howling, seconds later.

Keela sat on the floor, watching the empty driveway beyond the lobby doors and feeling more alone than the day she had arrived in this town without a friend to call her own.

No one spoke to her, although several people hovered nearby, their desire to be courteous and helpful battled with their innate fear of what she was, even though they could not have put a name to that fear had they been asked.

From the edge of her vision, Keela saw a slim tendril of mist snaking across the surface of the Delta River and smelled the familiar odor of sweetness and damp.

"Molan," she whispered. "Come out where I can see you."

He stepped out from the shadows beneath the walkway that bridged the river, striding directly towards her.

"I'm sorry," he said, coming to kneel beside her.

Keela shook her head, at a loss for words. "James..."

"I'm sorry about that, too. But I was apologizing for following you here, for spying on you."

"Yourself didn't need to do that. I've been fine for weeks on my own, you know."

"I was actually hanging about waiting for a good time to apologize for all of it. It's gone so very wrong between us."

Keela tore her eyes away from the driveway, confident, at last, that James's death would not be claiming him tonight. It wasn't far off, but it would not be before the show let out, that much she knew.

"Come to the Opry with me," she said to Molan.

"To the what?"

"The Grand Ole Opry. James thinks the *Oran na Céle* is there."

"He does?"

Keela nodded. "That's the last thing he said to me. He told me to go there and to find it. Something about the floor."

"The *floor*?"

"Any guess yourself could make would be as good as my own. But the show is just about to start and we've still got to go claim the tickets. The answer is inside, waiting for myself to find it. Let's go."

"Are you sure?"

"Aye. James was sure. And if himself was sure, so am I."

Molan helped Keela to her feet. His hands were strong and sure, without a hint of reluctance or fear. She hadn't realized how much she missed that.

In the shadow of his musty cloak, she saw tiny will o' the wisps blinking. He shrugged, helpless. "They wouldn't let me come after you alone."

Keela had to smile. "Very well, but let's just hope they won't need their own tickets."

Track 17

James's car still sat in its parking spot halfway between the entrances to the hotel and the Grand Ole Opry House. It was still so cheerfully blue despite the terrible goings-on with its owner. Oblivious, Molan pulled her along, his great, ground-covering strides caught them up with the last of the crowds filing towards the theatre.

Two walkways flanked a central area filled with tables and chairs, planter boxes, and a fountain. Two oversized guitars, one acoustic and one electric, pointed to each of the paths that came together in a courtyard just in front of the Opry House. It was as different from the Ryman as could be. Whereas the Ryman was a brick building with a certain flavor of late-Victorian Neoclassicism, the Opry House was an imposing structure of poured concrete and varnished wood that could only have been built in the 1970s.

Keela found herself tremendously disappointed that it was so ugly.

On the right side of the broad entrance breezeway was the gift shop and on the left was a set of doors labeled with a colorful banner that said "TICKETS." Once inside, Keela gave the smiling redhead behind the counter the confirmation number and just like that, she had the tickets. The woman never even asked her name.

She caught up with Molan as he nervously read over a sign admonishing against recording the performance. They entered through the set of doors on the left, tall and made of dark wood with large stained glass panels. The glass was cut into hexagons fitted together like a honeycomb, it matched the tiles in the lobby.

An impressive brick and wood staircase dominated the center of the lobby and a helpful usher pointed them upwards to the balcony. They raced up to the second level as a soft chime rang several times through the building. Each door was numbered with a section and they found the one that corresponded to their tickets: section 20, dead center. They hurried down the aisle to row A, seats 7 and 8; front row center. They were surprised, however, to find that this venue was just like the Ryman in one important way: there were no chairs or traditional seating, instead there were benches — pews, basically. They sidled to their seats, having to shoo the people who had filled in the gap back to their own numbered spaces. Molan had just settled his cloak around him when the lights went down and the applause came up.

"Ladies and gentleman," came a resonant male voice, "welcome to the Grand Ole Opry, the show that made country music famous. Tonight's show is broadcast live on WSM and heard all around the world on XM radio."

The thick red velvet curtain went up showing a handsome man in a suit at stage right and a stage set that looked like a barn. But what attracted Keela's immediate attention was the six-foot circle of golden wood set in the center of the stage. The lights glinted off of its varnish and there was a hint of a glimmer there, like something swirling beneath the surface.

Then the show began and singers came out to stand at the microphones arranged at the edge of that circle. She might have enjoyed the show more had she not been transfixed by the glow coming up from the floor every time someone walked over it. Had she not known any better, she would have thought it just a trick of the lighting. But as they sang, the glow warmed and spread across the stage, it seeped out into the audience.

"Are you seeing this?" Keela whispered to Molan.

He nodded, his mouth caught between awe and

concern. "So, is that it? Is that the song?"

"Aye, I think so." She looked around the theatre. It was an impressive space, nice seating, great acoustics, big video screens to give everyone the best view of the performers, and…something else, something intangible. "It's never been sung here, though."

"But it resides here," Molan said. He, too, was looking at the circle on the floor of the stage.

"It resides *there*."

"But what is it?"

Keela sat back against the velour padding of the seat and sighed. "I don't know. But I aim to find out."

The acts came and went throughout the show, a true variety of country music stars and newcomers, there was a comedian and a couple of skits that were far more silly than funny but still enjoyable. The lady in the flowered hat with the dangling price tag was really popular; they kept playing clips of her on the big screens between acts.

During the intermission, Keela and Molan meandered down to the stage level. The curtain remained up and folks were taking pictures of the stage and of themselves in front of it. Molan watched, his expression calm and somber, not like he was having fun at all.

"I'm sorry I dragged yourself out to this. It was good of you to come along."

"It's my pleasure," he said. "Why are you apologizing?"

"You don't seem to be enjoying yourself, is all."

His face softened into a smile that warmed her unexpectedly. "You don't know much about Gray Men do you, Keela?"

"I'm supposing that I don't, after all."

"The concert is nice. Not anything I have ever listened to before, but nice. And I wouldn't put you through this alone, sitting next to his empty seat."

Keela heard what she thought was some jealousy in his voice. "It's not like that."

"I don't think that it was. Or is. Or ever will be. Just the same, you do love him. That much is obvious."

She turned away but found herself unable to look at the stage, either, for Michael filled her mind. So she watched the audience members mingle and stretch and sip their drinks. "I love too freely, it seems."

"Some might say not freely enough."

She glared at him, but he too was lost in thought and Keela was suddenly unsure that he had spoken at all.

Finally, Molan glanced over at her then nodded towards the stage. "You think you'll ever be up there?"

"No."

"But you'd like to be, wouldn't you?"

Keela looked at all the people, the thousands of people in the sold-out show, appreciative fans every one of them. "I'd be lying if I said I wouldn't. But I don't think it would be right. Not without James."

"So get the song back and bring Michael here. He was a musician, too, wasn't he?"

"Molan! You do not understand! They aren't interchangeable pieces — today I'll have a fiddle, tomorrow the mandolin. These are people — creative, beautiful people who I loved, and who loved myself despite having every reason in the world not to!" She lowered her voice, afraid of attracting attention. If anyone noticed, no one acted like it.

He put his hand on her shoulder and squeezed it gently. "I'm sorry. I didn't mean it like that."

"Yourself doesn't understand."

"No, I do. I think it's you who doesn't. Keela, have you ever been bound?"

"To a soul to guard and follow and sing to his or her grave?" She shook her head, hating to admit to it. "My mother never thought I was good enough for a charge of my own."

"Good enough how?"

She shrugged. "Don't know, she never really explained. Not a good enough singer, not a good enough banshee, maybe a hundred other reasons. I thought my time was nigh, but then Michael…"

"Michael," Molan agreed.

"He still needs me. I still am sworn to free him."

"And James?"

"What about him?"

"Are you sworn to him as well?"

Keela thought about it. "No. I don't think so. Not formally, anyway. He's an O'Brien. I sang for him once. A banshee *sean-nós*, when we first met and I realized that he was dying."

"Did he know what you were doing?"

"Aye. He's clever, that James."

"I think we should go."

"What?"

Molan looked back at the stage floor. "It's here, it isn't going anywhere and neither are you. James, however…"

"I don't even know where the hospital is. And how can we even get there?"

"I remember the last time you tried to…travel." He smirked. "It didn't go so well. But I can help so long as you direct me where to go."

"Aye. They told me where they were taking him, I can look it up, I think."

"Then let's be away, they're about to start back up."

The announcer came back to his podium and the chiming sounded again, the cue for the audience to return to their seats.

Keela's feet felt rooted to the floor. That near to the stage, to the song itself, she found that she could not make herself walk away. "I can't," she whispered.

"Do you need my help?"

Feeling utterly defeated, utterly weak, Keela nodded. "Aye. Please, Molan."

"A guardian lives only to serve," he whispered and wrapped her up in his cloak.

He pulled her off of her feet and held her close while damp wool caressed her forehead and will-o'-the-wisps tucked themselves behind her knees and beneath her chin. He carried her up the aisle and through the lobby and finally into the dark, quiet courtyard.

Only then did he move to set her down, although he did not take his hands off of her waist nor unwrap her from his cloak.

"Are we not staying?" she asked, a little dazed.

Molan shook his head. "You have your answer. Let's go find your friend."

Keela took her phone out of her purse and stared at it, unsure who she should call to find out where the hospital was located. She turned it on and was surprised to find that she had voicemail.

There were three messages. They were all from Teri, although she had called from James's phone.

"I am asked to call you and tell you that James has been transferred to Vanderbilt Medical Center, seventh floor, room 722. And that Polly is on the way to pick up his car from Opry" The message ended abruptly.

The second one started with an exasperated sigh. "Visiting hours are over, long over. They ended at six. But I presume that won't be an issue for you. James would really like to see you. Tonight."

"If you ever check your fucking messages," was the last one.

Keela stepped out of the safe confines of Molan's cloak and walked down to the edge of the parking lot. It was quite dark already, but she could see the empty spot where a cheerfully blue car had once been parked.

Molan's touch on her upper arm was gentle. "We can do two things, you can fly and I can meet you there with your things."

"Or?"

"Or I can take you."

"How?"

"You have the stone, yes?"

She touched her purse, feeling the smooth density of the river stone there beneath the fabric. "Of course," she answered. He knew it, too; she wondered why he'd asked.

"I am bound to the land once more. And right now, Keela, you are my land."

"How can that be?"

"I told you, Radha released me. To come to you."

"Herself bound you to me?" Keela's voice rose sharply in pitch and she found herself caught between insult and flattery. "She had no right…"

"No. Not like that, at all. She *released* me. And the bond I was born into replaced where hers once stood. I am a Grey Man, Keela, I am bound to the land."

He had said that so many times but the meaning came clear, at last. She took the stone from her purse.

"This land. This *exact* piece of land."

He nodded, the ghost of a smile tugging at the corner of his mouth. "It is all that I have left."

"And you gave it to me. Why?"

At that he looked away. "I can't tell you, really, because I don't know. It was impulsive and probably stupid of me. But I knew you'd take care of it, I knew you'd need it. And…" He sneaked a shy glance towards her. "And I knew, I'd need you."

"Molan, I can't…"

"I don't need you to love me," he said, quickly. "And I don't need to love you. I just need to be your guardian. The Fae of True Telling has many Guardians. You have none. And you need one. *At least* one. And she bid me to go to you. To help you. To protect you. She sees danger for you, Keela. No one wants to have that to come to pass."

"Yourself can take me to James?"

"Yes. Easily. You're fae, you hold the land. Do you know where it is, this Vanderbilt?"

"Aye. Not too far from where I'm living now."

"Perfect. Take hold of the stone and picture it, wish us there, if you would." He wrapped them up in his cloak, much tighter this time.

Keela did as he asked, picturing the hospital on 21st Avenue. The pavement beneath her feet fell away and she felt as if she floated, incorporeal, through the night. Molan's arms felt strong and real as he held her close and the will-o'-the-wisps flickered and faded in their own rhythm.

"722?" Molan asked.

"That's what Teri said."

"Sure hope she's right, otherwise someone's in for a hell of a scare."

Beneath her feet, the ground came back, not ground, no, but linoleum-tiled floor. She peeled back the cloak, finding the room nearly as dark. Will-o'-the-wisps came pooling out around her feet.

A single bed dominated the room. It was elevated slightly and connected to a wall of machines by wires and tubes. Just beyond it, a figure stirred from the bedside chair.

Teri, her face careworn and morose, faced Keela in the greenish light of the oxygen meter and morphine drips.

"It's about damn time you got here," she began, then stopped suddenly. She looked at Keela a long moment, eyes squinted and mouth grim, as if she had suddenly caught sight of something. For a moment, Keela thought it might be Molan standing at her back, not touching her but just waiting for the cue to move. But the muse's eyes never left Keela, never noticed the shadowy man behind her. Then Teri's face, her whole posture, changed. "No. No, no, no, no." She shook her head and paced two quick steps away before abruptly turning back to try and loom over Keela, an impossible task with Molan standing there.

"No," Teri said again, her voice cracking in agitation.

From the bed, they heard a soft laugh. "Yes, Teri," James said, weakly. "She found it."

Music City

Side B:

"Honor Thy Music"

Track 1

"You have no idea what you've done," Teri broke the silence at long last.

"I told you, yourself would not be stopping me in this."

Teri swore and stalked away again. "You don't have it," she said at length. "I'd know if you possessed it. And let me tell *yourself*, Keela, that finding it is different than having it. Very different."

"She needs it, Teri," James whispered. He batted at the oxygen tube at his nose.

Keela saw him for the first time, his utterly hollowed cheeks and sunken, shadowed eyes. She stepped back, shocked.

Teri was forgotten. "Oh, James." She touched his leg under the thin hospital blanket and felt the tremors in the muscles there. She met his eyes and he did not look away. He didn't withdraw from her touch. She could feel his death there in that room with them.

"It'll be okay," he said, gravel in his voice. "We'll be singing at McNamara's again in no time."

"You don't have to make up stories for me, James."

"Maybe I'm just making wishes for myself."

"James," Teri reasserted her presence. "I think you

should rest now." She took Keela by the arm, grimacing. They stepped out into the hallway with Molan right behind them. Teri gave him a significant look. "You're not needed here, faerie-man."

He bristled but Keela reached out a calming hand. "Keep James company for a moment, please?"

Silently, he went back into the hospital room, sulkily flickering will-o'-the-wisps in his wake.

"Let me be clear," Teri began before the door had even shut. "James is very dear to me. Dearer than most have ever been."

"Then why…"

"Because he asked me not to. He asked me not to get involved in his professional life. So I stayed away. That's not my duty anyway. I deal in inspiration, not paychecks. But had I to do it over again, I would have insisted. Even if it made him hate me."

"I didn't mean it as an accusation."

"Doesn't matter, it was one. A logical one. Because he should have done better for himself. I should have made sure of it."

Keela didn't know what to say. "He's dying, in earnest now. It won't be but a matter of days."

"How long have you known?" Teri asked.

"Since the moment I met him. I'm a banshee. It's part of what I do." Keela thought about it a moment. "How long have you known?"

"I knew before he told me. The look was in his eyes. You meet enough mortals over the years and you get to know that look really well. When they know they're going to die, it changes everything."

Keela nodded, but really, she didn't know. She'd never had a ward of her own, and Michael didn't know he was going to die. She almost made a comment, but decided not to. Let the muse think of them as kindred in this regard for a little while longer, if not forever.

"He's known for a long time, he told me," Keela said.

"Yes. He's been lucky. Lucky and blessed with good friends who can pull strings here and there. But eventually, there just ain't enough string in the world."

"Eventually, everyone dies," Keela agreed.

"Everyone but us. We stay behind and write the

songs about them."

They stood there, in nearly companionable silence, for a little while longer. But Teri had mentioned songs and the silence finally grew tense once more.

"I don't want you to touch that song," Teri said, finally.

"I know," Keela said. "But it isn't yours to command. And neither am I."

The muse snickered. "It'd be far easier for me if you were."

A biting reply rose to Keela's lips, but she swallowed it when her phone rang. She scrambled to find it and silence it before it attracted unwanted attention in the hospital corridor long after visiting hours. She didn't know what thing she pressed but the bouncy music stopped and Keela saw that it was Ottilie calling. She let it go to voicemail.

"Disney?" Teri asked, incredulous.

"It came programmed already, myself didn't choose any of it."

The phone rang again. Ottilie. Sighing, Keela answered.

"Where have you been? You left hours ago! No call, no email, and it's late and you're still not home."

Keela couldn't tell if Ottilie had just been worried or if she was angry. She didn't like that the woman felt entitled to either. "I'm safe," was all she could think of to say.

"Where are you?"

"I went to the Opry with James O'Brien."

There was a long beat of silence on the other end. "You did, did you? What did you think?"

"I think it was everything I was hoping it would be."

The long pause on the phone coupled with Teri's darkening glare made Keela uncomfortable. "Don't worry yourself, Ottilie, I'll be home soon."

Ottilie's smile seemed to shine right through the phone. "That's just fine. Take your time, just enjoy yourself. I was just wondering where you were. And now I know."

Ottilie then said goodbye with a flourish and hung up, leaving Keela staring at the phone with a growing sense of dread. Teri was upset that she'd found the song, but Ottilie seemed to know something about it, too, and she was thrilled. There were a lot of things not adding up.

"Maybe you'd better scurry on home now, anyway. You've had a long day," Teri said. "Polly's on her way back and we intend to stay here with James all night."

"I don't want to leave him."

"Is he going to die tonight?"

Keela wanted to tell her a lie, just to spite her, but she didn't. "No. Not tonight. It won't be long but it won't be tonight."

"Thank you."

Teri opened the door but Keela stepped in front of her. "Can I say goodnight, then? Without you?"

She thought the muse might object, but she didn't. "Don't stress him out, okay?"

"Aye. I promise I won't. He's dear to me too, you know."

Keela stepped back into the dark room and knew what she looked like: hair silvery, flesh glowing. Molan sat in the chair previously vacated by Teri and gazed out the window while his wisps bobbed gently around James's bed. Some drifted around the machines, investigating the lights and buttons.

Molan rose when Keela entered. His lips parted and something like pleasure lit up his face. He touched her unbound hair, letting the sparkling silver locks spill through his fingers. "You're beautiful, Keela."

"Can I have a minute? To say goodnight?"

"Yes, of course." He might have been blushing, she couldn't tell in the darkness. But he certainly fell over himself leaving the room, making flustered apologies after stepping on Teri in the hallway.

The door sighed shut and Keela turned back to her friend. The wisps had stayed, gathering around his sleeping body and pulsating gently with light. James looked like a knight from an old story, fallen prey to the faeries, sleeping in an enchanted glen. There was no sídhe lover for him, and no cruel tricks that faeries might play, but his outcome and those of the stories would be the same: he would die, and soon.

"I came to say goodnight," she whispered, half hoping it might wake him but also wishing it would not.

His eyelids fluttered and he glanced up at her, obviously uncertain where he was. "Am I dead?"

"No, not yet."

"You look like an angel."

"No, I'm just Keela."

His forehead furrowed. "Keela?"

"Aye. We sing at McNamara's together. Does yourself know me, James?"

He smiled and nodded. "I was just dreaming about that. And I kept thinking, I know this is real, that it really happened, but I knew I was still dreaming. I got confused."

"'Tis a'right. Yourself's had a long day."

"I showed you the hotel," he said.

"Aye. You remember."

"It's so much prettier at Christmas."

"Oh? You'll have to show me then, too."

The shrewd look she knew so well came back into his eyes. "Keela, don't tease me like that."

"I'm trying to be nice. Teri scolded me already."

"Teri is very protective of me."

"She loves you," Keela said.

"I know." James relaxed a little and the wisps floated around his face. "You sure this isn't heaven?"

"It's as close as either of us is going to get tonight."

"So, it's still Nashville." He grinned and Keela's heart broke.

"Aye." She kissed his forehead. "James, I'm going to make you a promise."

His shadowed eyes lit up and he grabbed her hand with unexpected strength. "You're going to sing for me?"

"Aye. I'll sing you to sleep tonight and every night. Until the night I sing you away from this life."

He frowned again, confusion stealing back into his features. "Isn't that against the rules?"

"Aye, it is. And it's going to take a fair bit of doing on my end, but I'm going to do it. For you." She thought of Michael, but it was dimmed by her grief. James had been so kind and without him, she wouldn't have found the song. Well, she was reasonably sure she would have, eventually, but he gave her something, a beautiful gift unasked for: friendship, and the chance to sing. She couldn't decide which one was more valuable to her. "You gave me a voice again, when I thought all had been lost. Yourself is one of the few who truly understands what that means to one such as myself."

"You're a banshee. Your voice is yourself, your soul. I understand." He coughed. "But I didn't do that, I didn't make you into anything you weren't already, little lady."

"It had been locked away from me, James. You showed me the way back to it. You gave me the key."

"Because I was dying."

Keela started to disagree, but she couldn't. "Aye."

"Will taking the song back restore something lost to your people?"

"Aye."

James smiled, almost smug. "Well, then, there you go. Not everyone can say that, can they?"

"No, they cannot."

"Everything happens for a reason Keela." He squeezed her hands again. "I'm so glad I met you. I'm so glad I could be your reason."

The tears she'd been holding back broke free unexpectedly. She wiped her face against her shoulder so she wouldn't have to let go of him.

"I love you, James."

"I know."

"Good, because I didn't." She drew a ragged breath through her tears. This wasn't the burning passion she'd felt with Michael, but more like a little ember of warmth that she could carry. Like a river stone.

"Little lady, you've got such love in your heart, it touches everything you do. Everything." His eyes drifted closed and he twitched, then came back. "I'm so sorry, I'm so tired."

"Shhh, you rest. I'll sing."

"I'll know when it's real, won't I? When it's time for *the* song?"

She disengaged her fingers from his to stroke his forehead, running her long fingers through the greying streaks at his temples. "Aye, you'll know. Don't be afraid."

"I'm not. Not much, anyway."

She hummed the tune she'd sung that first day at the karaoke bar. It had been weeks ago only, but yet felt like a lifetime had passed. She murmured the words into it, singing them softly, just for James's ears.

Keela knew now what she must do, and quickly.

When she finished the song, James was sleeping peacefully. Molan, Teri, and Polly stood in the doorway, listening. She was embarrassed to have been caught singing. She wasn't sure why; she had sung that same song for the hipsters at Buck Wild, but this was different, somehow. She didn't want the others to hear what was meant for James alone.

"That was beautiful," Teri said, gently. "You have quite a gift."

"And quite an ambition to go along with it," Polly said with a sidelong look towards her sister. Teri silenced her with a nearly imperceptible shake of her head as if to say, *Not now.*

Keela watched them, perplexed. "You'll stay with him tonight, then?"

"We'll not leave his side," Teri assured her. "I promise."

"No matter what else, that's one thing we're in agreement on," Keela said.

Teri's mouth lifted into a slight smile. "Indeed."

Track 2

Keela was in Ottilie's office the next morning.

"I want to sing at the Opry. I don't know how yourself goes about arranging such a thing, but make it happen."

Ottilie took a long sip of her coffee. "That's a change of heart. Have fun last night, did you?"

"I just found out what I wanted."

"To sing at the Opry?"

"Aye. Even if it is only once. It's very important to me."

"Have you taken the tour? It's a lovely tour, takes you right backstage," Ottilie said.

Keela checked her phone. "Aye. I've got a ticket for the first one of the day, steps off at nine."

Ottilie looked amused. "You're way ahead of me, then."

"Can you do it? Can you book me for the Opry?"

"You haven't even recorded a single yet, how am I supposed to convince them to let you onto that stage and sing?"

"I have faith in your good self, Ottilie."

"How about I give a call to my contact there and see if they'll at least agree to talk to you. We can start with that, see where it leads."

Keela beamed. "Gorgeous!"

"I don't know what's gotten into you, my dear, but I like it. Keep up the enthusiasm and you'll go real far!"

"I plan on it," Keela told her. "And I'm going to be late for my tour. Ring me when you know something."

She walked out of the purple Victorian and across the street to her own building, in case Ottilie or anyone else was watching. Molan was waiting in her apartment and as soon as Keela arrived, he had her wrapped in his cloak and on their way back to the Grand Ole Opry House.

They stepped out of the shadows of the smaller Acuff theatre next door, unnoticed. The moment she was in that courtyard again, the pang of ambition returned. She wished once more that James could be there beside her.

She picked up the tickets inside the box office, this time from a handsome gentleman who smiled flirtatiously at her the entire time. Once, she might have been embarrassed or upset by the attention, but things were different now, she realized. When they had changed, she couldn't say, but things were definitely different now.

She mentioned it to Molan as they strolled around to the right side of the building where the tour would be departing.

He laughed. "It's called acclimating."

"What do you mean?"

"You're becoming American."

Keela frowned. "Is that good or bad?"

"I guess it depends who you ask, really. American girls are known to be bold and to speak their minds."

"Bold?"

"It's a compliment here."

"It *is*?"

"Aye," he said. "Boldness is not connected with inappropriate behavior here. To be bold is to be brave, to be an individual, to be daring no matter what the odds. In America, it is a very good thing to be bold. It is what makes them Americans."

"'Them'?" They came around to some benches where a few others were already waiting. "You're not considering yourself to be an American? After all this time?"

"I've lived under it, never *in* it. So I'm neither here

nor there. A hundred years or a thousand, it doesn't change the fact that I am no closer to becoming American, not like your cousins." Molan whistled through his teeth, chuckling. "They are something, those banshees. Bold."

"Bold," Keela agreed. They had mortified her when she'd met them. Not so long ago, really, yet that seemed like another life. She thought of them now, spirited and feisty and so very bold, so very American. And while Keela did not feel that she had become like them, she felt a kinship to them that had not been present upon their first meeting. "I'd like to visit them again, when I have more time to spend."

"Making plans for the future, are you?"

She shrugged. "Don't know. But I'd like to get to know them, hear their stories. Mother said there were banshees here, but it always sounded like that was a bad thing, or at least an improper one. 'They're not like us,' herself said. And I always wondered what that meant."

"Well, now you know."

"Aye. I do. And she was right. They are nothing like my mother."

"And you?"

Keela thought a moment. "Perhaps, a little like myself."

"But you're different."

"Aye. And it makes things difficult sometimes."

"That's what I first noticed about you. You weren't like them. But you weren't like the banshees from home either."

"I am myself, which has landed me in trouble each and every time."

"Some trouble is worth the trouble."

"Aye. Sometimes it is."

His somber face brightened with a smile that reached his grey eyes. It seemed so strange to be watching a Grey Man fill with mirth. But perhaps he was far more American than he thought, as well.

The tour guide emerged into the small courtyard and handed them lanyards. He was a tall, dark-complected youth with elegant hands and a sonorous voice.

"He's got a great voice. Think he's in a band?" Molan asked her as they passed him into the first room of the tour.

"Are ya new here?" Keela replied, laughing.

They watched the introductory video, but Keela was impatient to see the rest of the performance space. She could feel the song here, not quite in the same way as she felt it in the Ryman, but present just the same. The longing was keen, gliding through her soul like a blade.

"Are you all right?"

"That obvious?"

"You're bouncing your leg. Either you are really eager to see the inside of this place or you really have to pee. I'm willing to bet it isn't the latter."

"Yourself'd be winning that bet."

Finally, their velvet-voiced tour guide led them through the lobby and out the other side of the building, looping around to the stage door to start the meat of the tour. Even at that early hour, preparations were already being made for that evening's show.

The huge grated doors just off the stage were open and people were cleaning and tuning instruments. Someone had taken out all the WSM podiums and was tightening any that wobbled. Long tables had been set up and huge white boxes of fresh flowers were being opened and prepped for dressing rooms. A catering crew pushed in a pallet of bottled water and hauled several bags of rich-smelling coffee. The energy in the air was palpable, intoxicating.

Keela's desire to be a part of it sharpened and she drew a quick breath.

"Easy, there," Molan said. "You weren't quite this excitable in Boston."

"Something's happened, I can't say what exactly, but the very thought of getting up onstage, it's become a dream, an obsession almost."

"When did that start?"

Keela shrugged. "Don't know. Sometime after I started performing regularly. Banshees don't sing for others, you know. It's not allowed, to perform. But once I started, I haven't been able to stop. That night when all the musicians and artists came to McNamara's, that was when it hit me, really hit me, that this is what I wanted to do. Forever."

"Why were there all musicians and artists at McNamara's?"

"Teri's birthday."

Molan nodded. "The muse, right? Of music?"

"Aye, that's the one."

"Must be a sign that she approves of you, then."

Keela had to smile at that. "That'd be nice, wouldn't it? I don't think herself is too fond of me, though."

"She seems conflicted, I'll grant you that."

"We're at cross-purposes. Were it not for the song, we might be friends, I think."

"Yes, but were it not for the song, you never would have met."

"Good point."

They passed through the backstage area and came to a red-carpeted walkway. "This is the performers' entrance," the guide told them. "We can roll down these walls and give them some privacy while they come in to work. Follow me to walk in the footsteps of your favorite stars!"

The other tourists tittered and took pictures while Keela did her best to stay grounded.

"You're thinking about coming through these doors for real, aren't you?" Molan asked. It was a question to which he already knew the answer.

Keela nodded. "Soon," she said. "It has to be very soon. For James."

"And Michael?"

"Michael can wait. A little while longer, at least. James needs me now. And I need the song."

They entered a mini-lobby complete with a wall of post office boxes and a large desk.

"When our performers arrive, they are checked in here at security and assigned their dressing room for the evening. And just like y'all are doing now, they sort of wander in, lean on the desk, and have a look around. We feature our own post office extension here where Opry members can get their fan mail. The boxes are assigned alphabetically, except for Little Jimmy Dickens, his is down with the Ms 'cause he can't reach up here to the top row."

A wave of laughter followed and the guide then showed off Minnie Pearl's shoes and hat in a glass case among a wall of names.

"Once you are inducted as a member of the Opry, your name goes up here on the wall forever and you join a very elite group of performers. The Grand Ole Opry is the longest-running radio show in history but it also functions a little like a Hall of Fame as well, back before we had an official one."

More pictures, more excitement.

"And since no one is here yet, let me open up all the dressing room doors for you," the tour guide said as they started down the hall. "They are numbered one through nineteen, but there is no room thirteen."

"Superstitious," Molan said. "I like them already."

"You'll notice that the rooms are small, and only two contain bathrooms. Everybody wants to get assigned to one of those. Everyone else has to go down the hall."

"Old school," Molan said. "I like that, too."

"Careful, I'm starting to think yourself is encouraging me."

"Would I do that?"

On the far side of the greenroom was the last dressing room, all on its own it was the closest to the stage entrance.

"And this was Roy Acuff's dressing room, room number one. There's only one rule about room number one and that is that door must always remain open. That's how Roy did it and that's a tradition we still follow here at the Opry."

"Traditionalists, too. You'll love it here, Keela!"

And then they were passing through the doorway and onto the stage. There was something about the way it smelled: a little dusty, a little sweaty, a little like paint, and a little like dreams. It reminded her of Molan's cloak, in a way: musty, sweet, and comforting. She wasn't sure if she liked how much he was encouraging her, but she didn't want him to stop. If Ottilie could do what she promised, there would be no reason that she couldn't one day cross this threshold for real. If only that one day was soon enough.

The guide was talking about safety and the edge of the stage and something or other, but Keela and the rest of the tour had already forgotten about him and were focused on that circle of wood in the center. They were all drawn to it, every last one of them. Even Molan seemed to feel the pull of what lay within those boards.

Six feet across, a perfect circle of oak gleaming golden under the years of varnish.

Keela trembled as she approached it, unsure if she

wanted to be the first or the last to set foot into that sacred space. Molan nudged her towards it and decided for her: first.

She walked gingerly, reverently towards it, aware of the stares of the others on their tour.

"...came all the way from Ireland, just for this," she heard Molan explaining. There were murmurs of approval and the click of cameras. The rest of the tour gave her space.

Drawing a deep breath, Keela stepped into the circle.

It felt warm.

It felt bright, as if spotlights were gleaming down upon her even though there was nothing but the most basic of stage lighting. She heard, softly as if from great distance, the rush of applause and beneath that the strum of guitars and beneath that the trill of a fiddle and beneath that, just barely audible amid the other currents of phantom sounds, she heard the lilting sound of a man's clear, tenor voice. The words were hard to catch, but she recognized them. Older than language, they were the ancient lyrics to Eimear O'Neill's *Oran na Céle*, lost a century and more ago. The song was there, lodged in the oak floorboards of the Ryman, locked into the wood at the feet of the man who had stolen it and sung it all those years ago and brought here to the Grand Ole Opry House. They had known, somehow, all those years ago that those boards were special, sacred, and when they had torn them out of the Ryman, they brought a circle of them from center stage to sit at center stage here in this new venue. Its echo still reverberated at the Ryman, but the song itself was here, here beneath Keela's own feet. She was the first banshee to hear it in nearly two hundred years.

Keela began to hum along with it, softly at first, unsure. But she could feel it rising through the wood and wax towards her. She sang to it a little louder, coaxing it up through the years, through the layers of varnish.

She knelt, pressing her hands to the sacred circle of floor and realized her hair had gone silver and gleaming and that people were standing there, staring.

Keela stood up with some difficulty and met their disbelieving gazes. She twirled a lock of her hair around her finger, relieved to see that it was black once more. The song settled back down deeper into the wood and Keela smiled uncertainly at the rest of her tour.

It was as if they all awoke from a collective dream, at once they began to move and talk amongst themselves and start to take pictures again.

Some asked for pictures with her, other complained that it was their turn to stand in the circle. The song all but vanished again beneath her feet and Keela rocked on uncertain legs. Molan took her hand and helped her out of the circle. They must have looked quite a pair: Molan with his old-fashioned clothes and long cloak and Keela with magical color-changing hair that had been seen, but apparently not quite believed. At least the wisps were keeping out of sight.

They moved to catch up with the tail end of the tour, passing through the workshop full of stagehands. The tour had stopped in the audience and they were hearing all about the choice of pew-like benches for seating to remind people of the Ryman.

But before they got there, they were intercepted by a flustered middle-aged woman in a business suit and an equally out-of-depth older gentleman in an embroidered Western-style shirt.

"Excuse me," said the woman, "are you Ottilie Moisés's client?"

"Ma'am," the man added, inclining his head towards Keela.

Ottilie sure worked fast. Keela wasn't sure what to say so she decided to be bold. "Good mornin' to ye," she laid on the accent thickly and bobbed a little when she spoke. "Aye, I'm Keela O'Reardon and I'm with Vox Beata records. So Ottilie Moisés contacted yourselves about scheduling me for the Opry? Thought I'd take the tour and learn about it all since I just got here from the Old Country."

"Isn't that nice." The woman flashed a smile. "My name's DeeDee Russell and this here is Greg Swinn, *the* Greg Swinn."

Keela tried to look suitably impressed as the faded country star puffed out his chest at her and winked. He had a bit of a leathery tan and his teeth were very white, very straight, and very fake.

"And this is…?" DeeDee angled her head towards Molan. The full, blonde-frosted hairdo never moved.

"This is Molan MacLiath. He's my," Keela searched

for the right word, "bodyguard. 'Tis really just a formality, but my mother, she worries and Miss Ottilie likes to take good care of myself. Keeps everyone happy, it does."

Greg smiled paternally at her. "Can't be too careful, especially a pretty young thing not from around here. What did you say your name was again, miss?"

"Keela O'Reardon."

"Ottilie had mentioned she had some new talent last time we talked," he said to the woman. "But I thought we had one of her girls already scheduled for tonight. Marie Macula, that little cute one with the nice voice." He gestured at his chest when he said "voice."

"We need to get Ottilie back on the phone is what we need to do," the woman said, looking less flustered but still confused and unhappy about being so.

"She did call yourselves, did she not?"

"She spoke to my assistant. All I saw was a message to intercept you before left, that it was urgent."

"Urgent?" It was Keela's turn to be confused, now.

"Let's all go down to my office." DeeDee led the way back across the stage and through the greenroom then down the hall to the door behind the security desk. Past the mailroom area was a large and warmly furnished office. Framed autographed pictures lined every wall and a large russet-colored couch dominated one whole side of the room. The woman gestured to the couch and Keela took a seat. Molan leaned a hip against the back and crossed his arms, looking every bit the bodyguard type.

"Can I get you anything?" DeeDee asked. "Coffee? A Coke?"

"I'm fine," Keela said and glanced up at Molan who shook his head but didn't say anything.

"Well then, let's get down to business." DeeDee settled down into a nice leather office chair while Greg perched on the corner of the desk, his hip nearly knocking over a heavy glass award of some kind. "We are part of the Opry management and we are very happy to make your acquaintance," she said in that pleasant, Southern way that Keela already recognized as polite yet not entirely sincere.

DeeDee pressed a button on her desk phone. "Put me through to Ottilie at Vox Beata."

She smiled back up at Keela, her blue eyes would

have been prettier were they not so made up, but she was one of those Southern women with the hair and make-up done to extremes.

"Your presence on the tour caused a bit of a stir," DeeDee said.

"I don't know about you, but I for one enjoy a good stir," Greg said. He winked again and Keela couldn't help but smile indulgently back at him.

"I just wanted to see the circle, more than anything else I have ever wanted. That's all I can say," Keela told them. And it was the honest truth. "I'm sorry if I did something wrong, took too much time, or went out of turn."

"That's just somethin', ain't it, DeeDee? Precious is what that is. That's what's missing from these young stars, most of them got no appreciation of the past. Sure they respect the legends, but they don't seem to feel it, feel the history!" He slapped his palm to the table and the award fell over. "You felt it, though, didn't you, miss? You felt what's down in them there boards. The magic, the power."

Keela's mouth fell open. He could not possibly know. There was no way he could.

"The generations of voices that sang over the top of that wood, that stays with you, stays with all of us, it's why we brought it here, to remember our roots. You ain't nothin' without your roots! You know roots, don'tcha, miss? They got roots in Ireland like we ain't never seen. You look like a girl who's got a profound respect for that sort of thing."

Keela nodded. "Aye."

"I like her, DeeDee." But DeeDee was on the phone, speaking quickly and nodding a lot. She acknowledged Greg with a wave of her hand and when back to her conversation. "I like you," he said to Keela. "But can you sing? Ottilie's never taken on a singer that wasn't no good, so there's that, but I still like to let my ears do the deciding."

"Yourself's a wise man, Greg Swinn."

"Wouldn't still be in this business if I wasn't." He winked again. "Now give us a sample before Ottilie gets down here and makes me pay for the privilege."

"She's coming here?"

"Sounds like it to me."

Keela glanced over at Molan who shrugged. *It's up to you*, she heard him think towards her.

Giving Greg a shy smile, Keela pulled herself out of the deep cushions of the couch and got to her feet. She tugged at her blouse and smoothed her skirt. Then she opened her mouth and sang "Amazing Grace" for him.

The phone fell from DeeDee's manicured hands and clattered loudly to the desk. Molan simply leaned back and smiled while Greg whistled through his teeth.

Keela finished the verse and waited. The silence that followed hung heavy in the office before Greg stood up, clapping slowly, deliberately.

"Roots," he said. "Yup, miss, you know your roots."

Track 3

By the time Ottilie arrived, DeeDee and Greg practically had Keela scheduled for a full run at the Opry.

DeeDee swept across the room to embrace Ottilie in a polite and decidedly Southern hug. "We love her. What we don't want to do is make any waves with your other client we've already got scheduled."

"Oh don't you worry about Marie," Ottilie said and sank into the couch, crossing her long legs. "That's why I called, I was already on the way over. I wanted to come break the news to you in person that she was going to have to cancel."

"Oh no," DeeDee gasped. "Whatever for?"

"Terrible laryngitis." Ottilie shook her head. "I hate it for her, she was so looking forward to this!"

They sat around a minute, looking uncomfortable until Ottilie chimed in, "I'd be remiss if I didn't offer another client in her place, so y'all aren't left in the lurch. Did you like Keela? Do you want to hear her sing?"

Greg tried, and failed, to suppress his mischievous grin. "Maybe she could grace us with a sample."

"I think she could, don't you, darling?"

Keela nodded and stood once more, ignoring Ottilie's calculating stare and her curious sidelong glances at Molan, about whom she'd not said a word and for which Keela was thankful.

This time, Keela chose "Danny Boy."

"*Roots,*" she heard Greg murmur again.

"So, where does she sign?" Ottilie asked before Keela had finished the song.

"Does she have a band?" DeeDee asked.

Keela's throat tightened. She wanted to very much to say yes, to call James and tell him to get the others and come over to the Opry House. But she couldn't. And it nearly broke her heart.

She overheard them arranging some house musicians and noted that no one bothered asking her opinion in any of it. She wondered if there was a fee for using those musicians and if that fee would come out of her earnings.

Molan rested his hand on her shoulder. "Is this what you need?"

"Aye, all of it," Keela replied.

"What happens, then?"

"I don't know."

Molan raised an eyebrow at her but Keela could only shrug. "I haven't really thought that far."

His grey eyes flickered across the scene before them, the management types bent over contracts and talking numbers. His voice was barely a whisper, "I don't trust them. The fellow, maybe a little, but the ladies none at all."

"I just need them to get me onto that stage with a band and an audience. I don't care what happens after that."

Molan sat back, scowling. "Be careful what you wish for, Keela."

She shot him a look, but Ottilie interrupted. "Done," she said with a gleaming smile. "I think we should go get some lunch to celebrate and then you've got to head back here to get ready. I'll have Kristy bring some wardrobe choices to your dressing room once they assign you one."

"That's it? I'm singing? Tonight?"

"There's no formal rehearsal, but you'll get a chance to meet with the house band onstage beforehand just to work out your set list and whatnot. Stick to the standards, you'll get about three or four songs."

Keela rose to her feet. "I'm grateful," she said to no one in particular. "This has been one of the very best days of my life!"

"Welcome to the family," Greg said and almost hugged her, then stopped himself. "You keep going like you are and you'll be one of us for real in no time."

"'Tis an honor."

Ottilie opened the office door and motioned Keela though. She waved over her shoulder to DeeDee. "Don't you worry now, I'll have her back for her call time!"

Molan held the door for them and silently followed.

"We have some things to discuss, Keela," Ottilie said as they passed through the performer's lobby and out to the backstage area. "I'm parked in back."

"Do you want…lunch?"

"Hardly. But we need somewhere to have a chat." She perked up. "Let's go to the mall."

They ended up in the food court of the Opry Mills mall, Ottilie sipping expensive coffee, Keela nursing a tea, and Molan looking on like the cool, dispassionate bodyguard he now truly thought he was. Once a Guardian, always a Guardian.

Shoppers, mostly moms with young children, hustled by them, not paying them any attention. A small but charming carousel spun in the center of the food court, and the music it spewed covered any conversation that might be overheard.

"He's a friend from home, I take it," Ottilie said, tipping her Starbucks venti caramel macchiato at Molan.

"More or less," Keela told her. Molan nodded.

"I can't decide if I'm angry at you or impressed. Well, I'm impressed regardless," Ottilie said.

"I didn't mean for it to go quite like that."

Ottilie raised a perfectly curved eyebrow then laughed. "I should hope not. But it may work out in our favor. I just don't like this seat-of-my-pants business. I'm a planner, you know. I like things orderly."

"Sorry. Perhaps you should have mentioned you were calling them before I left for the tour. I did tell yourself what I was about, after all. Might have been polite for you to do the same." Keela sipped her tea. "Besides, it's all gone the way you wanted, hasn't it? Right from the very start this has all gone the way you've wanted it."

As if Keela had not spoken that last bit at all, Ottilie

said, "I'd asked you what happened while you were onstage, but I have a feeling you'd tell me something that while technically true, isn't the whole story. So let me cut to the chase. You found what you were looking for there, didn't you?"

Keela had expected that, somehow. She looked at Ottilie's face, at the calm around her eyes and the corners of her mouth, the way she leaned in for Keela's reply.

"Aye," Keela said to her. "You knew where it was all along, didn't you?"

Ottilie sat back and took a long drink of her coffee, leaving more red lipstick on the lid. She seemed to choose her words carefully. "I knew *something* was there."

Keela caught Molan's eyes for a mere instant and read his assessment: Ottilie wasn't telling the whole truth. At least that was in accord with her own thoughts. She nodded while keeping one eye on him.

Ottilie set her cup down and folded her hands primly on the table. "It is what you came here to find, isn't it?"

Keela hesitated, then lied. "I don't know."

Ottilie examined her nails, they were perfect, of course, but it didn't stop her from examining the color-shifting teal polish on each one. "I guess we'll find out tonight, won't we?"

Keela did not like the tack this conversation was taking. Something about Ottilie knowing about the song unsettled her and put her in mind of Cayden's warnings. Cayden, whom she hadn't seen in days. Fear kindled in her belly, gnawing and churning her insides.

"Aye," was all Keela could say.

"I may have to send Kristy out on some last-minute shopping," Ottilie said, bringing the subject to safer territory. "We don't have anything with nearly enough sparkle for the Opry."

"Banshees don't *sparkle*."

"Honey, are you new here? Don't worry, we'll keep it tasteful."

Molan coughed, conspicuously.

"You don't like her wardrobe, bodyguard?"

"No," he answered. "Not especially."

"Tough. It isn't you she needs to impress."

"Longer looks better on her."

"I'll keep that in mind." Ottilie pulled out her phone and sent a text to Kristy the stylist. "But everything's short this spring. I'll tell her to hit up Two Old Hippies first, though, that ought to placate you."

Molan stole a glance at Keela but Ottilie caught him. "I liked James better. He didn't interfere with me so much as this boyfriend."

Keela bristled. "Neither qualify as my 'boyfriend.' And James is in hospital right now."

"In the hospital? What, are you trading up already?" Ottilie laughed. "You've got the celebrity tabloid thing going on already, I love it!"

Keela stood, leaning over the table. "You have no idea what yourself is talking about."

"Calm down, little banshee. If you can't take some accusations about your love life, you've got no business being in the music industry."

"If yourself can't be professional, you've got no business being a manager."

That took Ottilie aback but the offense rolled away from her face and was replaced by a mean smile. "I was wondering when I'd see a real backbone in you." She checked her phone. "Ahh good, Kristy's on her way out to do your shopping. She'll have your wardrobe ready for you by three. Perfect!"

"If that's settled, I'd like to go have a visit with James while I have some time."

"I think that could be arranged after you and I talk about…"

"I wasn't asking permission from yourself. I was telling yourself what I was doing." Keela nodded to Molan who came to her side immediately. "I'm sure I'll be seeing yourself later today."

They left through the doors that led out to the parking lot and kept walking all the way to the far side where the Cumberland River curved right alongside the mall's main access road. Once safely in the shade of the trees that helped hold the levee together, Molan enveloped Keela into his cloak and they traveled back to Vanderbilt.

Keela found Polly in the bedside chair. She was scribbling furiously in a little notebook open across her knees, occasionally wiping tears from her cheeks. Her head came up the moment Keela's feet touched the floor.

"It's you," she said. Her perpetually sad-looking eyes were downright miserable now, red and swollen from crying. "We had a betting pool, Teri and I."

"I don't care to know which of you bet against me." Keela ignored her then and went to James.

He was sleeping, but not a natural sleep. His mouth hung slack and there was no flicker of dreaming beneath his eyelids.

"They had to sedate him." Polly touched Keela's shoulder. "It's been a rough morning around here."

"What happened?" Keela's voice betrayed her by breaking. She swallowed hard against the clenching of her throat.

"He seemed all right earlier today. But then he had another seizure, just a little one and only affecting one side of his body. But when he came out of it, he was raving. Paranoid, angry, thrashing around. He said horrible things, yanked out half his tubes, and then lapsed into incoherence. That's when they drugged him." Polly sighed. "It was for his own good. But it wasn't pretty."

"What were you writing?"

"Memories. Good ones. Of James. I needed something to clear my head, so I was putting some songs together, or at least things that will become songs one day. When you've lived as long as my sisters and I, it helps to write things down, so those things don't get tangled up with others. You must understand that."

"Aye." Keela touched James's hand, it was cool and a little clammy. A sheen of sweat still shimmered on his forehead. "We all want to remember James as he was."

"I don't know if we'll ever get him back," Polly barely choked the words out. "I think this is it."

Keela extended an arm towards the muse and brought her close in a brief and very awkward hug that lasted only a second before they both backed out of it.

"Where's Teri?" she asked.

Polly waved her hand towards the door. "She went for a walk. It was harder on her, seeing him this way. I can't even imagine."

"Were they lovers?"

"Yes. Once. It was complicated, what they had. And

I've had my share, but I never had to watch them die in agony and madness."

Keela went back to James and patted his brow with the corner of the sheet. "I won't let him suffer any more."

"What does that mean?"

"Listen to the Opry tonight. If things weren't like this, he'd be on stage with me. He deserved that. So I'll have to sing for us both."

"The Opry?" Polly sounded alarmed. She swore. "Teri said you'd found it, but I never thought you'd be able to get to it so soon!"

Keela pinned a cold stare on her and felt Molan step up behind her, silent and imposing. He was so very good at that.

"Yourself will not be stopping me. Teri, neither. I'm going to do it and I'm going to do it for him." Keela pointed defiantly at James.

"She underestimated you. We both did," Polly said. "She didn't know what she did. She thought you'd get rhinestones in your eyes and forget about taking the song. She didn't figure on James taking a turn for the worse. That's made a wreck of everything."

"Wait…who did what?"

Polly winced, realizing exactly what she'd said. "No one, nevermind."

"No, tell me."

Tears welled up in the muse's eyes. "I can't deal with all of this right now!"

Keela, with Molan at her shoulder, got between Polly and James's bed. "Tell me. What did your sister do?"

Polly shook her head. Angry, Keela grabbed the little book that Polly had left on the bedside chair.

"No!" Polly lunged for it but Molan intercepted her and managed to pin one of her arms behind her back.

Keela opened the book and thumbed through page after page of Polly's exquisite handwriting. She couldn't read the words, but they practically shone from the pages. Which was why it pained her so much to rip one of them out.

Polly choked back a scream as the thick, cream-colored page bent sharply before it finally gave way and tore with an awful sound. The tear cut across several sentences, severing a handful of words. Keela thought she saw sparks as they were torn, but it could have been her imagination.

"No! Stop!" Polly struggled against Molan, but it was obvious that she was in no condition to put up much of a fight. Her exhaustion and emotional pain were plain on her face.

Keela crumpled the page and dropped it, reaching for another. "What did your sister do?"

Polly glanced around, as if Teri might return at any moment. "She blessed you, all right? At her birthday party. She thought if she fed your ambition enough that you'd run straight to Ottilie, forget about the song and be done with this whole thing. And you did. But it's all gone so very wrong now."

"Why is the song so important to you? That's the one thing I've not been able to understand. What do the Greek Muses want with a banshee song?"

"It holds it all together," she said through her tears. "I don't expect *you* to understand."

Keela didn't, that was for sure, but she was irked at what Polly had implied. "I am a being born of music, same as yourselves. Save your high and mighty act for another. Nothing has changed: a banshee song was stolen and I am here to have it back. As is my right and my duty."

Polly's shoulders slumped and Molan eased his grip on her. "Just promise me you won't let Ottilie know about the song or where it is. Promise!"

"I think she already knows both of those things."

The color drained from Polly's face and she closed her eyes. "She can't… She can't get to it. You can't let her."

"I have no intention of letting her have that song, trust me. Not after all this trouble getting it myself!"

"Will she be there tonight with you?"

"I assume so."

"Then it's over," Polly murmured. James was forgotten. Keela, even, was forgotten. She said something in a language that Keela had no hope of understanding and sat down hard, right on the floor. "And we've failed."

Track 4

Keela walked into the Grand Ole Opry House alone. Molan would be nearby, but she wanted to savor the moment on her own. He left her in the small courtyard of the performers' entrance, right beside the little fountain that had once belonged to Minnie Pearl.

The large dividers had been rolled down, making a private passageway between the glass doors and the lobby with the mailroom. A broad-shouldered security guard with a military haircut assigned her to room number eleven which turned out to have a dark wood paneled floor with some kind of hide on the floor in lieu of a throw rug. The far wall was mirrored and there were a smattering of angular, not-quite-comfortable-looking chairs and one trim loveseat. It was elegant, if a bit impersonal. Walking by the other rooms, Keela noticed some were already occupied, but all were filled with elaborate arrangements of flowers in tall vases.

Except hers.

A coatrack with two garment bags waited for her instead. She unzipped the first one and found a bright red sheath dress made of sequined fabric, then zipped the bag back up again. The second bag held a longer dress made of stretchy, midnight blue velvet that had been embroidered with silver and gold threads strung with glittering glass beads at the neckline and up the sleeves. Dark blue velvet shoes, a near-perfect match to the dress, had been tucked into a drawstring bag at the bottom.

Keela was in the midst of shimmying into the blue dress when there was a knock at her door.

She was pleasantly surprised to find Greg Swinn, his white hair now arched back over his head in an architectural bouffant and his embroidered Western shirt had been replaced with one sewn with spangles and beadwork in rose and guitar motifs that had been repeated down both legs of his pants. He held a modest bouquet out to her.

"I noticed that no one signed in any flower deliveries for you. Can't have your Opry debut go unmarked. It's bad luck."

"Oh Mr. Swinn, how very thoughtful of yourself!"

He showed those perfect teeth in a wide grin. "We're family here, my dear, I hope you'll be with us long enough to learn all about it firsthand." He placed the simple vase in her hands and gave her a quick nod of the head. "I'll see you out there. Break a leg."

Bells of Ireland arced out of a base of white and pink roses bordered by shamrocks. He obviously had it made especially for her. Keela stepped out into the hall, but he was already gone, vanished around some corner or another. She put the vase on her makeup table and looked at it from all angles, admiring its reflection in the mirror, too.

A second knock. This time a stagehand dressed all in black waited in the hall. She had a clipboard and looked impatient.

"O'Reardon?" she asked.

"Aye," said Keela.

"They need you to post your set list for the band."

"Oh." Keela hurried back to the vanity, looking for that piece of paper she swore she'd seen there earlier. Ottilie had left it and she was to take it to the house band. It was nowhere in sight now. "D'you have a pen?"

The stagehand, annoyed, brought over a basic stick pen and Keela wrote on the back of her welcome letter: 1. "Danny Boy," 2. "Wild Mountain Thyme," 3. "The Parting Glass," 4. *Sean-nós* (unaccompanied). It was a slow, sad set of songs. She hoped for the best.

The stagehand looked dubiously at the paper but led

Keela out to the band's warm-up space anyway. They were kindly fellows, encouraging and smiling. None of them were like James, though. They had a fiddler and a drummer, a man on guitar and steel guitar which looked a lot more the some kind of electronic dulcimer than a guitar of any sort. They read over the set list and made a few notes among themselves. They had Keela hum a few bars here and there and made more notes about key and tempo.

They kept her list and went back to their warm up. The stagehand was gone. Keela wandered back to her dressing room, a little unsteady in the blue velvet heels, but determined to make walking in them look as natural and easy as possible.

When she opened her dressing room door, the woman sitting at the mirror did not immediately surprise her. Then Keela realized it wasn't Ottilie.

"Shut the door, I want to speak to you." Teri turned to face her. She looked as disheveled and careworn as her sister had. Her face was tearstained and her eyes swollen with grief.

Keela hesitated, then drew the door closed behind her.

"You were cruel to Polly."

"Yourself came all the way here just to tell me that?"

Teri stood, her hands clenched at her sides. "No. I was just letting you know that I was adding it to the list."

Keela glanced at the clock. It was getting close to showtime. She put her hand on the knob behind her. "This might should wait until after the show."

"There won't be any after the show, Keela. I can't let you go out there."

"No, you have to let me go out there."

Teri shook her head, a few trailing curls fell loose from her bun. "I know what you're going to do, or at least what you're planning on trying to do. I have to stop you. The song isn't yours to take."

"Says you. Yourself is no banshee, what do you know?" She turned the knob, but it wouldn't budge. More than just locked, the doorknob was entirely stuck in place. "It'll take more than just locking the door."

Keela stood tall, the bluff brave on her lips, but Teri stood between her and her purse which contained the two things she could really use right about now: her cell phone and the river stone. She called for Molan in her heart, hoping against hope he would hear her.

"I plan on doing more than that. I'd like to think that, had things been different, we could have been friends you and I. But I am not going to let you single-handedly destroy what I have spent nearly two centuries protecting." Teri was quick, advancing on Keela in the span of an eyeblink. She carried about a yard of rough-hewn chain, black as night and bearing a peculiar and earthy metallic odor.

Keela screamed the moment she recognized what it was. Ottilie's table had been one thing — wrought iron, smelted and shaped in an industrial factory — but what Teri had was something else entirely. The links of chain were ill-formed, imperfect circles of barely crafted cold iron. Heated only to the point where the metal could be worked, cold iron was raw and elemental and deadly to fae of all kinds. The chains wouldn't kill her, but they would bind her in unbreakable bonds for as long as Teri saw fit to have her, which given the circumstances would likely be forever.

Keela yanked on the knob, nearly tearing it off. She shouted and beat on the door.

"Scream all you want, no one can hear you, I've made sure of that."

"MOLAN!!" Keela cried, frantically thinking of what options she had. The room was little and narrow and there was nowhere that she'd be out of the range of that chain should Teri decide to swing it.

Teri took the ends of the chain in each hand and attempted to sling the loop over Keela's shoulders. Keela ducked and did the only thing she could: she changed into a crow. The beautiful dress fell to the floor atop the matching heels and Teri was briefly off her guard. Keela swooped down and raked her face with her taloned feet, flapping away before the muse could grab her.

There was nowhere to land near the ceiling, though and the lights were far too hot to perch on. She alit on the top of one of the chairs, then fluttered to the lamp on the end table, and bounced off the sprinkler jutting down from the ceiling.

Teri swung the chain in wide arcs, one pass took out a couple of lightbulbs on the mirror and another smashed the vase Greg Swinn had brought. Keela cawed in dismay and make another attempt on gouging the muse's eyes out.

This time, Teri was quick and got a hold of Keela's leg. She managed to keep Keela within range of the chain, but the frenzied flapping of Keela's wings kept Teri from making contact with the iron. The impasse lasted several agonizing minutes before the stagehand returned with a sharp rap at the door.

After another long moment, the stuck door flew open under the shoulders of the big security guy from the desk and Molan. They stumbled into the room as Teri let go of Keela's foot, allowing her to fly into the hall. Shouts went up around the entire backstage area and dressing room doors up and down the hall slammed shut to keep the crazy bird out of them. Someone swung a broom at Keela and she made for the back hall, cutting through the locker room.

Keela swooped into a utility room and tucked herself into a shelf of black three ring binders, hoping to blend in. She could hear the pandemonium in the hall. Two separate groups were running around, one calling her name, the other looking for the rogue crow that had somehow flown into the building.

She shivered and her feathers stood on end. The awful stink of iron coated her nose and the back of her throat. She wondered where Teri was. There had been no shouts from security about a chain-wielding madwoman, so Keela assumed the muse had exited the way she'd come in: secretly and magically.

"Keela," she heard her name whispered from the shadows and froze, ice cold panic drenching her with fear. "*Cadhla.*"

"Molan," she croaked and hopped forward to peer over the edge of the shelf.

He reached his hand towards her and she gratefully flew to him, wrapping her talons around his strong fingers. He stroked her feathers gently, smoothing them back into place.

"They're calling for you, you need to get backstage right now."

Keela swore. "I can't! I need to get back to my dressing room. If I change back now, I'll be naked!"

"You'll be bumped if you don't! What happened?

They were looking for you for quite a while."

"Teri," she said. "Long story. What do I do?"

"Change back," he told her. "Quickly."

As she did, Molan turned away then held his clothes out for her. She hopped into his wool breeches and shrugged into his linen shirt. They were both damp. With an amazing efficiency, he twined his belt around her waist, drawing in the clothes to they wouldn't sag or fall off. Finally, he swirled his cloak from his shoulders to hers and when the wool had settled, he was nowhere to be seen.

There was no time for hair or shoes; Keela ran through the greenroom on bare feet with her black hair streaming behind her. She nearly collided with the stage manager who frowned at her attire.

"You're kidding, right?"

"Do I have time to go get my dress? There was this huge raven in my dressing room!"

"That was you? Damn, girl, you've got awful luck tonight!" The stage manager shook his head. "No time to change, they're about to call you on. Tell them you're doing you're hobbit impression or something."

"Isn't she a little tall for a hobbit?" asked the stagehand Keela had met earlier.

"Just get out there!" The stage manager gave Keela a shove then recoiled in disgust. "You find this stuff outside in the gutter or what?"

Keela had no time to reply, she came around the side of the stage to find dozens of people briskly working. The stagehands and techs were rushing about, and musicians and singers were pacing, drinking water, shaking out their hands, and whatever manner of warming up one did before an Opry show. They all stopped and stared at Keela

She ignored them and followed the beckoning of another stagehand who pointed at the circle in the center of the stage then the podium where the host was introducing the sponsors of tonight's performance.

"And now, ladies and gentleman, direct from the Emerald Isle, making her Grand Ole Opry debut, our new favorite newcomer, please welcome Keela O'Reardon to the stage!"

She closed her eyes and took a deep breath. The scent of Molan's cloak gave her strength. She imagined James standing behind her with his guitar. She could see the look on his face, the goofy, incredulous grin as he realized what she was wearing. How he'd smack Lisa the fiddler's shoulder and they'd both be pointing and shaking their heads in good-natured teasing and someone would crack a joke about the whole thing. Probably James. And it would have been really funny.

Instead, the house band, aware that some bizarre emergency had happened backstage, stood quietly without looking at Keela, their faces carefully arranged bland masks. She squared her shoulders and walked out into the stage.

The crowd gasped, then giggled, then murmured a shared confusion. Keela had to hitch up the pants legs as she went, since Molan was quite a bit taller than she. Embarrassment burned through the cold terror as uncomfortable quiet settled down on the audience. Keela never thought she'd reach the circle in the center of the stage.

With the lights blazing down, she couldn't see where the circle began. It blended too well into the oaken floorboards of the rest of the stage. But the moment her bare toes touched that old varnish, she knew she'd made it.

She wrapped her fingers around the microphone stand to steady herself.

"Good evenin' to yourselves," Keela said. "Strangest thing happened to me tonight. There was a crow backstage and it made off with m'dress! True story," she added with a laugh. "And I'm not even tellin' you one of them old Irish yarns. I had to beat up a street urchin for his clothes else I'd be up in front of yourselves naked!" She felt the cold of panic within her loosen as the crowd soaked up her accent and her ridiculous story. Still unsure if it was part of the act or not, they were warming to her anyway. "At first I thought to m'self, what've you got to hide, lass? But then I thought, I already made one debut in this world in my birthday suit and that's enough for me."

That got a laugh and she giggled along with them.

"This'll be a night I'll remember for a long, long while," Keela said. "Always, even."

Someone in the audience shouted "Us, too!"

The announcer laughed. "I don't know, might have been even more memorable if she had come up here naked."

"You, hush!" Keela scolded him.

He mimed turning a key against his lips and the audience laughed a little more. Keela turned to the band, who were waiting, patiently. She gave them a nod.

"I honestly didn't come here to tell jokes. I'm a much better singer, I assure you," she said as the fiddler opened up with the familiar tune of "Danny Boy."

Keela pressed her toes to the floor, feeling the warm stirring of the song beneath.

Barefoot. She could never have tried to plan for this.

As she sang, she reached down through the ages, through the layers of performances laid one on top of the next for generations and generations. By the time she'd made it through the haunting end of "Danny Boy," the crowd was hushed and attentive, their energy, their focus all on her. It took them a moment to applaud.

Keela breathed, relaxing her body and feeling the magic beneath her. She was connected now, connected the way so many had been before. She could feel that, the electricity of that coupled with the applause coming from all around her. She took hold of the microphone stand once more to steady herself.

She flashed number two to her band and they started "Wild Mountain Thyme." It was hard to disengage from the audience enough to draw the song upward. She wanted to pour her energy outward, into their waiting souls, but instead, she balanced it carefully, letting some flow but using the rest to forge the connection with the *Oran na Céle*. And it responded in kind. It was as if the song itself knew what she was and had been waiting for her, or someone like her, to come back for it all this time.

They reveled in each other, the banshee and the banshee song, lost for so many years in a country so far away from home. Keela opened her arms wide to it, beckoning it to her.

Her voice sailed through the sweet and melancholy chorus, "Will you go, lassie, go? And we'll all go together, where the wild mountain thyme grows among the bloomin' heather. Will you go, lassie, go?"

She gave the band the signal for number four and segued into the *sean-nós* right away. It was a simpler one even than the song she'd sung that first night in Buck Wild, somewhere between a basic mourning song and the *puirt à beul.* It was a traditional, the first song all young banshees learned, the song of introduction. And it was not unlike the *Oran na Céle* in many ways. The *Oran* surged upwards at the sound of the banshee tongue being spoken.

Keela thought she might fall, but the power of the song bore her up, it strengthened her trembling legs and filled her to bursting with its light. She wondered what the audience saw and what they thought because she could tell without looking that her hair was gleaming silver.

Without a sign to the band she went right into "The Parting Glass." The band stayed silent and Keela was glad. With the *Oran na Céle* inside of her, she didn't need their music, she had her own. Whether just in her head or if it could be heard by the whole world broadcast on WSM radio, she didn't know, but there was a symphony of accompaniment for her. It was as if all the banshees and all the angels and all the spirits of the dead had come and stood on that stage behind her and sang with all their hearts.

She sang to them, this eager audience, moved to tears now, she sang, "I gently rise and softly call, goodnight and joy be with you all."

She furled Molan's dark cloak around herself and dropped to her knees, just as the spotlight on her went out. But before she touched the stage floor, Keela had disappeared.

Track 5

Keela lit up the enveloping darkness of the hospital room. Teri had been dozing in the chair and Polly was stretched out on the floor, her head pillowed on her arm. On the bedside table, the little radio played the wrap-up of Keela's set. The announcer called her "mesmerizing" and "unforgettable" and said, "I'm sure we'll be seeing more of her…just not right now since she seems to have vanished. What a performer! Let's have another round of applause for Keela O'Reardon, she is handsome, she is pretty, she is the belle of Music City."

The crowd cheered heartily and the announcer went on to talk about health insurance. Keela switched off the radio.

"I was listening to that," James said. His voice sounded strong, like its old self. She knew that was a very bad sign and that she had come just in time.

"Did you hear me, James? Did you hear me sing?"

"Yup," he laughed. "And what was all that about having your dress stolen by a bird? Whose clothes are you wearing?"

"Molan's and it's a long story, really. One I'm afraid we don't have time for right now."

James nodded, "I figured as much. But it was funny.

You were great up there Keela. I'm sorry I couldn't be there in person for you."

"I wanted you there, James. You and Lisa and Joseph and David. It wasn't the same without you there, my friend."

He sat up and reached for Keela's hand. "I heard you. It was enough. It was beautiful. I'm so proud of you, Keela."

Tears prickled her eyelids. "That means the world to me."

"You found it, didn't you? You found the song. That's why you're here."

Keela squeezed his hands. "Aye, I found it."

"You look different, I can't place it, but you do. It's like I am seeing you, but there's something else there, another version of you." He gazed at her a long while. "This means I'm dying, doesn't it?"

"Aye. I'm not going to lie to you."

"I knew waking up feeling this good was too good to be true."

"When did you wake?"

"When I heard you on the radio. You sang that last for me, didn't you? The banshee song and 'Parting Glass.' It was almost like you were right here, like the time you sang to me, the day we first met. You sang a song, not the same song, but one just like it. That's how I knew you realized I was dying. That's how I knew what you were."

"And you've never been afraid of me."

"Death comes for us all. Not everyone gets theirs as a beautiful Irish gal who sings such wonderful songs just for them, and not everyone gets to perform with her either. I knew what I was getting into, and I haven't a single regret about any of it." He looked over the muses, still asleep. "Can I say goodbye to them? They've been beside me the whole time."

Keela shook her head. "We're not there anymore, James."

"Will you tell them for me, then?"

"Aye, provided Teri doesn't try and kill me this time."

He raised an eyebrow. "I had hoped you two would get along."

"Myself as well." She shrugged. "But I will tell them, you have my promise on that, James."

Keela could feel the change in the room around them, planes shifting, doors opening. "It's time," she whispered through her tears.

She began to hum, at first, then brought in the words, forming them carefully and with great love. She had never learned the *Oran na Céle*, but it was there inside of her and the words brought themselves to her lips of their own accord.

The room doubled in brightness.

"You are death's beautiful companion," James murmured.

She helped him from the bed, his body strong and straight, untouched by illness. He started to look back towards the bed, towards the husk he left behind, but she turned his attention towards the other side of the room. Where the window had been was now a doorway of light.

"Where does it lead?"

"I don't know," Keela answered honestly. "I've never been through it, that's not my duty. I stay on this side and escort others."

"That must be incredibly lonely."

"Perhaps. But it is what the banshees do, what we were born to do."

"Will the O'Brien's be angry at you for this?"

Keela shrugged. "I don't know. And I don't care. If they want to hate me for looking after an Irish soul when there was no one else to do so, let them. I've had about enough of them, of everyone."

"I am forever grateful to you, Keela." James put his arms around her and held her close. "Why have I never hugged you before?"

"Because humans find us repulsive, until they are dead."

"Maybe that's to give us each a little joy in the passing."

Keela's breath unexpectedly hitched. "Perhaps," she squeaked out.

They stayed there in that embrace for a long while, until finally James stepped back from her.

"Do you hear that?"

Keela shook her head.

"I hear music! Sounds like the pub on a Saturday night. Can't you hear it? They're singing along to 'No, Nay, Never,' don't tell me you can't hear it!"

"That's your own heaven, James." She took his hand and walked towards the doorway. She thought she could hear something in the distance, something like a revel with singing and clapping that sounded indeed a lot like McNamara's on a Saturday night.

"You wish you could come with me, don't you?"

"A little bit, aye."

"But you have much yet to do here."

"Aye."

"If I see your Michael, I'll tell him you're on your way for him."

"Thank you, James, for everything. I am in your debt, always."

He gave her hand one last squeeze. "From where I'm standing, we're even." He hesitated at the threshold. "Even with company, this is still a daunting task."

"Go on," Keela urged. "They're waiting for you."

"I'll never see you again, will I?"

"No, I don't think so. But, really, you never know."

"I never thought I'd see you to begin with and I did. So I'm holding onto hope that we'll meet again, Keela."

"You do that, James, and I'll do the same."

"Deal." He put out his hand and she shook it. "Until next time, then."

"May the road rise up to meet you. May the wind always be at your back. May the sun shine warm upon your face, and rains fall soft upon your fields. And until we meet again, may God hold you in the palm of His hand."

James laughed. "And may your heaven be filled with music and pints glasses that never run dry."

"Have a Guinness for me, James."

"Every damned night," he assured her and he stepped through the doorway.

For a moment, she could see his silhouette. He looked back over his shoulder and waved. It looked like someone handed him a guitar. Keela could hear the music clearly now: "Whiskey in the Jar." James strummed right into the chorus and started to sing along.

Keela took a step towards him, but what had been an open, inviting doorway to him felt like nothing but cold glass to her. She could see him, she could hear him, but she could not go to him. The song would allow her, it insinuated. But no, the time for goodbyes was past.

With the heaviest of hearts, Keela sang the doorway closed and left James to his heaven of music and laughter and rounds and rounds of whiskey, always on the house.

Track 6

Ottilie was waiting.

Keela knew this without any magical assistance. Whatever Ottilie's game was, it also hinged on the *Oran na Céle*. She'd been conspicuously absent from the show and had Keela been any less nervous, or any less scared for her life, she might have noticed it then.

She slipped backstage, unnoticed, amid the murmurs of complex reactions to the show. Everyone seemed to have enjoyed her set, but everything else, they said, felt flat somehow. But no one could put his or her finger on why.

Moving unseen through the backstage, she heard the same over and over again. The other performers chattered amongst themselves in the halls as they packed up to head out. Yes, something was weird tonight, something was wrong, something wasn't right.

Guilt tingled down Keela's spine.

She made herself walk calmly to her dressing room. The vase had been replaced and the flowers salvaged. Someone had also replaced and cleaned up the broken lightbulbs. Her dress had been hung nicely back up on the coatrack. She caught her reflection in the mirror, she looked disheveled, but her hair was black once more.

Ottilie sat in the same seat Teri had used, only Ottilie

had a bottle of wine with her.

She rose when Keela entered. "You're lucky I didn't decide to open this while I waited. Where have you been? Your set finished up over an hour ago."

"I had something that needed doing," Keela said.

"I presume it's done now?"

"Aye."

"And you can focus on your career now?"

Keela shook her head. "That…still needs doing."

Ottilie rolled her eyes, but she popped the champagne cork and poured two tall flutes of mostly foam. "Well, here's to you, anyway. Congrats on your Opry debut."

They touched glasses and drank. Keela had never had champagne and didn't know how to rank this one. It was tasty, fizzing in her mouth and it had a very celebratory feeling to it. She decided she liked it.

"Now you're going to explain just what the hell happened in here."

"I can't, well not the whole of it."

Ottilie frowned. "I don't like that answer, dearie, let's try again."

Keela put down her champagne and crossed her arms. "Teri was here. She wanted to stop me from performing. She didn't. End of story."

"What was she stopping you with? A sledgehammer?"

"No. A length of iron chain."

Ottilie whistled long and low. "She was serious, then."

"Apparently."

"But she didn't stop you and you've found what you've been searching for. I can see it in you, hear it. You're going to be fantastic tomorrow."

"Tomorrow?"

"Well, in theory. See, they had Marie scheduled for two nights and still need to replace her on tomorrow night's show. I have submitted you to the committee for a repeat performance. Provided they don't take umbrage to the collateral damage. If they say yes, try not to destroy your dressing room this time, okay?"

Keela declined to voice the seething comment

she thought at that moment. In the mirror, she saw that a shifting aura of darkness had materialized around her though. She took a deep breath and tried to relax. The aura diminished somewhat.

"You're going to have to watch out for that," Ottilie said to her reflection. "It's going to get you into trouble if you aren't careful. And you haven't been careful. Not careful at all thus far."

"I'd like to get changed now," Keela said.

"Are you asking me to leave?"

"Aye."

For a moment Ottilie looked like she might argue. But she only topped off Keela's glass and picked up the bottle of champagne. "Come by Vox Beata in the morning, I should know something by then."

The door had just clicked closed when a swirl of mist rose up into the center of the room.

"Hello there, Molan." Keela took off the cloak and held it out to him, averting her eyes.

The mist coalesced into a man's shape beneath the cloak. Keela dropped his pants, relying on his shirt to keep her nudity covered. She pulled on her street clothes under that shirt and handed the rest of his clothing to him.

"Thank you," she said and meant it. "Thank you for coming to my rescue and for giving me the shirt off your back."

"And the cloak. And the pants. Don't forget about the pants."

Keela laughed. "Of course, the pants." She gathered her costumes back into their garment bags and flagged down one of the stage hands to request a locker. "Maybe tomorrow I'll get to actually wear some of this."

"The blue dress looked beautiful on you."

"Saw me, did you?"

"I did. While you were talking with the band."

She took her garment bags to one of the lockers down the hall. Molan stayed by her side.

"Did you go to James?" he asked.

"Aye." Keela locked her costumes safely away and turned to face him. "He's gone."

"I'm sorry."

"Aye. Me, too."

"Now, Michael."

Keela nodded. "Tomorrow, I think."

"Here?"

"Aye. 'Tis the only place I think I could really do it. The song is powerful, but I am going to need the crowd."

Molan escorted her to the performers' entrance and out into the night. Clouds had rolled in and a steady rain had begun to fall. "What now?"

"I need to make a stop in East Nashville."

"To see who?"

"The muses," she said.

"Are you sure that's a good idea? One of them tried to kill you tonight."

"Herself had no interest in killing me, just stopping me."

"Still…"

"You don't have to come along. But I owe it to them. I took their friend away tonight. I need to make my condolences to them. And deliver his last message."

"Lead on, my lady."

The muses' house was just as Keela remembered it: artsy, charming, at the end of Electric Avenue right before the entrance to Shelby Park. Tonight it was somber, though. Candles burned in all the windows.

Keela and Molan stepped onto the wide porch and knocked. Teri answered, her mouth set into a hard line. For a long moment, none of them spoke and the pattering of the rain on the roof filled the silence. Even the wisps didn't show themselves.

Finally, Keela said, "I've come to tell yourselves that James was safely escorted to the other side. And that he says goodbye and sends his love to you."

"You could have woken me." Teri's voice was flat, but her eyes betrayed the depth of her pain.

Keela shook her head. "No, I could not. When I arrived, he was already slipping from the living world. We couldn't get to where you were. I'm sorry."

"I thought that the song would make you all-powerful."

"The song just gives me my powers back. They were stripped from me."

Teri raised an eyebrow. "How'd you manage that?"

"'Tisn't important right now. I just wanted to come tell you that James said goodbye and that his last thoughts in this world were of you. And Polly. But mostly you."

"I appreciate that."

Thunder rumbled in the distance and Molan's head turned sharply to listen to it.

"Is anything wrong?" Keela asked him.

"Don't know yet. There's something not exactly *right*, but I'm not quite sure what it is."

"Seems like it's the night for that sort of thing," Teri commented. "Or hadn't you noticed, Keela?"

"Aye. I noticed."

"Then maybe you will begin understand why my sister and I have worked so hard to keep that song right where it belongs."

"It *belongs* to the banshee."

"Not anymore!" Teri took a step forward and Molan intercepted her.

Polly came running to the door. "Oh, it's you," she said, obviously disappointed in seeing Keela. "We're in mourning, here."

"And I'm not?"

"Talk to me when you've known and nurtured someone for forty-six years," Teri snapped.

"Years mean nothing to immortals, Teri. I can't say I had the same sort of relationship with James, but he meant a lot to me."

Teri shut the door on them. Through the large windows on the porch, Keela watched them sit down together on the couch and gaze into the flickering fireplace.

"Let's go," Molan whispered. "I don't like being out in this rain."

Keela let him wrap her up in his cloak and take them both to her apartment. It was Friday night. She should have been at McNamara's. With James.

"Everything's wrong, Molan. I feel like I've succeeded, yet lost everything. How can that be?"

"Tomorrow, you'll call Michael back from the dead and then we can think about what to do next."

"Aye. Michael," she said, nodding absently.

Molan sat her down on the corner of her bed and began to brush out her hair. His wisps tumbled free of his cloak with every brushstroke. "Yes, the very thing you came here to do in the first place? Don't tell me you've forgotten."

"No. But things weren't so…complicated… when I arrived here."

"Life is complicated, Keela. Under the barrows, concerned with the dead and never the living, that's easy. But you didn't choose that life."

"Because I took up singing when I got to Nashville?"

"No, because you fell in love with a mortal lad in Galway." He set the brush down and leaned into her field of vision. "I meant what I said, that you are nothing like the other banshees. And I meant that as a compliment."

Keela fell back onto the bed and let out a pent up sigh, sending will-o'-the-wisps twirling in all directions. "Never have been. I've never been like them."

"But in Nashville, you can be anything you want."

She looked over at him. "Within reason."

"What reason? You shouldn't limit your dreams. This is Nashville. It's kinda like Hollywood with a twang."

She laughed. But it made her wonder. "D'you think I could? Stay, I mean. After I bring Michael back?"

"Unless you want to go off with him?"

Keela thought about that, as well. "I don't know. I don't think so. For him, it will be like no time has passed at all and nothing has changed…"

"But for you, everything's different now."

"Aye. Everything." Tears welled up and Keela crushed her eyelids closed to try and stop them. But it was no use, they ran over her cheeks. But the wisps touched them with warm light and dabbed them each away.

"No more tonight," Molan said, gently waving his wisps back under his cloak. "No more talking, no more thinking, no more fretting. Get yourself to bed and relax, you've earned it. I promise your problems will still be waiting for you come morning, they're quite patient that way."

"All right, then." She let him turn back the bed and tuck her in.

After he had turned off the lights he came back to her side. In the rainy light, his skin glowed softly like a silver pearl.

"Molan MacLiath," Keela said, "Servant of the storm,

son of thunder."

"That I am."

"Guardian."

He smiled down at her. "Guardian to Keela, beautiful voice of the O'Reardon clan, and lately death's companion." The rain pounded against the window and the thunder growled. He glanced up and scowled.

"Yourself has done that twice now, is anything wrong?"

"That's for me to worry about, not you. But I won't be far away from you tonight, I promise."

"Oh. Good." She watched him stand up and settle his cloak around his shoulders. "Molan? How far away?"

"Would you like me to stay?" he asked. "Like where you can see me?"

"Will yourself think me a coward?"

"Keela, you're one of the bravest beings I have ever met." He sat back down on the bed. "How about I stay right here?"

"That would be…lovely."

He stretched out and draped his cloak over himself like a blanket. Keela rolled over and breathed in that familiar scent of sweet, damp wool. She moved in a little closer, pulling a corner of it over herself as well. The wisps snuggled up against her side, blinking in contentment.

"It's been a very long day," she said.

"Yes, it has. And I fear tomorrow will be even longer." He rested his hand on her shoulder.

The thunder eventually gave up grumbling and faded away, but the rain fell hard all night long.

Track 7

Come morning, it was still raining. Molan was nowhere to be found, and it troubled Keela a little. She held the stone and waited as the rain pelted the windows. Finally, she dressed and walked across the street to Vox Beata, hopping over the swiftly moving water that flowed down both sides of the street. It was a little after eight, and she wondered how early that committee got up in the morning.

Keela found the door closed but unlocked when she stepped onto the porch. She knocked, then turned the little key that rang the bell, but there was no answer.

"Hellooo?" she called as she stepped inside.

She hung her jacket, already dripping just from the short walk, on one of the decorative hooks that ran along the foyer wall.

The first floor was empty, even Ottilie's office. There was no one in the kitchen and the coffeepot was off.

"Cayden?" She peered out the kitchen window into the small parking lot in back. It was devoid of cars.

Keela headed up the back stairs only to find the second floor as deserted as the first. That only left the attic. Keela had never been up there and but it was where Ottilie had mentioned keeping her truly rare music so naturally Keela had been curious to see it. After a good deal of hunting, Keela found that the door in the corner, which she had taken to be a closet, hid the small staircase that led to the attic.

The third floor had been converted from an unfinished attic into a loft. The eaves and architectural details remained, but the rest of the space had the same feeling of Edwardian luxury as the downstairs. One long room, it had been divided somewhat into sections using furniture and some Japanese folding screens. The windows were all filled with stained glass, mostly abstract designs in blues and greens but the front and rear windows were figured. The one that looked out the rear of the house was of a mermaid sitting on a large rock. It would probably have gleamed in the morning light, but the heavy clouds and rain totally so obscured the sun that the whole attic was very dark.

She wondered again where Molan was, and momentary thought of running back to the apartment and leaving him a note. But that would mean going back out into the rain once again.

The area where the stairs came up was organized like a sitting room of sorts, reminding Keela of a lobby. Two loveseats sat facing a pair of chairs that backed up to the railing of the steps with a mahogany coffee table between them. A dish of tumbled sea glass and shells had been placed artfully off center on the tabletop. A matched set of lacquered folding screens set off this area from the rest of the space, and Keela had to walk between the two loveseats to move to the next section. It had definitely been designed to encourage anyone coming up to this floor to stay right there and wait.

Keela followed the sounds of quiet classical music playing from the front of the house. She moved carefully in the heavy shadows, passing bookshelves built into the angled walls, as well as freestanding shelves used to delineate the different "rooms." Whoever had laid out this space knew what they were doing.

The front window came into view, finally. It depicted a beautiful woman holding up what looked like a giant pearl portrayed in an Art Nouveau style. It reminded Keela of the Vox Beata logo. The music was louder here, coming from the westernmost corner of the attic, an area that had been set off by shelving the way much of the rest of the floor had been, but these shelves were open. They formed a vaguely circular enclosure with a single passageway into that room. The shelves themselves were about seven feet tall and reached nearly to the crossbeams in the ceiling. Each and every one was filled with a profusion of glass jars and bottles. Some were ornamental, colorful, with interesting shapes while others were basic mason jars and the like. They all had two things in common, however: they were all sealed with some kind of wax, and they were all labeled in the same scrolling handwriting.

Keela hesitated in the opening to this area. She could feel magic here, she could smell incense and sage. On a tall, round table in the center of the room sat a beautifully restored antique Victrola and a decorative box of records. The music stopped. This part of the house was so dark that Keela couldn't see far at all into the space before her. She could only guess at its dimensions, but where she stood seemed to correspond to the small turret that whimsically jutted from the side of the third floor.

Keela heard a single footstep on hardwood before it was muffled by a thick throw rug. She became aware that she was glowing and stepped away from the shelves, hoping to remain unseen.

"So good of you to come, Keela," Ottilie said. "I want to talk to you about tonight's performance."

"So, they answered you?" Keela asked, remaining just shy of the threshold to that strange little room. "I'm on for tonight?"

The music started up again, this time some lovely vocal piece from an opera that Keela didn't recognize. Ottilie was nothing more than a shadow in the dark, indistinct.

The Victrola sounded clear, gloriously so, impossibly so. It reverberated the glass on the shelves, making it sound like hundreds of tiny voices were trapped inside and trying to sing along. It was unnerving.

"So long as there aren't any problems like there were last night." Ottilie came toward her, the soft light coming off of Keela's skin and hair illuminating her like a ghost. "For your sake, I hope not."

"For the sake of everyone," Keela said.

"Where's your bodyguard? I want to get some

assurances from him on that, to pass on to the committee."

"I'll let him know."

"Where is he? I'm surprised he let you come here alone. He's barely let you out of his sight since he showed up."

"He's very diligent."

"Except for today."

"What are you getting at, Ottilie?"

She smiled, as if she knew a great secret. "Nothing. Just seems odd, that's all. Do you even know where he is? You don't sound like you do."

"I don't, but I don't see how that matters. 'Tisn't like I'm in danger here, is it?"

Ottilie smiled at that and crooked her finger towards Keela. "Of course not. Come here; I want to show you something." She turned away and switched on a little Tiffany lamp on a nearby table.

In its small circle of light, Keela could see that the standing shelves butted up against built-ins that lined the curved walls. Aside from the tables which held the Victrola and the Tiffany lamp, there was also a tea cart and a chaise lounge in the enclosure. The bottles and jars lined every shelf, some shelves held dozens, others only a few.

Ottilie stood in the center of the room and stretched her arms wide.

"What is this place?" Keela asked, venturing a few steps in past the ring of shelves.

"My workshop."

"I'm afraid I don't understand."

"I know," Ottilie said. "But you will."

Keela didn't like anything about what she felt up there in that garret. "Have you seen Cayden this morning?"

Ottilie sighed. "I had to let Cayden go."

"Oh?" Warning roared in Keela's ears. "That's a pity. I rather liked him."

"I did, too, and it pained me to do it, but he just wasn't working out for me any longer. He had to go."

"Do you have a replacement?"

"Oh, yes. Training one right now, in fact."

"I see."

Ottilie's smile was not reassuring. "Tonight is going to be very special, Keela. It is going to change everything for us."

"Us?"

"Nothing will be the same for either one of us after tonight."

The song on the Victrola ended and so did that ghastly reverberation, leaving only the steady beat of the rain on the roof. Keela swore it was raining even harder now.

"Is this usual?" She pointed up at the ceiling.

"The rain?"

"Aye."

"Don't you know the old song? 'Lord, it sure rains hard in Tennessee.'"

"Never heard it before."

Ottilie lifted a shoulder in a shrug. "No matter, it does."

Keela looked around at the strange collection of glassware. "What are all of these?"

"My collection. Each one is unique, you know, no two are exactly alike."

"Is that so?" Keela backed out of the enclosure, suddenly unwilling to be there within those walls a moment longer. "Was this all yourself wanted to speak to me about, then? I should get going, prepare for tonight. "

"Keela…"

"Because I promised Molan I'd meet himself for breakfast." It was a lie, one they both recognized but it served to put distance between then.

Ottilie's smile surprised her. "Of course," she said, pleasantly. "I'd hate to keep you. I just wanted to let you know about tonight and make sure you were ready. How's your voice today?"

"Fine," Keela said. "It's never been better."

Ottilie's pleased smile broadened into a grin. "Perfect."

Keela fled as calmly as she could. There was not a staircase down to the second floor at the front of the house, so she navigated back through the warren of furniture and folding screens, bumping into just about everything in her path. From the corner of the attic, she heard the Victrola start up once more, another aria which stirred whatever was inside of all those glass jars.

The purple Victorian was still devoid of people as Keela left it. She grabbed her jacket and shut the front door firmly behind her. The water in the gutters had deepened and met in the middle of the road, making it look like a shallow but swiftly moving river. It was a challenge to get back across to her apartment without getting her feet wet. She looked back up at the building, at the turret window where the only light shone, and felt chills race through her.

One more night, she told herself. *After tonight, Michael will be restored and I can put everything to rights again.*

But the thought of leaving Nashville pained her, almost as much as the thought of Ottilie scared her. Keela ducked into her apartment and for the first time in days put on her green wool dress and her cloak. She then turned herself into a crow and headed for familiar territory.

Nashville was subdued today, whether solely on account of the rain or not, she couldn't tell. It was quiet though, the undercurrent of music that permeated the place had gone silent.

The City Cemetery was solemn in the rain. The whisper of the raindrops in the grass was soothing, however. Keela sat in the branches of her favorite magnolia and tried to ignore the water splashing through the leaves. It was raining too hard for the poor tree to offer much shelter.

The ghosts didn't seem to mind the weather and milled about as was their custom, day or night, rain or shine. They didn't acknowledge her, though. Already they seemed to have forgotten she'd been there.

She sat still and quiet, watching the shimmer of rainfall, thinking on the days and nights she'd spent here. Thinking on Michael. On James. On Molan and where he could possibly be.

It was unsettling to have woken to find him gone. No note, nothing to let her know where he'd gone to or when he might be back.

The restlessness returned. The ambition that had come as a gift from the muses, a gift to occupy her and keep her from her task. The *Oran na Céle* burned deep inside of her, roiling and powerful and difficult to contain. It had lived in the whole city until last night. It had been lodged in the circle of oak at the Opry, but that space had not confined it. Now it chafed at the bounds of Keela's banshee self, unable to flow in and out of all the places it had been accustomed. It hurt.

Keela finally took off, stretching her wings through the rain and flying for the very last place she wanted to see today, but yet the only place she wanted to go: McNamara's.

The doors had just opened when she arrived. She hung her cloak by the door, remembering to take the stone from the Liffey in its little bag out of the pocket. She walked straight to the music room.

On the stage was a framed picture of James on an easel draped in black fabric. A bouquet of lilies stood on the big Jameson barrel beside it. This room would never hear his voice again. She wondered if it would ever again hear hers.

"Ah, my dear lass, I'm so glad to see you." The owner's wife surprised Keela. "You've heard about James?"

Keela nodded and needed to marshal her strength before she spoke. "Aye. I was there."

"When he passed?"

Keela nodded again.

"Bless you, bless you for being there with him in his final hours." She gave Keela a heartfelt hug that ended abruptly with a shiver. "Apologies. None of us have been ourselves since we heard he'd taken ill."

"It's all right." She made herself smile. "D'you mind if I sit here for a little while?"

"Mind? Of course not! Keela, my girl, you're family. You're welcome to sit, sing, do whatever you want."

"That's sweet of you."

"That's the truth." She ducked behind the bar and came back with a shot of Feckin' Spiced, James's favorite whiskey. "For his memory."

The tears came back as Keela took the glass. "Did you hear me last night? On the Opry?"

"We did. Teri told us all about it."

"She did?"

"She said you were singing for James, so of course we all tuned in. Your rendition of 'Parting Glass' was inspired. Will you be on again?"

"Tonight," Keela said.

"Then we'll be listening. We'll put it on here in the music room."

"No band?"

She glanced over at the stage with its lonely picture. "We're having a wake tonight. Nothing formal, so there's no one scheduled to perform, although someone will, I'm sure. Lots of someones, probably."

Keela smiled through her tears. "He's going to be so disappointed to have missed that."

"I'm sure he's got better things to worry about now, doesn't he?"

Keela nodded. "He does."

"Take your time, dearie, I'll be up front if you need me." She squeezed Keela's shoulder and left her alone with her thoughts.

Keela sipped the whiskey, letting it warm her.

She was still there an hour later when Molan found her.

"I didn't even need to check with the stone to know where you were," he said. His own cloak had been hung in the lobby, but his clothes were still more than damp. "This was my first guess and I was right."

"Where's yourself been?"

"Out," he said and didn't elaborate. "Are you ready for tonight?"

Keela decided not to press the point. "So long as no one comes to kill me, aye."

"I'll make sure of it."

"You've taken this bodyguard thing awfully seriously."

"Guardian," he reminded her. "And it fits. So here I am. No one will be getting anywhere near you tonight."

"I'm afraid, Molan," Keela whispered.

"Afraid of failing?"

"Aye. And afraid of success."

"Then there's only one thing you can do about that."

"What is it?"

He went to the bar and fetched back the entire bottle of Feckin' Spiced. "Drink more whiskey."

Track 8

The night went much more smoothly this time
around. Keela had no visitors and she had no problems with
her set list. She was to sing "Danny Boy" and "Amazing
Grace," "Tell Me Ma" and "The Star of the County Down,"
a good mix of upbeat and melancholy, all sure to be crowd
pleasers.

Molan lingered patiently about, but his mind was
obviously elsewhere. Had this been Keela's debut night,
she would have sent him away for infecting her with her
nervousness. He paced, mostly, and that would have been
fine would he not suddenly stop and listen, then go back
to pacing with renewed agitation, leaving a trail of equally
agitated will-o'-the-wisps in his wake, each bobbing and
blinking sporadically.

"Yourself is going to be kicked in just a moment
if you don't stop or tell me what's going on," Keela said,
stepping in front of him as he made a return trip towards
the dressing room mirror. He stopped short and the wisps
scattered to either side.

"Wear your green dress tonight," he answered.

"What? This? You can't be serious!"

"Yes, that, and I am. Something's very wrong Keela,
you need to be ready to go at a moment's notice and I don't

want you showing up naked wherever we may end up."

"Ready to go? Why?"

Molan's grey eyes flickered up towards the ceiling. "The rain," he said.

"The rain? We're from Ireland, we're used to rain, Molan."

"Not like this."

"So fix it, Servant of the Storm."

He sighed. "I can't. This is no natural storm and it isn't a spell of my doing. So I am useless. And trust me, I have tried to avert the disaster that is heading straight for this city."

"Disaster?"

"Just be ready to run when I tell you, okay? I don't care if you are in the middle of a song, there will be no noble 'the show must go on' sacrifices, either. People will die."

That gave Keela pause. "Just what's happening out there?"

"The rain. The river. The levee." He wrung his hands. "There's flooding upstream and stress on the whole system. Something's got to give. And when it does, Nashville is going to drown."

His words took a minute to sink in. "Drown?"

Molan nodded. "That or be swept away."

The knock at the door startled them both. "Miss Keela? Time to go," one of the stagehands called from the hallway.

Molan caught her in a quick hug. "Listen for me."

Keela stepped out into the corridor and passed Ottilie in the greenroom. "Oh, tell me that's not what you're wearing!"

"Why not?"

"I've worked so hard!"

"I don't have time to change now."

"I'm so disappointed in you," Ottilie said and shook her head.

The friendly stagehand from the night before tugged on Keela's cloak. "They need you, now."

Keela walked away from Ottilie and forced a smile onto her face. The host was just finishing his charming introduction as Keela stepped out onto the stage. The song surged within her, nearly knocking her off of her feet. She almost missed the witty banter he was making about her dress.

"It came from Ireland," she responded, pretty certain he'd said something about where she'd gotten her outfit.

"It must have, you'd never see anything like that around here."

"Of course not," Keela said. "Where else but Ireland could yourself find green sheep?"

He was stunned a moment before falling into a fit of giggles. "Nowhere," he said.

"Besides, I dressed up for everyone tonight!" Keela hitched up her hem. "I'm wearing *shoes*!"

An appreciative "Ooooohhhh!" went up from the audience followed by a round of applause.

The host said, laughing, "My dear, you're missing a price tag."

Keela didn't get it, but she winked at him anyway and walked towards the center of the stage. The circle of oak looked barren now, flat. The *Oran na Céle* writhed as she neared its erstwhile resting place. It was a fight to stay standing, not to mention to smile and even try and think about singing. She all but clung to the microphone stand, glad of the long dress so they couldn't see how badly her legs trembled.

Holding the song within her was like keeping a tempest bottled up. Over the years, it had been fed on all manner of music, passion, stardom, sweat, tears, laughter, joy, and despair and it had grown impossibly strong, impossibly large. Too much for Keela to contain for long.

This wasn't a song about death's companion anymore, it was now *music's* companion and it was shouting at her that it wanted to go home. She understood Teri a great deal better all of a sudden and wished that the muse could come to her aid now.

Instead, she saw Ottilie standing at the foot of the stage with a strange, satisfied smile on her face. She caught Keela's gaze and nodded enthusiastically in a *get on with it* way.

"Before I start my set tonight," Keela said, ignoring Ottilie's scowl, "I would like to say a word of appreciation to the good people of the Opry for giving me this chance and to you fine folk out in the audience, near and far, for not only opening your ears but opening your hearts to an Irish lass living out her dreams."

She was interrupted by applause.

"And I couldn't have gotten here without the help of a great many people. I'm not going to mention them all, but I am going to tell you about James. James O'Brien was my first friend in Nashville. And a good friend he was, d'you know he bought me a shot of Jack my first day here, aye, a very good friend indeed."

Someone whooped out in the audience, followed by a wave of laughter.

"James should have been playing up here with me this weekend, but he'd taken very ill and he passed away last night," she paused through the collective gasp. "He got to hear me sing last night, though." A lump found its way into Keela's throat and she swallowed it down. "They had the show playing in his room, I know he heard," the last came out as barely a whisper and the crowd sighed and sniffled with her.

Ottilie impatiently circled her finger, indicating she was running out of time. Her posture was stiff, uneasy now. She kept looking towards the west.

"I sang 'The Parting Glass' for him last night. And I was wondering, if yourselves wouldn't mind, if you'd all be so kind in singing 'Amazing Grace' with me for him tonight?"

The swift, affirmative applause answered her and someone brought the houselights up a bit so Keela could see them all, these people who were going to help her. For James. For Michael.

Ottilie retreated from the edge of the stage, her mouth bent into an ugly frown. She had something in her hand that gleamed under the houselights but that Keela couldn't identify.

Ignoring her, Keela nodded to the band and they started the song. They were a good band. James would have liked them; they took their tempo cues from Keela and didn't rush her or drag her down. She had barely sung out the first syllable before the audience poured in. They didn't know James and would never meet him, but they knew Keela, or at least felt like they did. They sang from their hearts, from their individual senses of loss, disappointment, heartache, and pain. The *Oran na Céle* touched them all as they sang along with Keela, along with it.

Ottilie made a disgusted face and left in a hurry. Keela watched her go and almost gloated. Whatever Ottilie was about, she was deeply unhappy with this performance and anyone who could take umbrage to something like this was not someone for whom Keela had any respect.

Things would be different for them both, Ottilie had said that morning. *Different, indeed,* thought Keela.

The verse ended and she considered starting up the second when the crowd got to their feet, applauding. Keela let out a long breath and felt something like peace settle over her. The applause washed over her, steady as the rain outside. Even the host was standing at his podium, clapping. There were tears shining on his cheeks. The moment stretched on and finally the audience started to settle.

But she had them, now.

It was time, finally time to sing Michael back from the dead.

"You have no idea how much this means to me," Keela said into the microphone. She felt strong, stronger than she ever had before, but also deeply humbled. "If James were here, he'd say-"

"Can't any of y'all hear me? EVACUATE!" A man stood at one of the section doors, he wore hip-waders and a reflective coat and he was dripping wet. "It's coming and we're running out of time!" He stepped further into the theatre and swore, his eyes growing wide with shock. "I can't believe anyone at all is still in here, much less a full house!"

He pulled a radio from under his waders and began to bark orders into it.

The spell Keela had woven fell apart and she stood there, mouth open, watching the pandemonium erupt before her. People who had been singing in unison, even harmony, before were now pushing and climbing over one another, scrambling for the exits as *it* came, whatever it was.

It turned out to be the Cumberland River.

Backstage also erupted into a flurry of activity as doors were opened and dividers rolled back to allow people to get out. But they saw, too late, that it was letting the water in. Panic reigned as the floodwaters began to pour down the aisles and gather at the foot of the stage. Rain blew in through the open doors backstage and soaked everything.

Keela watched it all from her vantage point, standing on the circle of oak on the Opry stage. Announcements started coming in over the address system, urging people to move safely to the exits. But the water still rose and the atmosphere became like that of a sinking ship.

The entire Opry complex rested in a hollow beside the river. If the water had gotten here, then that meant the mall next door must also be flooded, along with the parking lot full of cars and the only road out to Briley Parkway. They were really and truly trapped.

Through the rain, Keela heard helicopters and shouting.

She stayed on that circle of oak, unwilling, *unable* to leave. The song wove itself around her, digging itself into the wood once more. It wanted to stay and fight.

"Can't fight this," Keela murmured. But she didn't move. Instead, she began to sing. She knew a banshee song for the dying, one to ease the fear of the coming death. No one here was about to die, she hoped, but keeping them calm could only help.

The bottom level had been mostly cleared, but they had backed up getting down from the second tier. The water was coming swiftly into the theatre now, climbing the stairs one step at a time. People were afraid to step down into the rising flood. The water had collected at the foot of the stage now and was threatening to lap up over the lip.

The lights flickered once, twice, a third time, then faded to half strength for a few minutes before glowing with blinding intensity and then going completely dark. The acrid smell of hot wiring filled the building.

Keela knew she was glowing before she saw her shimmering reflection in the floodwaters. The pew-like seats were starting to float. Already cushions were drifting on the currents and eddies like so many tiny icebergs.

Still Keela sang. She had no idea where anyone was, not Molan, not Ottilie, not the host, not the band, not any of the stagehands. In all of the chaos, she appeared to be forgotten. Even the people up in the balcony, still waiting to get out of the doomed building, didn't seem to notice her.

Finally, Molan appeared. He splashed through the

few inches of water that now covered the stage, his wisps in tow, fanning out across the water's surface to encircle Keela.

"Happened so fast," he panted. "Levee's down. So many people here."

"Ottilie," Keela said.

"Haven't seen her."

Keela shook her head. "She knew. She left directly before everything began. She's involved in this somehow: the storm, the fact that no one knew we were still here."

"They thought you'd been evacuated already. I thought you had, I've been looking all over for you." The corners of his mouth twitched.

The water lapped up to Keela's ankles. She looked up to the upper tier, squinting in the darkness. She didn't detect any movement in the seats, but she could see flashlight beams and silhouettes in the upstairs lobby beyond.

"We've got to go, Keela, I don't know how deep this water is going to get."

She looked down at the circle now underneath a good six inches of water. She swore Molan would hear the shrieking of the *Oran na Céle* from within her. Through it, Keela could feel the moisture starting to seep into those old boards, saturating the wood fibers and warping them, ruining them. So much history, so much magic, all being washed away.

"Keela!" Molan took her by the shoulders. "Stay with me!"

"I can't leave."

"Is this like before?"

"No. Not quite. The song, Molan, it wants to protect this place, it wants to stay here. It won't let me go!"

"The *song* won't? It's…sentient?"

"Aye, near enough. This isn't a banshee song anymore."

"Which is exactly what I've been telling you this entire time!" Teri surprised them, wading over from stage right, followed by Polly. "It. Isn't. Yours." She threw up her hands. "And now look what you've done!"

"This?" Keela looked around at the water, now swirling around her shins. "I had nothing to do with this!"

"You brought that Sea Witch in here. You know, I had just gotten her ousted from the Opry committee, but now that she's got this *stunning new talent…*" Teri mimed putting her finger down her throat.

"I want to help you!"

"You can help by getting out of the way," snapped Polly.

"Keela, let's go," Molan tugged at her sleeve. "I'm sure the muses can handle this."

"You really want to help? Stop her," Teri said. "I don't know what Ottilie thinks she's doing, but it's bigger than anything she's ever tried before. This water, it reeks of blood. Can't you smell it?"

Keela began to protest, but she recognized the faint trace of death here. "Sacrifice," she whispered. As soon as she said the word, she knew it to be true. There was the echo of ritual across all of it. And she realized she knew who'd been done in. "I know how to stop it. And I can."

Teri's face went from scoffing to serious as realization dawned on her. "*Oipho*, I'll bet you can! Spoil the sacrifice, spoil the spell."

Keela smiled. "Aye, exactly."

Molan said, "Even if he or she is already dead, this sacrifice?"

"Are you new here, Fae Boy?" Teri asked. "You do know Keela's a banshee, right?"

"But she can't call just anyone back from the dead… can you?" he asked.

"With this," Keela pressed her hand to her chest, nodding towards the oak circle on the floor. "Aye, I think I can, indeed."

"Then let's find her and let's stop her before Nashville gets washed right off the map," Molan said.

"That puts us on the same side, then. At the moment, anyway." Teri reached out her hand to Keela.

"Aye, I suppose it does."

"About damn time," said Polly.

"*Kali tihi*," Teri said.

Keela clasped the muse's hand firmly at the wrist. "I'm going to need it."

Track 9

"You haven't forgotten about Michael, have you?"

"Of course not, Molan." They sheltered on the porch of Vox Beata, the ground was soggy and the street a river, but no flooding touched this neighborhood, yet. "I think this might serve both purposes, but I have to make certain what herself might have been about, here."

The front door was still unlocked.

"Do you know what you're looking for?"

"Aye." Keela pushed the door, letting it swing open before she stepped inside. It hadn't been so long ago that Cayden had met her there. Sweet, silent Cayden who had worried so much about her. "He warned me," she said to Molan. "He thought I was in danger from her, he urged me to leave. But it was him…"

"Who?"

"Cayden. The young man who worked here. He was Ottilie's assistant. I think he's the one she sacrificed."

Inside, the stately Victorian was dark and empty, just as Keela had left it that morning. It was eerier now in the dark with the terrible rain falling, still falling, and the floodwaters rising, still rising.

Keela led the way to the back stairs and up to the second floor, then directly to the smaller staircase up to the attic. They didn't bother turning on any lights. Keela shone enough for them both to see their surroundings, and the wisps helped light the way. Weaving through the maze of the top floor, they finally came to the circular area of the turret. Here, Keela hesitated.

"I don't blame you," Molan said. "This doesn't feel right at all."

She said nothing in return, just took a deep breath and walked into the room. Ottilie wasn't there. Keela switched on the little lamp on the table next to the Victrola, which she avoided touching. Molan stayed nearby, shadowing her. On the tea cart were several of the glass vessels, seals broken. They sat empty, discarded, but like the Victrola, Keela was loath to handle them. She bent down to peer at the labels and was surprised to find they were names. She looked up and found the same thing on the shelves. Each of the bottles and jars was labeled with a single name.

"I don't understand, what's it mean? Heather, Gretchen, Monica, Roz, Nat, Brad, Gabe, Renee, Kadee, Lira," Molan read down the length of one shelf.

"I'll know as soon as I find his."

"Cayden?"

"Aye." She skimmed each shelf, but there were so many, far too many. It gave her a headache.

"Here," Molan said. He reached under the chaise lounge and held up what looked like a large inkwell of cobalt blue. Written in that rococo script was the name Cayden.

Keela stared at it, almost unwilling to believe her suspicions had been correct.

"What was in here? His soul?"

She shook her head and looked out at the dimly illuminated front stained glass window. The one with the woman holding up the pearl, her mouth slightly open, her posture triumphant. The image that reminded Keela so much of the Vox Beata logo, the woman with the jewel coming out of her mouth.

"No. Not his soul. Listen." Making as little contact as possible, Keela turned the key a few times on the Victrola and dropped the arm onto the thick record waiting on the turntable. The unearthly aria began again and within moments, the jars on the shelves began to hum. "It's his voice. It was anyway. I don't know where it is now." She jerked the arm off the record and the humming faded away with the song. She noticed the label on the record: Marie M.

"Um, Keela?" Molan brought her another empty jar, the largest in the room. It was a tall, green glass cylinder with a lid that fit snugly on top and sealed, like something to be used storing flour in a pantry or candy on a countertop. Its label had already been applied. It said *Keela*. She backed away from it. "It was on the bottom tray of the tea cart. Along with some sealing wax and a stack of uncut records. What's she been doing up here?"

Keela held Cayden's empty jar cupped reverently in her hands. A part of her lamented that she would never hear his voice. "She takes things that don't belong to herself, that's what."

"Voices." The word hung there between them, Keela shivered and Molan put an arm around her shoulder. "Not yours. Not ever yours."

"I'm going to end up singing for her, you realize. To get this done, to stop this terrible flood, I'm going to have to sing."

Molan hefted Keela's jar and threw it down with all his might. It shattered onto the hardwood floor. "Not taking any chances," he said.

"She planned this all, very carefully. The rain, the flood. She wanted to destroy the circle. Once I had the song, she had to keep it with me until she could harvest my voice."

"Why didn't she burn the place? That'd do worse damage, don't you think?"

Keela paced, her boots crunching the broken glass. "Water is her affinity. She mentioned it to me once, called herself 'a waterbaby in a landlocked state.'"

"Tennessee's not landlocked anymore."

"If Teri can't intervene and save that circle of wood, I don't know what's going to happen, Molan. And I feel that so much of this is myself's own fault."

"Keela, look at this place. These jars, they go back years. She's been feeding off of Nashville's brightest talent for who knows how long. She would have found a way to the song without you, I know she would have. Maybe you hastened her plans a bit, but she's been plotting something like this for a while now."

"But…why? That's what I don't understand. The jars, the voices — that, I get. It terrifies me but I get it. But the rain, drowning the city. It couldn't be all for the sake of keeping the *Oran na Céle* in me until she could take it, could it?"

"Perhaps. But the question to ask is why does she need the song? I'm willing to believe that she would take these steps, blighting the whole town just to corral you, but what we ought to be thinking through is what does she intend to do with the *Oran na Céle* once she has it? What could she do with it?"

"Run this town," Keela said. "It would put her on par with the muses. It would make her the power center of the whole industry."

"But could she use it?"

"She wouldn't have to. She'd have my voice."

"That means she's waiting for you, somewhere out there in that storm."

"Aye. We'd best go find her, then." Keela went to the one window in the turret's wall, which opened easily outward. She could see the bands of clouds moving slowly west. The Opry had to be entirely inundated by now, she figured, but the storm still raged and now it was bearing right into downtown. Headed straight for the Ryman Auditorium.

Keela's body had shrunk into a crow's by the time her feet touched the window ledge.

"Wait, where are you going?" Molan was already climbing out the window after her, disintegrating into mist as he went.

"Ryman," she squawked and spread her wings.

She could have traveled with Molan, but she needed to see for herself. As she neared downtown, streets everywhere were flooded, the running water met with the rising river around 4th Avenue. The flood's depth was only a few inches, but it was rising quickly as the bulk of the rainwater was now coming down the tributaries and swelling the Cumberland to impossible depths. Riverside Park was covered, the Music City Star train station was flooded to the tops of its benches, and the Red Grooms carousel was likely ruined.

The Ryman still stood high and dry, halfway up the

hill on 5th Avenue, but the inundation had reached the north side of Broadway and was building around Legend's Corner. She flapped hard through the falling raindrops, looking down over the Cumberland where it had spilled its banks. Already the stadium across the river was losing ground, and the Shelby Street Pedestrian Bridge ended in several feet of water over on 3rd.

Police officers and firefighters directed traffic and people out of the danger zone while the shopkeepers and business owners of Broadway were sandbagging and praying. But it was too dark and the water was rising too quickly. Fort Nashboro's rustic timbers stood valiantly against the dark tide, but it was losing.

Keela watched the swell come down river like a slow moving wave. Somewhere upstream a dam had failed or been opened. What was already bad got so very much worse. Cars were lifted and knocked into buildings. The huge front window of the Buck Wild Saloon shattered and the water gushed in, pulling with it tree limbs, newspaper boxes, and all manner of debris. The barstools were pushed over by the tide and it seemed like her meeting with James had just been erased. Next door, the old, mullioned windows of Mulligan's fared better, but Keela knew the water would eventually win.

She landed on top of the pedestrian bridge, exhausted and soaked to the skin. She fought the urge to shake out her feathers, which would only make matters worse. Even from her vantage point, the sheets of rain made it difficult to see. Molan's foggy form drifted directly beneath her, watching and waiting. The river churned with a ferocious new current only yards below the deck of the bridge, and Keela watched that force moving steadily westward even though the east side of the river was flatter and a more logical place for the water to spread. But it didn't. As if it had a mind of its own — which Keela was now convinced that it did to some degree — the floodwaters pressed into downtown. The storefronts on Second were flooded to the tops of their doorframes already, and the shops of Broadway were not far behind. The rain, too, changed direction, now coming in from the east and pelting the buildings with renewed vigor. The Ryman's lobby faced east, with its spacious courtyard. It was raised up a bit from street level, but at this rate, Keela wasn't sure that would protect it.

Then Keela saw Ottilie.

She had climbed out onto the large sculpture installed on the river's east side, directly across from the park. It was called "Ghost Ballet" but the locals called it the "roller coaster" because it consisted of two overlapping semi circles made in red tubular metal that looked more like a thrill ride's track than art. Ottilie had climbed atop the thing, now an island jutting out of the dark water. She leaned against one of the struts, her legs clasped around it while she held her arms aloft.

The glow that emanated from her reflected off the water in whorls and eddies that built up strength and speed and rushed ever westward, elevating the flood level inch by inch as the rain continued to pour.

Keela had to act or else Music City would be no more.

She leapt into the air and battled the buffeting wind to swing out and come up behind Ottilie's position. As she neared, Keela heard Ottilie singing. Not in her own voice, but a resonant tenor, warm and sweet as whiskey. Underneath that, softly, barely heard, was Ottilie herself, her voice threading through the spell.

Keela landed on the supports that held up the sculpture and looked human once more. She drew her cloak up over her head to cover the shining silver of her hair. The sting of the iron scalded her hands, but she held on. The mist followed her, as she knew it would, wrapping the bottom of the beam and caressing her white-knuckled hands.

The *Oran na Céle* had been subdued since the water had overtaken the Opry, but it raged now, furiously trying to escape, to take its vengeance on Ottilie. Keela did the only thing she could think of: she began to hum. The song within her settled, grudgingly, and allowed itself to be bidden.

Keela clutched the metal frame, took a deep breath, and began to sing. It was not timidity that she started out singing low and soft, but tactics. She had to gather her strength, build her own spell woven note by note, and it had to be ready to hold up to Ottilie by the time the witch noticed. It was a tall order, Keela thought, but the comforting scent of Molan, of wet wool, gave her courage.

The *Oran na Céle* responded, warming to her, coiling within her and readying itself to burst free. She hoped she'd have the strength to reel it back in when it was all said and done. Keela wondered if it had missed being a banshee song. She had used it once already to open the gates of the other side, but this was going to be quite different.

If she was to challenge Ottilie, it had to be now, before she lost the element of surprise.

Keela got to her feet, wind and rain threatening to knock her into the river. There was nothing to hold onto, nothing with which to even steady herself. Only fog and music. It would have to do.

For the first time since taking possession of the *Oran na Céle*, Keela gave it free rein. It nearly consumed her, but she fought through the blaze of light and fury, keeping her eyes on Ottilie and the strange and exquisite tenor voice incongruously coming from her mouth.

Cayden, Keela realized. Yes, the song, the sacrifice; Ottilie had used them both, his voice and his blood.

Keela stood straighter now, the *Oran na Céle* steeling her against the storm and against Ottilie's spell. The rain fell gentler here, no longer stinging as it struck her. It felt almost like a natural rain, like an Irish rain.

She sang out, letting the song ride her, take her voice and shape it, use it to cut through the worlds. From high above, Ottilie took notice. There wasn't much she could do, perched as she was at the top of the curved structure, slick with rain and swaying in the wind. If she was going to fight Keela, she was going to have to come down to her.

In the meantime, Keela focused on her task. *Spoil the sacrifice, spoil the spell.*

She sang down to the river, pulling apart the worlds at the seams, using the river as a conduit. Ottilie's song faltered and Keela pressed on, straining her voice to drive more power behind her song.

Still singing, Ottilie was now scrambling down the sculpture, occasionally slipping and breaking off her tune. Keela saw the round glass bottle dangling from the belt at her waist. Just about the size and shape of the thing she'd seen Ottilie holding at the Opry.

Keela focused, eyes on the swirling water turning faster and faster until it formed a whirlpool. At first it was no more impressive than a bathtub drain and Ottilie laughed, far too nearby for comfort.

"Little banshee," she said simultaneously in Cayden's voice and her own. "Trying to play at being a sea witch. Amateur! I thought I trained you better than that?"

The vortex widened, little by agonizing little as Ottilie closed the distance between them. Still, Keela sang on, tapping into everything the *Oran na Céle* had to offer her. She could taste Cayden's blood in the air; it grew stronger as the whirlpool widened. What should have been the riverbed was nothing of the sort. In the center of the swirling water was nothing but light.

It even gave Ottilie pause, but only for a moment. She reached the bottom of the ladder-like curve and yanked the bottle from her belt. Her tone changed now, chanting more than singing, strange words that made Keela's head spin. She held the bottle towards Keela and a tiny shimmer coalesced inside of it.

Turning her back, Keela focused on the water, on the gateway at the bottom of the vortex. The lightheadedness interfered with her balance so she crouched down, reaching for the support beam under her feet. She started to feel a tickle in her throat. The *Oran na Céle* blazed out of her and she formed his name inside of it: *Cayden*.

From the depths below, something stirred, interrupting the light.

"Rise, rise, rise!" Keela sang.

The tickle turned to tightness and her voice grew hoarse around the edges. The strength in her was failing, even the *Oran na Céle* was fading.

She fell to her hands and knees, grabbing desperately to the iron supports that both chilled and burned at once. A silhouette appeared in the hollow of the whirlpool and rose out of the churning water.

Keela didn't pay that any mind, though, her eyes remained on the gateway still open and the last vestiges of power she had held in reserve. For this, the one thing she had come here to do.

Before her voice gave out, lost and locked forever into one of Ottilie's shining jars, Keela cried, "*MICHAEL!*" into the river.

Then all went dark.

Track 10

Reela came to in a flash of confused terror. Someone held her, someone shouted, and the patter of rain still splashed down on her face. The throbbing in her head nearly outweighed the rawness of her throat. She sat up, aching from the cold burn of iron.

Molan helped her, shielding her from the worst of the contact with the metal with his own body. In front of her, Cayden and Ottilie squared off. Ottilie held onto her bottle with a death-grip. It looked maybe half full of something shiny.

"You won't stop me," Ottilie yelled. But already the rain had tapered off to something like a normal shower and the river was retreating a bit. At least it no longer flowed uphill.

"I loved you so much." Cayden's voice came from somewhere between them. His mouth moved, but the sound did not emanate directly from his lips. "I could not care less about the damned music. I loved *you*."

"But you were so talented…" Their exchange had the feeling of an old argument falling into well-worn ruts.

"Li," he said, sadly, "you'll never understand passion, only ambition."

She held up the bottle. "And power. Don't forget

power."

"How could I?" Cayden's ghost voice asked. "Look what you've done to me. I can't believe I thought you loved me once, too."

"Cayden…"

"Don't. Don't say another word to me."

Ottilie looked wounded, just for a second, but the fleeting vulnerability passed. She held up the bottle of Keela's voice. "I can do better than speak."

Keela was on her feet in an instant and on the wing a moment after that. She caught the bottle in her taloned feet and tugged but Ottilie resisted, holding fast to it. As a crow, Keela did not have the strength to take the bottle from her. Ottilie yanked it free of Keela's grip and backhanded her away from it. Keela fell, half flapping half tumbling towards the water. She changed back in time to catch the concrete foundation of the sculpture, her legs dragging in the river. She looked for Molan, but he was nowhere to be seen.

She called his name, her voice weak and hoarse, it barely carried over the gush and rush of the swollen Cumberland. Above her, Cayden lunged at Ottilie, grappling with her, looking like he wanted to throw her over the side as well.

"Molan!" Keela croaked, the voice of her human form sounded now like herself as a crow.

She pulled herself up, dress and cloak soaked and heavy, and got her knees under her. The water in the river was rising again as the flood pulled back to its natural course, no longer angling up the hill towards the Ryman but now pouring into the flats on the east side, inundating the stadium and the scrap yards, heading towards the highway. Keela scrambled up onto the metal part of the supports just as the water lapped up over the concrete.

From her position, she could see Molan. Illuminated by his cadre of wisps, he helped a bedraggled and confused young man into the sculpture.

"Michael," Keela whispered, hardly daring to hope. She saw in Molan's hand the glint of silver. Molan had Michael and her comb.

She stood up to see Ottilie push Cayden and knock him off balance long enough to bring the bottle to her lips. She seemed to drink it in and inhale it at once, drawing the shimmering essence into her mouth.

Keela screamed. The song within her thrashed furiously as its power was divided in half. She staggered; the pain of holding the song was nothing compared to it being rent from her, even just part of it.

Ottilie flung the bottle away, smiling. A glow filled her, infusing her features with otherworldly light. Her caramel complexion paled and her dark hair streaked itself with glints of silver. She rose up on her toes and it looked like there were waves crashing all around her, like a cloak of water.

"And now all I have to do is sing you all into the underworld where I never have to look at you again." Her voice boomed with this new power with the sound of waves and thunder inside of it.

"What makes yourself think you can do that?" Keela forced vigor into her voice, drawing on the remnant of the *Oran na Céle* within her. "Yourself's no banshee, Ottilie!"

"Try and stop me, Keela. You're sounding a little hoarse, dearie, I doubt there's much you could do. A banshee without her voice, such a tragedy."

Keela climbed up into the bottom of the sculpture and used it as a bridge to the other support. Michael, still groggy and confused, lit up when he saw her.

"Keela!"

But she didn't spare him more than a momentary smile. Instead she turned to Molan. "The comb! I need it!" She couldn't quite reach them, though. As she started to climb down, something stirred the air beside her head.

The owl swooped down, long talons razor-sharp aiming for Michael's hand. He curled back in on himself, raising his other hand to shield his eyes. Molan caught his right wrist, the one holding the comb, and lifted it.

Michael fought for all that he was worth. "No! No, please don't take it, you can't take it!"

"Michael, please," Keela rasped.

His green eyes widened in panic, darting between Keela, Ottilie, Molan, and the enormous owl circling back for another pass.

When the owl came close again, time seemed to stand still. Her amber-barred wings swished in ultra-slow motion as she hovered over Michael's body. She lowered her head and uttered a low, melodic, and utterly un-owl-like cry. Transfixed, Michael sat forward and elevated both of his hands to her. Time snapped back into motion and the great owl's talons curled securely through the comb's decorative scrollwork. Michael relinquished the comb to it and the owl banked sharply back towards Keela.

The owl swung by Keela, bringing the comb within her reach. Hoping she'd read its intentions correctly, Keela made a grab for the comb and the owl let it drop nicely into her hands.

As the silver touched her fingers, Keela felt her power renewed within her. It almost made up for what Ottilie took and she prayed fervently that it would be enough. The owl glided past, screeching something down at her. It was neither pleasant nor reprimanding, but it was stern and absolute: *Don't mess this up.*

"Aye, my lady, I won't let you down," Keela said, watching it head for the pedestrian bridge. It landed on the railing in front of two figures. Teri and Polly, Keela guessed.

That must mean that the circle is safe, she thought, hoping against hope, and the song rejoiced, bubbling through her.

Keela got to her feet at the same time Cayden regained his own footing and swung at Ottilie. He had no magic of his own but his determination to destroy her gave him remarkable strength. He managed to knock her down this time. She fell, laughing, off of the sculpture and landed on top of the river as if it was solid.

"Idiots, all of you," Ottilie said, still laughing.

Keela twined her hair into a knot and slid her comb into it. It felt good; she felt almost whole again. She stared down at Ottilie who got to her feet and stood, hovering just above the water's surface.

"You can't control the song, Ottilie, it was never meant for yourself."

"Watch me," she said, but Keela could read her bluff.

Keela's half of the song rebelled against the whole thing, it tried to pull itself back together. The power it leant Ottilie was never meant for her to tame; it was meant for no one to tame, not anymore. Keela walked to the very edge of the sculpture's foundation.

"You can't wield it, it won't listen to you. Not

without this." Keela pointed to the edge of her comb rising out of the bun on her head. "Yourself can't control banshee magic without a banshee comb." She said it as a taunt, daring Ottilie to come after her to get it.

Ottilie sang out a note, it hit Keela keen as a blade. Keela countered, belting in her lower register where some power remained. It shook the witch, but she remained standing. They traded attacks, howling melodies at one another, but were evenly matched.

Ottilie's frustration grew; Keela could see it in her eyes and in the pinched set of her mouth. Teri appeared near the top of the statue where the curving track made a little platform.

"I sure hope you know what you're doing," the muse said to Keela.

"Aye. But you're going to have to trust me."

"I ain't got much choice," Teri replied, dryly.

"The circle?"

"We've done what we can, but it's still touch and go."

Keela swallowed back the lump in her throat. "I'm sorry."

"Don't be sorry. Just win." Teri helped Cayden up to her vantage point and Polly appeared down where Molan and Michael stood. "We're going to minimize the collateral damage. You just do what you gotta do, Keela."

Ottilie came at her with another note and Keela blocked it then parried with her own onslaught of music. Her brittle, injured voice made her banshee howl even more haunting and terrifying. It reverberated off of the brick walls that lined First Avenue, casting strange echoes back at them. It threw Ottilie off more than once, but none of it fazed Keela. This is what she had been born to do, and there would be no stopping her.

"You have my birthright," Keela said, arching her words over the top of the notes she sang.

Ottilie's concentration faltered and her feet dipped below the water.

"The song doesn't belong to you. And it doesn't belong to me, either, I've realized. It belongs to Music City."

The song inside of Keela rolled over on itself, she could feel its other half doing the same. Keela rode out the sensation, nearly used to holding such power inside of her, but Ottilie bent over in obvious distress. She came up again, screaming, dumping everything she had into that one breath, her mouth distended and bizarre. It struck Keela fully in the chest and dropped her to her knees. She hardly noticed the sting of the iron now, but she knew there'd be marks all over her in the morning. Provided she lived through the night.

She stayed there just a little longer, hoping to let Ottilie think she'd been harmed. Then, getting slowly to her feet, Keela looked out at the sea witch perched above the rolling waves of the river. She began to sing low and soft, the coaxing song she had sung to draw the *Oran na Céle* out of the wood at the Opry House.

Ottilie came closer, compelled. Keela sang the other half of the *Oran na Céle* to her, feeling the attraction of the two parts pulling together like magnets. Nearly within arm's reach now, Ottilie smiled suddenly.

"I thought I could just incapacitate you and take what I wanted. But you're making this really challenging and I'm tired of this game." From her belt, she drew a thick, black stiletto. A railroad spike. "I've learned so much about faeries from you, dear Keela, I am in your debt."

The words reverberated through Keela, it was her turn to smile. "Not nearly enough, it seems."

Ottilie raised the knife and brought it down swiftly towards Keela's heart. Keela had only one chance.

"I command you stop!"

Ottilie's arm froze.

"As you are in my debt, drop the spike."

"You conniving bitch!" But her hand opened and the deadly iron tumbled free of it, lost to the Cumberland.

It was a last ditch effort, a bullet dodged, but it would only work once. What followed, Keela prayed, would be entirely up to timing and a great deal of luck.

"Luck of the Irish," she whispered to herself and began to sing again.

Ottilie came ashore to the sculpture in a frenzy. "You could have made it easy for yourself. We could have run this town. But no, you had to go and challenge me."

Keela sang, sang to the *Oran na Céle*. "Trust me," she said in the banshee tongue, "I will not imprison you again, I will not tame you, I will not harm you, I will give you to this city and give this city to you, trust me, I am your kinswoman, I am your blood, upon my true name I swear, *Cadhla O Riordain.*" She ground her hand into the iron strutting until the metal burned a wound into her palm. Lifting it up towards Ottilie, she said, "This is the blood pact I offer you, banshee blood for banshee magic."

Ottilie's skin began to glow, softly at first then with shining force. She reached out and clasped Keela's bleeding hand and drew her forward, close enough that the two halves of the song met and mingled once again. Keela could feel it swimming through her body and into Ottilie's and back again.

"You're out of tricks, banshee."

"Aye, that's a'right. This one last is all I need."

"Don't bet on it!" Ottilie yanked Keela's comb from her hair.

In an instant, the renewed vitality she had felt left her and her throat clenched. The *Oran na Céle* pulled free of her soul, tearing her apart from within as the ravages of the iron and Ottilie's spell came to bear on her body.

Keela heard Molan's anguished shout and Teri's shrill cry as she crumpled to her knees. Ottilie held the comb aloft, her face triumphant. Just like Michael's had been. Only months ago, yet it seemed like a lifetime. So much had changed, so much was still changing.

Ottilie took one step back onto the river's surface, her flesh glowing white-hot now as the fullness of the *Oran na Céle* coursed through her.

Then, as if the water had opened to swallow her up, she was gone.

An after-image of her flickered on the surface of where the witch had stood, then it dissipated.

Keela held fast to the sculpture's foundation, the very last of her life, her energy bleeding out of every pore. The metal behind her groaned as one of the concrete pilings gave way, pulling the two semi-circles apart.

Bubbles came up to the river's surface, popping little flashes of light into the darkness. Then in a rush, a fountain of silvery light burst forth from the dark water. It reverberated with sound: steel guitar, banjo, fiddle, applause, and two voices singing in its very core. One was a man's voice, a rich Irish tenor, but it soon faded and the other came through strong and proud, a banshee voice. Keela's voice.

"I will give you to this city and give this city to you, trust me, I am your kinswoman, I am your blood, upon my true name I swear, Oran na Cadhla."

The light came and settled over Keela, enveloping her, lifting her from the cold, damaging iron. She looked like an angel, beautiful and terrible in her banshee form, floating above the waters that had ravaged the city she had come to love as her own.

Molan reached out his arms and Keela lowered into them. She leaned against his chest. "Take me home, Molan."

"I think you *are* home, Keela."

Track 11

Teri passed around the ouzo — it was so cold that
ice crystals were forming across the surface of the clear
liquid. Polly brought out a plate of feta and tomatoes and
pita and made sure the humans had something to eat with
their liquor.

"Here's to living to fight another day." Teri raised
her glass and the rest of them followed suit: Polly, Cayden,
Molan, Michael, and Keela.

Keela raised hers slowly and gingerly. As the feeling
started to return to her body, it was beginning to hurt and
badly. She would heal, at least she hoped so. She took a long,
savoring sip of ouzo and carefully set down her glass. Molan
had wrapped her hands, paying special attention to the
one she'd cut open for blood. It itched deep inside and she
rubbed her palm against her knee to keep from scratching it.
That one might very well scar, she thought.

Michael and Cayden were wrapped in the muses'
bathrobes while their clothes tumbled in the dryer. On any
other day, there might have been some mirth about the
menfolk wearing ivory silk stenciled with laurel leaves and
Greek key patterns, but not tonight.

A fire had been laid in the hearth and Keela and
Molan sat side by side in front of it, letting the warmth dry

out their clothing. Polly had brought out the small television from her bedroom so they could monitor news of the flood. The rain had stopped falling at long last, and the river was due to crest sometime in the morning.

"We were supposed to get about four inches this weekend," Polly said, "until Ottilie interfered. Where is she, Keela?"

"Same place Michael and Cayden were, somewhere on the other side."

"Where am I now, Keela?" Michael ventured to ask. He'd been so quiet, and they had all left him alone while he processed his situation.

"Nashville," she reminded him. "We're in the States."

"And your comb, it's gone?" Hope battled with doubt in his eyes.

"Aye."

His face fell. "Then I'll never be able to marry you."

"Marry? Me?"

He nodded, looking miserable. "Maeve told me if I took your comb, you'd marry me. That it was the only way."

"Maeve was…incorrect. In fact, I think she may have been playing a trick on you. And me." Keela sat back and sipped her ouzo, letting his confession sink in. She'd known, in her heart she had known that was Maeve's ploy. But to have the proof of it from Michael's own mouth. That was different.

She did not and likely would not ever know why, though. Simple malice, perhaps, or jealousy. Maeve O'Neill was not used to coming in second to anyone.

The song stirred within her at the very mention of the O'Neills. She hummed to herself to settle it once more.

They were all looking at her.

"What happens now?" Michael asked her. "We should go home, shouldn't we?"

Keela took a deep breath and let it out slowly. "I think yourself should go home, aye."

"What about you?"

"I think I am home."

"But Keela, you're a banshee."

"Aye, and still without a comb," she said. "Nashville is the only place I'll ever be whole."

He stood up, unsteady and upset. "That's

ridiculous."

"Let's step outside," Keela said, carefully setting
down her ouzo and keenly aware of Molan's gaze on her.
She shot him a glance and he stayed put, thankfully, as she
escorted Michael to the wide porch.

Michael still did not mind her touch. Something
about that made her sad.

Once outside, they sat in silence of the damp night.
She had to make herself take a breath, exhaustion and pain
were battling over who was to make her more impatient and
short-tempered and the song was laying bets.

Water dripped off the branches and pattered every
so often onto the tin roof of the porch. There was no sound
of traffic, and the usually silent river in the distance rumbled
like a much larger and more dangerous waterway. It was
like a whole different world, not quite the Nashville she
knew.

For a while neither one of them spoke, although
Keela could feel all the questions he had.

"Tell me what it was like," Keela said.

"While I was dead?"

"Aye."

He shrugged then leaned forward bracing his
elbows on his knees. "Don't remember much. One minute
we were at my flat in Galway and I had your comb in my
hand. The very next thing I really remember was himself,
the tall, serious-looking fellow, dragging my arse out of that
river. Somewhere in the middle I remember singing with
you, I think. But that was like a dream, if I think straight on
it, the memory's not there. I have to try and remember it
sideways."

"There was a song, indeed," Keela whispered.

"I hope I sounded good."

"Aye, you did."

Michael sat back and looked out at the grassy hill
that sloped down to Shelby Park. "I don't remember things
ever being this…awkward with you, before." He looked
like he might reach over and touch her leg or maybe her
shoulder, but instead he just put his hands in the pockets of
the robe.

"A great deal has changed."

"I can see that," he jerked his chin back towards the

house.

"Michael, what we had was grand, it was beautiful, and I wouldn't trade it for the world…"

"Ach! Yourself's breaking up with me, aren't you?"

Keela bit her lip. "Well, I…um…"

"You are!" He stood up and paced the long porch. "Faerie women! My mum warned me, she warned me but good"

"If it makes yourself feel any better, my mother warned me the same about humans."

Michael threw up his hands. "Doesn't change the outcome."

Keela went to him and put her hands on his shoulders. "Michael, I was a fool to fall for you. But a happy one. Yet we both knew, or we should have, how much trouble we were in for: a human and a banshee, from two different clans at that! This ending has been waiting for us."

"Why did you go through all this to save me, then?"

"Because you deserved it. Because I owed it to you."

"Nothing more?"

"Oh, at first, aye. When I started this quest I was as lovestruck as I was the day I met you."

"What happened, Keela? Was it that tall fellow?"

"Molan?" She shook her head. "Nah. To tell you the truth…it was Nashville."

Michael looked skeptical.

"Before coming here, I had never performed for fun."

"Of course not. You're a banshee. That's practically blasphemy."

"Aye, so you see what I mean, then. Before I came here, I was nothing but a lousy banshee who fell in love with a mortal warded by another of another clan. Nothing more."

"And what are you, now?"

"I'm myself. Finally. I'm Keela O'Reardon and I've sung at the Opry. Twice. I belong to a motley crew of musicians that plays at the local pub. I was part of a record label."

"And that's *important* to you?"

She was surprised by the vehemence with which he asked that. "Aye."

"That does make you a lousy banshee."

"Aye. That's my point."

"You're telling me you're willing to give up your home, your family, your birthright, just to be a rock star?"

"Michael, this is my home. Here is my family. I have found my birthright, and if anything, I'd be a country star."

He pulled away. "It's like I don't even know yourself anymore."

Keela shrugged. "How could you have? I hardly knew myself."

"Your friend Teri said she could get me home. Can she?"

"Aye, whatever you need. Clothes, ticket, passport, she can make it happen. You could probably leave in the morning, if you wanted."

"I do," he said and went back inside.

Keela stood a long while on the porch under the irregular staccato of droplets hitting the roof, staring at the door. That was it. She had hoped he could be let down easy, sent home to live his life as he should have from the beginning: without her. And that's what she got. She just never expected him to be so angry about it.

"He's hurt. Give him some time. I mean he's been dead for a couple of months now. He's going to need a little while to sort out his emotions." Molan materialized on the far end of the porch, out of view from the windows.

"Was yourself here the entire time?"

"No. But I saw him come in upset and ask to speak to Teri about a passport and a plane ticket. Said he wanted to leave first thing."

"Aye, that he did."

"Which he won't be able to. The airport's going to be closed a couple days while they pump out their basement and drain the runways then check them for damage."

"Maybe there's still time, then."

"Time to talk him out of it?"

Keela looked at Molan with surprise, then remembered he hadn't heard the conversation on the porch. "No. Something else. I might not be planning a return to Ireland anytime soon, but someday I might like to see the old place again, plus I don't like having a *geis* on my soul. I've got the second half of a promise to keep. And I think I know just how to do it."

Molan smiled. "I'll help in any way I can."

"You're a good friend, Molan. I appreciate you."

"I'm your Guardian, Keela."

"I want some more ouzo."

"Better hurry, then, Teri poured Michael a tall one, can't imagine there's much left after that." Molan opened the door for her.

There was, it turned out, plenty of ouzo to go around. Teri's bottle never seemed to run empty. Michael retreated to the guest room with a book from one of the shelves and his impressively full glass.

Keela found Cayden waiting for her. "Seems everyone wants a word with myself tonight."

"I won't make you go out on the porch."

"We can if you'd like."

"Not necessary." He spoke haltingly, still not completely certain of his voice. "I know you're not supposed to thank the fae, but I want to thank you, Keela."

"I should be doing such to you, for all the warnings and the worrying."

Cayden laughed, it was good to see his blue-green eyes merry. "I should have known you could take care of yourself." The mirth faded. "So many of her other victims couldn't."

"What are we going to do with the place?"

"That's what I wanted to talk to you about." He gestured for her to sit beside him on the couch facing the fireplace.

"Does yourself want it?"

He looked into the flames for a long while. "I don't know," he said at length. "There was a time Ottilie called Vox Beata *ours*, as in hers and mine."

"Is that in writing anywhere?"

"It could be," Teri chimed in from across the room. "If you want it."

Cayden shot Teri a look. "Don't get ahead of me, muse."

"There's something else, isn't there?"

He nodded. "She killed me. I was dead. Really and truly dead. She bled me into the Cumberland… But you brought me back."

"'Twas the song that brought you back, Cayden."

"It had to be you, Keela. You said yourself, only a

banshee could control that song and that magic. Ottilie never had a chance." He brought himself around to the point. "Do you know what's to become of me? What am I now? Alive? Undead?"

"I honestly don't know," Keela said. She turned to the muses who both shrugged.

Teri came over to the couch, her dark cheeks rosy. "Ottilie held a lot of power in this town, no matter how much we tried to keep her contained. When word gets out of her…untimely death, or disappearance, or whatever we're going to say happened, the industry's going to go through a power grab. And I'd rather not deal with all of that if I can help it. Getting one of the two of you situated to take her place would be the most helpful."

"One of the two of us?" Keela asked.

"I assumed you're staying, Keela? Else I don't think that boy would have been quite so put out tonight."

"I had intended to stay as long as needed to put the song back where it belongs."

Both Teri and Polly looked at her. "Put it back?" Polly asked. "Really?"

"You could have mentioned that a while back, you know," Teri said.

"I just decided tonight. The song belongs to Music City, and I now belong to the song. I thought it was the other way 'round, but I was wrong."

Teri smiled. "The music is bigger than all of us, even me." She turned to Cayden. "But you never cared for music, did you?"

"I cared for her. But she betrayed me and took everything I had, my voice, my life, everything. I don't know what I care about now."

"With the label, you can make amends," Teri told him. "You can undo the evil she perpetrated in this town. That's got to be worth something, right?"

"Let me sleep on it. I can't tell you now how I'm going to feel come morning when this all sinks in."

"Fair enough," said Teri. "Keela?"

"Let me finish my quest. And then I'll come back and tell you my decision."

"Everyone wants time to think and no one is committing to anything that might get used against them later. You're losing your touch, sister dear."

"Polly, hush." But they were both smiling.

"Yourselves will let me know before Michael leaves? I want to say goodbye. Of course, I'm not sure how best you'll contact me…"

"Oh, yeah, about that. Your dressing room was wrecked, again," Teri tossed Keela's waterlogged purse onto the hearth and pulled out her phone. "But this came through just fine."

"Amazing!" Keela grinned and slipped the phone into the inside pocket of her cloak.

She froze.

"Keela? What's wrong?" Molan came to her side.

Keela yanked off the cloak and laid it on the floor, digging into the pocket. It wasn't all that deep and after removing the phone it was most certainly empty. She sat back on her heels, the color draining from her face.

"Molan," she couldn't bear to look up at him. "Molan, the stone's gone. It must have fallen out sometime during the fight with Ottilie."

He blinked several times before speaking. "Oh."

"What can I do? How can we retrieve it?"

"It's a river stone. It's just found a different river, that's all."

"But your binding!"

"I guess that binds me to the city now, too, is all." His serene smile surprised her. "I've always told you, a Gray Man is bound to the land."

"But you didn't ask to be bound to this land."

"I can think of far worse places, I assure you. This country stuff, it's kind of growing on me. Maybe I should get me a hat…some boots." Molan barely kept a straight face.

"I think not."

"Keela, when I made the decision to follow you, I did it of my own accord. I stand before you today, no conditions, no expectations, just as I did that day in Boston." He took her hand and a few of the wisps caressed the backs of her fingers, comfortingly. "I sent you my protection because I wanted to, because I thought you might need it, need me, someday."

"Turned out the whole town needed you."

He looked away. "It wasn't enough."

"I think it could have been a whole lot worse had you not been here, Servant of the Storm." She squeezed his hands. "Swear to me this: may we both be bound to this city, me to the music and you to the land. And we shall stand side by side here and defend it, always."

When he met her gaze, his grey eyes were blazing. "Done," he said.

The surge that passed between them, beginning from their clasped hands, could be felt throughout the city.

"You and I, Molan, we are Nashville."

"We are Nashville."

"Does that mean Polly and I get some time off?" Teri asked. "Because that would really rock. Haven't had a vacation in nearly two hundred years."

"I'll volunteer to housesit," said Cayden.

Keela wasn't sure whether to laugh or cry. "Let me see this to the very end. And then we'll work out schedules for vacations and housesitting and whatnot. But right now, I just want to go home and sleep for a very long time."

"You heard the lady." Molan wrapped her up in his cloak where the wisps greeted her with barely contained glee.

Mistress, she thought she heard them giddily whisper.

She fell asleep there and then with their warmth all around her, holding her tight, right where she belonged.

Track 12

The Ryman was open for tours again on Monday and set to host the Grand Ole Opry that week. No one was quite sure how long the Opry House would be out of commission, but at least several months was the conservative guess. The airport opened back up Monday as well.

Keela's first stop, though, was the Ryman.

She'd taken the bandages off all but her right hand, the deep gash in her palm was half healed and would certainly leave a mark in its wake. *Something to remember it by*, Keela thought. Remember the flood, remember the quest, remember Ottilie and just how close she'd come to consuming Keela's voice. Keela shivered and the song caressed her from within before flouncing about wildly at the prospect of being inside the Ryman once more. It took her a moment to get everything under enough control to just walk through the doors.

The charming Cathe, the tour guide Keela had met on her first visit, was leading a group through as she entered. Keela waved, a smile on her face. So this was Nashville, where nothing could stop the music or the music lovers. She passed the display cases along the back side of the auditorium, grateful to still have them there to see, and made her way to the little recording studio.

She tapped on the window. "I was told you have an opening for a recording this morning?"

The sound tech nodded and waved her in. He was a tall guy, and so broad through the shoulders he looked like a giant in the recording booth. "You got a track picked out, miss?"

"This is an unaccompanied song, if that's okay."

"So long as you've got the rights to it, I'll make it sound perfect."

"That'd be lovely," she read his nametag, "Corey."

"You sound familiar."

"Did you listen to last week's Opry?"

"The one that got interrupted by the flood?"

Keela smiled. "Aye."

"You're the Irish girl, the one that had everybody singing," he smiled back as recognition dawned. "It's my honor to record for you. Is this for the Opry?"

"No. An old friend came to see me this weekend, but he's headed home today. I wanted to send him home with a little something."

"He picked a bad, bad weekend for a visit. Tell him he needs to come back when we're not under six feet of water."

"I'll tell him, and who knows, maybe he will, someday."

"At least he didn't miss the best part of the weekend," Corey said, flirting.

Keela smiled again and put the headset on and waited until he gave her the signal to begin.

She sang.

She sang the *Oran na Céle* and she sang the segue into what it was now, the *Oran na Cadhla*. It was such a different song now and it held such different powers. If she hadn't prefaced it with the original, she doubted anyone back home would have recognized it.

It took a little over ten minutes to get through it all, carefully, holding back in places to not fry the equipment.

When she finished, Corey gave her the thumbs up. "When's that getting performed?"

"Every day," she answered. "All over this city."

He nodded. "Good. 'Cause that's a helluva song."

"Good," Keela agreed. "'Cause it's a helluva city."

Corey put a label on the CD and closed it up in a nicely packaged case showing the Ryman on the front with a little about the building's history written on the back. "I didn't know what to put on the label, so I just left it blank. I hope that's okay."

"Aye, perfect. You've been very helpful."

He beamed. "Will you be on the Opry again this week?"

"As of right now, no, I don't think so. But that could change."

"Would sending them an email help?"

"It wouldn't hurt, I don't think."

"Then I'm gonna. You were awesome Miss Keela. And funny. That doesn't happen that often, you know. I don't think there's ever been anyone quite like you on the Opry."

"I'm going to have to agree with you, there," she said.

She took the CD and waved to Cathe again on the way out.

Broadway had dried out, but water damage was rampant. A few businesses near Fifth Avenue were still open, but the closer Keela walked towards the river, the worse the devastation became. People were bailing out basements and taking down broken windows. On Second, a jumble of cars, furniture, and junk made the road nearly impassable. Keela paused in front of Buck Wild's shattered storefront and said a prayer for James. She peered through Butler's Run, the breezeway that cut through the block and opened out onto First Avenue. It too was clogged with debris, but she could see the red sculpture across the river, listing badly but still standing.

A metaphor for the whole city, really. Still standing.

With no one there in the Run to see her, she shifted into a crow and flew for the airport, the CD clutched in her feet. The enormous mess broke her heart to see: knocked down houses, burned buildings, debris of every imaginable variety, and river sediment left nearly a quarter mile in each direction.

She went to the A terminal and landed on a plane taxiing up to the gate. She hopped down into the jetway and hid until the passengers began to disembark, then walked out with them in her human guise. Michael was not hard to find. Not for her, anyway. He still bore the faint trace of death in his aura. It would fade over time, but at the moment, it still shone darkly.

She sat down beside him and handed him the CD. "This is for Eimear O'Neill."

He frowned. "She wants a souvenir?"

"Aye. A very specific souvenir. Promise me you'll get it to her."

Michael hesitated, then took the case from her. "I promise."

Keela's spirits lifted for the first time in weeks.

"What do I tell them?" he asked. "About you, I mean?"

"Tell them the truth, tell them whatever you'd like. When they hear what's recorded there, they'll know all they need to know."

Michael nodded and didn't press. There were things, it seemed, he had learned to take on faith when dealing with banshees. He put the CD in the front pocket of his small rolling bag and zipped it up.

They sat for a few minutes longer, neither sure of what else to say.

The gate attendant called the pre-boarding for Michael's flight.

"I hear yourself is staying here for good."

"Aye. I told yourself that Saturday night, did you not remember?"

"I remembered. But just the way Teri said it this morning, sounded, I dunno, different than what you told me then."

"Aye, I suppose 'tis a little bit different."

"You look beautiful, Keela. More beautiful than I have ever seen you, more beautiful than I have ever seen any banshee."

"Go on, you flatterer!"

"It's the truth. And I never could have imagined it. Never could have imagined this."

"You could have stayed longer, Teri said she'd have gotten the guest house out back set up for you."

"I know. But I need to get home. My family will be worried."

"Aye," Keela nodded. "Mine, too, I wager. Tell them…tell them I'm okay? And that I'm happy?"

"I can do that."

"And the O'Briens, can you tell them I sang one of theirs to his rest last week?"

Michael's brows rose in surprise. "You did *what*? No wonder you're not going back, they'd have your hide for certain over that."

"It needed to be done, so I did it. And that's the way it's going to be from now on."

"You're going to sing over the entire city, one by one, when they die?"

"Perhaps."

"You're a madwoman, Keela O'Reardon."

"Just being myself, Michael O'Neill."

They called his boarding group.

"I guess this is goodbye," he said.

"Until next time. Safe travels. May the road rise up to meet you and all of that." They embraced. "Oh, I almost forget!" She pulled a silver chain out of the inside pocket of her cloak. "Give this to Maeve, or to the next banshee girl who takes your fancy. Just leave their combs alone from now on, d'you hear me?" Keela slipped the claddaugh pendant into his hand.

Michael smiled a little and closed his hand around the necklace. "Goodbye, Keela, I'll never forget you."

"Nor I you."

He turned away and wheeled his bag towards the gate. The gate attendant scanned his boarding pass and waved him through. He only paused a moment on the jetway to cast a single glance over his shoulder. Keela raised her hand in farewell. He turned back and disappeared from her sight.

She sat in the slowly emptying gate area until the last of the passengers were loaded. Then she watched as the big white plane pulled back from the gate and taxied away. Crossing to the other side of the terminal, she tried to keep an eye on it as it joined the line of planes waiting to take off. When she was reasonably certain his had gone, she started the long walk out of the airport.

Even here, every restaurant and bar had a band. Small stages were set up around the terminal and the ticket counters and the baggage claim. All the signage proclaimed "WELCOME TO MUSIC CITY" and "HOME OF THE GRAND OLE OPRY" and "THE HEART OF COUNTRY MUSIC."

Keela walked down the wide corridor towards baggage claim. She touched the words "Music City," "home," and "heart" as she passed.

Outside, the sun was shining and there was so much work to be done.

Bonus Track:

"Let the Circle Be Unbroken"

The purple Victorian had been repainted in a soft, sage green and most of the opulent furnishings had been sold and replaced with things more quaint and cottage-like. The interior had a familiar, homey feel not unlike McNamara's and they'd replaced Ottilie's stained glass windows with ones depicting a claddaugh and the other an owl in deference to the city's patroness. The new motto of Vox Beata became "Friendship, Love, and Loyalty" and they put the claddaugh on their business cards.

There had been some worry from the muses whether or not people would think they only dealt with Irish music, but Keela assured them they wouldn't. Cayden backed her up on that.

"They already know Keela," he said, "but our next talent acquisition will be more mainstream."

Teri could only laugh. "Well, it isn't like I don't trust you two."

And so it began.

Keela moved into the muses' guest house and Cayden into her old apartment. He had no desire to go back to his old place. Too many memories, he'd said.

They fell into a pleasant routine. First thing every morning, Keela flew out across East Nashville, landing on streetlights and treetops in the early hours of the day and just watched the city come to life. Then onto Vox Beata, where Cayden was waiting, usually with paperwork or a demo to hear. Playing the music was perhaps not his passion, but no one could deny that he was brilliant at managing it.

Sometimes Molan tagged along, sometimes he went wandering, gliding over the Cumberland and creeping along hills and hollows, a Gray Man getting to know his new land with his will-o'-the-wisps in tow.

And the song flourished. No longer bound, it blanketed the city with its energy using Keela as its conduit. Although it looked forward to the day it would be reunited with the oak floorboards of the Ryman, it would remain forever connected to Keela and her to it. They had changed one another.

As spring rolled into summer, Nashville recovered from the flood little by little. By June, Broadway was pretty well open for business from the riverfront all the way up to the arena. Teri helped organize a grand opening street party for all the bars and shops downtown. It was just what they all needed.

Keela finished up at the label, switching off the lights and checking all the doors. She'd sent Cayden and their student interns ahead to help Teri set up hours ago. She hesitated at the back stair, looking up towards the attic. They had packed all of Ottilie's jars and bottles into boxes and stashed them in another corner, far from the "workshop." Another problem for another day. Tonight, a party waited for her.

Keela opened the back door. The heavy, humid air hit her like an over-warm blanket after the crisp air-conditioning inside. She needed to figure out how to alter her gown for summer wearing, or somehow acquire a new one. Keela couldn't imagine wearing long-sleeved wool in Nashville in August. But that too was another problem for another day.

Taking wing, Keela headed for downtown, where streets were closed and bands were playing on every block and in every bar. She could hear the delightful cacophony as soon as she crossed highway 40. The *Oran ne Cadhla* rejoiced, sending silvery shimmers down each of her feathers.

The tall, curvaceous Greek woman stood out from the crowd in her sleeveless linen gown and hair piled up so artfully. Keela landed on Teri's shoulder and nipped playfully at her earlobe. In a twinkling, they stood side by side with the early evening sun behind them, casting long shadows down Broadway.

"October," Teri said with a grin.

"October?"

"The rededication of the Opry House."

Keela turned to face her, a grin of her own lighting up her face. "So, it's saved then? The circle is truly saved?"

Teri nodded. "There's some work yet needs to be done, but it's going to be okay."

"Bless you, Teri!"

"It's all in a day's work, for me anyway." They started off for the heart of the block party, walking slow and taking in all the sounds. "Soon to be all in a day's work for you. Sure you can handle it?"

"Aye. I've got help. Molan, Cayden, we've got a good bunch of youngsters interning for us. Plus yourself and Polly. Aye, I know you won't be here full time anymore, but this is the Athens of the South. I don't think you'll be able to stay away for too long."

"Maybe not Polly, she's the sentimental one, you know."

"Of course." Keela winked and Teri laughed.

They had to weave and wander through the crowds, bumping shoulders and elbows and hips. All around them was celebration, affirmation.

"We are Nashville!" someone shouted.

Yes, Keela thought, *we are.*

The music spilled out into the evening, soaring through the pulpy summertime air.

"You'll love it here in the fall," said Teri. "My favorite time of year here. I'll definitely come visit in the fall. In October, for the dedication, of course."

"We'd love to have yourself, anytime."

They reached Second Avenue and looked towards the huge stage set up at the waterfront, where the headliners played.

"Stop by the Opry on Monday," Teri said, casting a sidelong smile at Keela. "DeeDee left me a message. She has no way to contact you anymore."

"Do they want myself back? First I got a dressing room destroyed, then was part to blame for taking down the entire place!"

"I'm sorry about that, by the way." Teri looked away, gazing at the bats dipping and gliding in the setting sun, feasting on mosquitos by the river's edge. The next band was readying to play and the bats were grabbing some supper before the noise chased them away again. "I honestly didn't want to harm you, but Ottilie had to be stopped."

"I understand." Keela touched her chest and the song did a backflip within her. "This is worth protecting, at all costs. I knew that when I came here, but I truly understand it now."

"Good," Teri said. "I have something for you."

From seemingly nowhere, she brought out a leather bound book, a journal of some sort.

"I think we ought to begin thinking about you branching out into original work. This might be a good place to start. Until you get the feel for writing your own." Teri's voice quavered. She handed over the book with slight hesitation.

When Keela opened the cover, she understood why. Inside, the simple but beautiful handwriting spelled out an equally simple and beautiful inscription: *For James— I believe in you. –Teri.* She nearly marred the words with her falling tears.

"James," she whispered, wishing that he could be here.

"We argued about giving it to you. Polly was against it, on account of what you did to her book."

Keela felt ashamed. "I didn't like that, didn't like myself for doing it, but I didn't have a lot of choices."

"I think if you take good care of this, she might forgive you. She might even let you read hers. When you're ready for that."

"Tell her, I'll make her proud."

"Tell her yourself," Teri smiled. "She's meeting us for dinner at Jack's BBQ in an hour."

"Should I call Molan? What about Cayden?"

"Already taken care of. Think of it as our going-away party."

"We should have held it at the pub!"

Pain crossed Teri's face. "Not yet," she said. "In the fall. After I get some distance from his death. That's one of the reasons I gave you his book. He loved me, but in life he never wanted to belong to me. It isn't right that I should demand it after his death." She touched the book with reverent fingertips. "You were better for him than you'll ever know, Keela. Better for him than I wanted to admit. You gave him back his passion for music, for the love of it not for the career of it. Seeing it new through your eyes, he realized what he had been missing. When you get burned out, it's so easy to forget how much you love your job."

"Which is why yourself is going to take a nice long vacation and not worry a bit about Nashville while you're gone."

"Yes, ma'am." Teri saluted Keela. "I leave Music City in your capable hands. Yours and that Guardian of yours."

"He isn't mine. Not *just* mine. He belongs to the city now, all of it, just as I do."

The band on the big stage started up, just as darkness began to descend.

"I'm not happy about the flood," said Teri, "but sometimes we all need to almost lose what's dearest to us to remind us how important it really is. And the flood set the song free. There's no telling what amazing talent will come out of this city, now. So, I guess, in a roundabout way I should th—"

"No! You never thank a faerie!"

"When you mean it, you do." Teri clasped Keela's hand. "Thank you."

They strolled back down Broadway, towards Jack's, with the music all around them.

Always.

Liner Notes

This book was a labor of love right from the start. I wanted to capture my seemingly unlikely love for this kooky little city called Nashville. I hope that it has worked its magic on you as it has for me.

I have been as true to the history and geography and flavor of the city as possible. That said, I have obviously taken a few liberties (although not as many as you might think…truth is indeed stranger than fiction!) so please don't send me hate mail because I got something "wrong." Chances are better than good that not only do I know, but I did it on purpose.

A note about the flood. The Nashville flood occurred in May of 2010. It cost people their homes, their jobs, their pets, and their lives. When I first started writing this book, it had not yet happened. But once it did, and it was nearly supernaturally potent, I knew I wanted to make it part of my story because it was part of Nashville's story. It was an event that brought the whole city together. The saying "We Are Nashville" rallied all of us through those dark days of spotty electricity and strict water rationing. If you get a chance, check out the song "Tennessee's Not Landlocked Anymore" on YouTube, written by a local on Sunday of the weekend-long storm. And Google some of the blogs from that time. Cellblock 303 (a hockey fan blog for the Nashville Predators) actually coined the phrase "We Are Nashville," but no one seems to remember that.

I mean absolutely no disrespect to the families and folks affected by that weekend's devastation.

Although only one name is on the cover, no book is ever written alone. I'd firstly like to thank my amazing husband, Matthew Schwartz. He's an author too so he really understands what it means to need the time and space to work. During the push to finish this thing, he took on all the household duties, including making dinner and bathing our daughter and getting her into bed, all after his own full day's work at his day job. It was a wonderfully supportive and caring thing to do and I am eternally grateful for his partnership. He also makes an amazing sounding board and was the person who lit the fuse on this story. Without him, you would not be reading this and I do not hyperbolize that one little bit. His influence is woven into every syllable of this book. After all, he's the one who brought me to Nashville in the first place, so this is all *entirely* his fault.

I'd also like to thank Janet Harriett, editrix extraordinaire (www.janetharriett.com). She has the amazing ability to see the big picture and tweak and snip and rearrange but make it seem like nothing has changed, yet it is magically a million times *better*. She is an amazing partner in (writing) crime and by far my favorite editor to work with! I don't know exactly how she does what she does (mutant superpower maybe?) but I am so glad she does it and I look forward to doing it with her for a long time to come. (Uhhh, you know what I mean…)

And on the visual side, the inestimable Johnny Lee Park (www.johnnyleepark.com) put his talents towards a stunning book cover, taking in all my crazy (and occasionally contradictory) requests to create an image that was nowhere near what I had initially envisioned but yet everything I wanted. He's beyond talented and I recommend that you check out his work. It never ceases to amaze me with its beauty and depth.

Melissa Gay (www.melissagay.com) provided the lineart for the frontispiece because as we all know it is just NOT a Sara Harvey book without some art by Melissa Gay in it, right? She continues to be awesome and has the ability to STARE DIRECTLY INTO MY BRAIN AND SEE WHAT I AM IMAGINING! Usually, I'd say that's creepy, but when it's Melissa, I just sit there and let it happen because she always creates something <u>stunning</u> that looks *exactly the way I envisioned it*. And really, who WOULDN'T be all over that??

Last but not least, the biggest and warmest round of thanks to my Kickstarter folks. They came together with funds, with support, with cheerleading and here I stand with a book that I am putting out there in the world myself. A book that would still be quietly languishing on my hard drive, homeless, without them. If you are reading this book out there in the wide world and you love it, you have them to thank for that opportunity. And if it gave you pleasure,

please pay it forward and support a campaign on Kickstarter
or IndieGoGo or any number of crowdfunding platforms.
The internet can be a beautiful thing that helps people
like me reach goals otherwise impossible due to monetary
constraints. Thanks, y'all. I quite literally could not have
done it without you.

  There's only one name on the cover, but I didn't
do this alone. And for that I will be eternally grateful and
humbled.

April 28th 2014
Nashville, TN
(with another big storm rolling in…of course.
Springtime in the South!)